Message of the Crow

By

Ellen Dugan

Message of the Crow
Copyright @ Ellen Dugan 2015
Edited by Katherine Pace
Cover art designed by Kyle Hallemeier
Cover image: fotolia © Alexandr Satoru
"Legacy of Magick" logo designed by Kyle Hallemeier
Copy Editing and Formatting by Libris in CAPS

This is a work of fiction. Names, characters, businesses, organizations, places, events and incidents either are the product of the author's imagination or are used fictitiously. Any resemblance to actual persons, living or dead, events, or locales is entirely coincidental.

Excerpt of: Beneath An Ivy Moon
Copyright © Ellen Dugan 2015
Edited by Katherine Pace
Copy Editing and Formatting by Libris in CAPS

Other titles in the Legacy of Magick Series
by Ellen Dugan

Legacy of Magick, Book #1

Secret of the Rose, Book #2

Coming in 2016

Beneath An Ivy Moon, Book #4

Under the Holly Moon, Book #5

ACKNOWLEDGMENTS

Thanks to the friends, family, and fans who have enthusiastically supported me.

A few words of appreciation to Mimi and Ro for the on the spot information on Hoodoo and Root-working. A very special thank you to my Beta Readers: Shawna and Tess.

For Kyle, thank you for the bewitching cover art! You are so creative and talented. I guess you must get that from your mother. LOL

To my editor Katherine, who is always a pleasure to work with; and for the brilliant suggestion of adding the sneak peek of *Legacy Of Magick* Book #4— Ivy's story to the back of this book!

1 crow sorrow,

2 crows joy,

3 crows a letter,

4 crows a boy

5 crows silver

6 crows gold,

7 crows a secret that should never be told...

-Familiar Saying

PROLOGUE

The nights always seem longer, colder and darker during the month of December. Before the wheel of the year turns back towards the light at the Winter Solstice, the Wild Hunt rules, spirits roam, and darkness reigns. Therefore it was only appropriate, the Witch decided, to do the binding in the normally peaceful cemetery of William's Ford.

Walking confidently forward, the dense fog made the Witch practically invisible while moving between the tombstones. In the dead of the night, work could be done at the graveyard privately. For in the light of day too many people might see, would wonder and ask questions… Pulling the dark cloak closer, the Witch stopped and stared at the remnants of the funeral flowers arranged over the recent grave of Gwen Bishop.

"Damn you, Gwen," the Witch's voice echoed hollowly in the fog. "You didn't have to die. If only you would have been more reasonable." With only a shake of the head at the loss of a worthy adversary, the Witch shrugged over Gwen Bishop's death.

The Witch pulled a small fabric bag full of herbs from a cloak pocket, planning to hide it among the faded flowers. Intending to bind the spirit of this latest victim forever to the grave, the Witch reached out confidently, and with a power-laced voice. "With blood and baneful herbs, I will bind you to your grave..."

Unexpectedly, a blast of bright white magickal energy pulsed from the ground. Startled, the cloaked figure fell back. "Protected," the Witch hissed softly in disbelief. "Your grave site is *protected*. I wonder which one of the little Witchlings in the family had the foresight to do that?"

In frustration, the Witch spun away from the grave and gave in to rage. *So close. So close to assembling the pieces of the Blood Moon Grimoire. After all the work I have done, the role I'd been forced to play. Even after all the years I've waited, plotted and planned... the grimoire still remains frustratingly out of reach.*

"Why," another voice, a familiar and once-loved voice, whispered in the night through the cold mist. "I loved you so much... Why have you done this?"

The Witch stopped and turned towards the voice, watching as a spirit began to take shape from within the fog. Now confronted by the ghost of yet another victim, the Witch lashed out with angry and dark magick. "Be gone from this place!" With a gesture from the Witch, the spirit melted back into the night.

"Love," the Witch practically spit. "I have no need

for love. What I need is power... *Power is everything.*"

CHAPTER ONE

I had always wondered what drove people to lay wreaths or fresh flowers on a grave. Standing before what was left of my aunt's funeral flowers— I suddenly knew exactly why they did.

I was a little surprised to find myself here. I hadn't planned this trip, nor had I even realized that I was running to the cemetery— I usually jogged to the riverfront and back in a route I had set up months prior. There was no thought process involved; it was like a sort of auto-pilot for me. However, when my shoes had started to crunch on the gravel path of the old graveyard, I'd snapped out of wherever my mind had been and had slowed my pace out of respect. By the time I had approached the established graves of my grandparents and the new grave of my Aunt Gwen, I was walking.

I studied the large double headstone that marked the place where Morgan and Rose Bishop lay, and my breath puffed out in white clouds against the cold air.

To my right, a mound of dirt covered with old, withered and frost-burnt floral arrangements— marked where my Aunt had been buried only four weeks ago.

Even though I was dressed for the cold weather in thermal running gear, I shivered. Not from the temperature, but in reaction. It was almost as if I'd been compelled to come here. *Something* had drawn me here to the graves of my relatives. I tugged my red knit hat down farther over my ears— which I'd for worn more for warmth than holiday cheer— and considered what, if anything, I should do.

While hard, grinding rock blasted in my ears from my iPod, I focused on my breathing and visualized my connection to the earth. The winter grass beneath my feet, the old oak trees that were near by... After a few moments of concentrating, I felt steadier. The music helped.

My playlist today was a sort of defiance to the neighborhood homes all around that were decorated for the winter holidays. Christmas trees sparkled in front windows, and white or multi-colored lights accented the roof lines of the romantic Victorian style houses. Pine roping and lighted holiday characters adorned many front porches, and my hometown of William's Ford, Missouri looked almost picture perfect.

You'd never guess that here in this picturesque little college town dark magick fought against good magick, and that murder surrounded us all.

Now, as I reflected upon the dead flowers heaped

upon my Aunt's grave, I struggled with grief. I felt tears come to my eyes and let them roll down my face. I couldn't have cared less if anyone saw me.

I knew plenty of people, my Christian mother for example, who would think that Witches never cried, never felt remorse, and never grieved. However, I, Autumn Bishop, Seer and newest addition to the Bishop family line of Witches, could emphatically state that—yes, they grieved. Witches lived, loved, and laughed as any other person would. And when death came to a loved one, they mourned like anyone else.

I paused the playlist on my iPod and stood in silence, studying the site. This was the first time I'd been back to the cemetery since the day of the burial. And while I knew it was much too soon for a headstone to be placed, I still didn't like that there wasn't one.

For now, the only marker for Gwen Bishop's final resting place was a small plastic card holder. A piece of paper had been clipped to it, but the printing had run from rain. The edges had curled, and between that and the dead, faded flowers, it was thoroughly depressing. As I gazed out over the old cemetery where generations of Bishops and other founding families rested, I noticed evergreen wreaths on easels against many of the headstones.

I crouched down and ran my hands over the faded flowers and ribbons from an arrangement. "I'm going to call Violet today at the flower shop and have a wreath made up for you." I hadn't meant to speak out loud. But once I had, it seemed right. I shifted my gaze to my grandparents' graves, and amended my decision. "I'll have two wreaths made."

I looked towards the east and hoped for a glimpse of the sunrise. But, I was disappointed. There wasn't even a hint of color to the sky, only a lightening of the gloomy, cloudy gray. Crows were calling loudly, and a group of them circled the cemetery. As I crouched down between the graves of my grandparents and my aunt, I felt as if I needed to stay there and guard them somehow.

The protection holds... A voice whispered in my mind, and I shivered.

"Protection?" I asked quietly. "Protection for who, or from what?" I waited, but there was no response. It made me wonder, though, *why would a grave site need protection?* Before I could puzzle out the unexpected message, a crow swooped in and landed on my grandparents' headstone.

Kaww, kaww. The crow called out.

I couldn't say that I was surprised by the avian visit. This was William's Ford after all— and I'd given up hoping for normal. Still, I'd been having random close encounters with crows for the past few months, and I was starting to suspect that it might be the same bird at each meeting.

I had good reasons for my suspicions, *magickal* reasons. My grandfather Morgan used to have a pet crow named Midnight. It was his familiar, technically.

I'd never had the chance to find out from Aunt Gwen what had happened to the bird after my grandparents' passing all those years ago. Hunched down between the graves of my relatives, the waste of those lives seemed to weigh heavily down upon me.

I'd promised myself that I'd find out the truth about Gwen's accident one way or another, and whoever was responsible would face their karmic justice. I caught myself, and tried to banish any thoughts of revenge. It simply didn't seem respectful considering where I was. As if in agreement, the crow called out again.

"Hello there," I said to the crow. I took a calming breath, pulled out an earbud, and studied the bird as I stayed crouched down. "Are you Midnight?" I asked, following my hunch.

The crow's head bopped up and down in response.

I knew it. I smiled a little even as I sniffled. "I have a picture of you sitting with my grandfather," I said to the crow, wiping at my tears with gloved hands.

The bird looked at me with bright and intelligent eyes. He seemed to be waiting.

"You gave me a feather the last time you paid me a visit at the manor." The crow shook itself and tucked up its wings. I waited to see what he'd do next, but he stayed put and studied me every bit as thoroughly as I did him.

Curious as to what would happen, I took a deep breath, placing one hand on the winter grass to help keep my balance and held out my other arm in invitation. The bird gave a flap of his wings and hopped over, landing on my outstretched arm.

"God, you're beautiful," I whispered to the crow. He'd settled in above my elbow and turned his head, regarding me steadily.

"Did Grandpa Morgan send you to me somehow?" I asked.

In answer, the bird shifted and tugged at my red knit hat with his beak. He then pulled on the purple plastic cord of my dangling earbud.

"Ah, okay." I took that as a *yes*. I stayed crouched there with the crow, softly cooing over the bird and enjoying his company. After a couple of minutes, my arm started to tremble from holding it straight out. Apparently the bird could feel it, and he launched off my arm to perch back on my grandparents' tombstone.

Slowly I stood up. Midnight seemed unfazed by my movements. "Maybe next time, you'll allow me to pet you," I said to the bird.

The bird bobbed his head up and down again as if he was answering me. And I found myself smiling in response. In the distance I heard the sound of an engine. I saw a gator type of vehicle zipping along the gravel pathways of the cemetery.

When the driver pulled up along side of me, Midnight launched up into the sky. "Good morning, Miss," the man said, giving me a kind, sympathetic smile.

"Good morning," I answered back.

"One crow for sorrow," the man said.

"Excuse me?"

"You know, the old rhyme? One crow for sorrow, two for..." he trailed off, clearing his throat. "Are you family?" he asked, tilting his head towards the grave.

"Yes, I am." I took a breath and tried to keep my voice steady. "I'd like to bring back a wreath this afternoon. Can you clear out all the faded flowers for me?" I asked, gesturing towards Gwen's grave.

"I will be happy to," he said.

"Thanks."

"Good day, Miss," he said kindly.

I nodded at him and tucked my earbud back in place. I turned my music back on and hit shuffle. To my surprise, Annie Lennox started singing about a winter wonderland. I'd forgotten I'd had that song. As I walked away from the graves of my relatives a group of crows called back and forth to each other from the cemetery. I could hear them clearly over the holiday music.

The sun peeked through the clouds for a moment, and I took that as a good sign. Not feeling as down as I had earlier, I psyched myself up and picked up my pace. I exited the cemetery and jogged home to the manor.

***

"Holly, let's move!" my cousin Ivy shouted up the

back stairs.

I let myself in through the potting room, chucked off the outerwear and my hat, and headed straight for the kitchen fridge. I passed Great Aunt Faye, who was brewing a pot of tea at the stove, and grabbed a bottle of water. "Problem?" I asked, as Ivy continued to holler up the stairs.

Ivy stood with her coat on and scowled. "She's stalling again," she said of her twin sister.

"Again?" I raised my eyebrows. "You two have been late to school three times this week already." And it was only Thursday.

Aunt Faye took down a mug from the cabinet and poured herself a cup of tea. She squared her shoulders that were currently covered in a plush burgundy robe, and deliberately set the tea pot down on the stove. "I've had just about enough of this..." she grumbled.

I stepped back. Call me psychic, but I could see that a full blown family argument was brewing. The old Witch might be in her seventies, but she could pack a wallop with her magick— and I'd prefer to be out of the line of fire when everything hit the fan. "You gonna bring the hammer down?" I asked her.

Great Aunt Faye calmly added a dollop of milk to her tea. "Why yes... I do believe that I am," she said in a pleasant tone that had Ivy eyeballing her.

Holly finally came down the stairs. Her curly red-gold hair was pulled back from her naked face in a severe ponytail. There were deep circles under her eyes, she wore a pink sweater, khakis and carried her coat over one arm. Holly paused at the bottom step, taking her sweet time digging car keys out of her purse while Ivy urged her to hurry up.

Oh, jeez. I thought, and wondered why Holly was so determined to play the martyr.

"This martyr-like behavior stops *today*," Aunt Faye announced. I jolted a bit, realizing she must have picked up on my internal monologue.

Holly's head whipped up, and she glared at the old woman. "I have no idea what you are talking about."

"Then let me be clear," Aunt Faye said, crossing her arms over her chest. "Acting as if you are the *only* person that's mourning the death of your mother— is insulting."

Silently, I agreed. Everyone was hurting, and Holly's behavior only added stress to an already awful situation. Holly said nothing at Aunt Faye's chastising. She simply stared at the old woman.

Bran had come down the stairs, looking as worn out and sad as the rest of the family. He stopped and listened as the drama played out.

"Young lady," Aunt Faye's voice was soft but stern. "We have all had a hard time over the past month, but behaving this way does not prove that you loved her more than anyone else."

Holly mutely nodded her head.

"We've got to go— right now, or we'll be late again," Ivy said, and pulled a black knit cap over her brown hair. "Give me the keys— I'm driving."

"I said that I'd drive," Holly argued.

"Listen Blondie," I said to Holly, "I don't think you are in any shape to drive."

"Gimme the keys," Ivy repeated.

"I really think Ivy *should* be the one to drive," Bran said, and laid a gentle hand on Holly's shoulder.

Holly shook her head no and stubbornly held onto the keys. "I'm perfectly fine to drive."

Suddenly, with a sharp jingle of sound, the car keys flew out of Holly's hand and into Ivy's— via telekinesis. "And *I* say I'd prefer to get to school in one piece," Ivy snapped.

Silence hung in the air for a good five seconds, as Ivy realized her poor choice of words.

Holly's bottom lip started to quiver, and tears spilled over, running down her cheeks. "How could you *say* that?" she whispered to Ivy

"Holly," I tried to smooth things over. "She didn't mean it the way it sounded."

"Mom *died* in a car accident! How could you say something that stupid?" Holly's voice broke as she stared at her twin. She dropped her purse and coat, shoved past Bran, and ran back up the stairs. A few seconds later we heard a door slam.

Now Ivy was crying too. Aunt Faye was swearing under her breath, and Bran ran an aggravated hand through his hair. I motioned towards the kitchen stairs. "You take Holly," I said to Aunt Faye. "I'll get Ivy to school."

"Right." She nodded.

"Do you want me to talk to Holly?" Bran asked.

"No, I will." Aunt Faye sounded irritated, but as she passed Bran on the stairs she gave his arm a reassuring squeeze.

"Come on, Shorty," I said to Ivy. "Let's get you to school."

I had to warm up my truck and scrape the windows first, which is why it took even more time to get Ivy to school. Finally, I drove Ivy to the high school while she repaired her makeup. Sitting next to me on the bench seat of my pickup truck, she somehow managed to re-apply black eyeliner neatly and quickly.

"I'm going to be late again. Will you walk me in?" Ivy asked.

"I'm still in my sweaty workout clothes," I pointed out. *Damn, the last place I wanted to be was in the high school principal's office.*

"I don't care," Ivy said.

"What if they think I'm the gym teacher?" I joked.

"Then make them run laps." Ivy tucked her makeup bag back in her purse. "Please, Autumn, I'm tired of facing down the principal."

So, I found myself walking my cousin into the school office to explain why she was tardy for the fourth time that week. A sympathetic secretary wrote Ivy a hall pass, and as I tried to slip out, I was cornered by the school guidance counsellor.

"Your aunt, Miss Bishop, called a moment ago to inform us that Holly will be coming in later today." The woman appeared to be in her early thirties. She was a pretty blonde, wearing a red holiday sweater with gold stars scattered across it.

While I flinched at hearing the words, 'your aunt,' I knew she was speaking of Great Aunt Faye. I stood there slightly sweaty, with no makeup, and tried to answer the woman as politely as possible. "Holly's been having a tough time dealing with her mother's death," I finally said.

"I've spoken to the girls' brother, about grief counselling," she said.

"That's probably a good idea," I admitted, then excused myself and tried to walk away.

She caught my arm before I could get too far. "How are *you* doing?" she asked.

I frowned at the woman. "As well as can be expected."

"You think I'm being nosey?" she asked, smiling at me.

"Ah..." I wasn't sure what to say.

"My husband, Kyle Jacobs, was a cousin to Gwen. I believe you met him and our daughters at the manor while they were trick-or-treating?" she asked.

I thought back to the two little Witches that I'd met on Halloween. "Sleeping Beauty and Cinderella? Those are your girls?"

"Sophia and Chloe," she said.

"They were great." I smiled back and meant it.

She pressed a business card into my hand. "If you, Bran, or Faye need anything. Anything at all, please let me know."

"Thank you," I checked the card, "Shannon." Then recognizing the hyphenated last names from *two* of the founding magickal families, I blinked.

Shannon Proctor-Jacobs stuck out her hand, and I automatically took it. I felt a low sort of energy, warm and pleasant, when we shook hands. My gaze jumped to hers. That energetic buzz could mean only one thing.

"Blessed be," she whispered, confirming my hunch that she too was a Witch.

***

After returning from Ivy's school I showered and changed into jeans and a green sweatshirt. I secured my long hair back in a smooth ponytail and put some mismatched holiday socks on. The red and dark green stripes of my left sock clashed with the lime green and cherry red polka dots of the right. But they were cheerful, and they were probably the most holiday-like thing I'd seen around the manor in weeks.

I remembered to text Violet about the cemetery wreaths as soon as I'd returned home, and she had messaged back telling me the wreaths would be ready first thing in the morning for pick up. I stretched out on the family room couch, watching as a fire snapped in the fireplace. The manor felt gloomy, dark, and far too quiet, as Holly had finally gone to school. So, that left my brother, me and Aunt Faye to hold down the fort.

Bran sat brooding with a cup of coffee in an overstuffed chair. As he was on winter break from his position at the university library, Bran was dressed casually in dark jeans and a sweater. He sipped from the mug and crossed his feet on the coffee table. Great Aunt Faye was, as her habit, impeccably groomed in a gold sweater and black dress pants. She sat regally in a chair across from me, sipping at her tea. Merlin was sprawled across my chest, purring away. Or maybe he was snoring. The radio in the kitchen played quietly in the background. I heard Elvis crooning about a blue Christmas, and internally, I cringed.

"It's too dark in here," I said, setting Merlin aside. He complained at the disturbance, as I got up to turn on a couple of lamps around the room. To my surprise, it did little to dispel the melancholy atmosphere of the late morning.

"The days before the winter solstice the light gets less and less," Bran said absently.

"Your mother taught me that the winter solstice, or Yule, was when we celebrated the return of the light." I said. "It's the time of the sun's rebirth." An idea was brewing in my mind on how I could help cheer things up around the manor. "I have an idea," I said. "The sabbat of Yule is this weekend, right?"

"It is," Bran said.

"And there isn't any holiday cheer, decorations, or trim in sight," I pointed out. Then I said what I was thinking. "I bet Gwen would be pissed if we all sat around here feeling sorry for ourselves, and didn't even celebrate the sabbat."

"What do you want to do?" Aunt Faye asked setting her tea cup aside.

I walked to the fireplace and considered the bare mantle. "Halloween— I mean Samhain at the manor was styled like a magazine photo shoot, so you can't tell me that Gwen didn't take her Yuletide decorations any less seriously. She'd talked to me about how she decorated for Yule before the accident."

Bran and Aunt Faye studied me, so I continued. "Maybe we don't have to go all out, but I really think we should do something to brighten things up around here."

Bran sat up straight. "There's a ton of decorations for Yule up in the attic."

"I bet it would cheer the girls up to come home from school and see some sparkle, holiday lights, and a little magick," I said.

"I could bake cookies." Aunt Faye stood up smiling at me. "I'll run to the market and get some supplies."

"Okay." I glanced over at Bran. "Are you in?"

"Yeah." He actually smiled at me. "Let's do this."

An hour later Bran and I had assembled a slim-line, eight foot tree. It sat in the main foyer, tucked behind the curving banister— similar to the black tree that had been decorated for Samhain. Only this artificial tree was a traditional pine green.

While the classic music of the Sugarplum fairy danced from the CD player, Aunt Faye whipped up some culinary magick in the kitchen. Two thirds of the tall tree were lit, and Bran stood on a ladder, handing me an end of a light strand. "This should do it," he said.

From my place on the staircase, I took the end from him and plugged it into to the top section of the tree's lights. "This is so much faster with a pre-lit tree." I said, and, like magick, the entire tree was lit.

Bran tugged at a couple of branches, making adjustments to the top section of the tree. "It looks good," he said smiling a little.

This was the first time Bran and I had ever done anything *together* since I had discovered that he was actually my half brother— and not my cousin. After everything we'd gone through, I couldn't say we were closer, but we had rallied together during the crisis and tragedy of Gwen's death, and at least we weren't sniping back and forth as much as we used to. A perverse part of me missed the sniping. However, he seemed as determined as I was to make the holidays as cheerful as possible for the girls.

I fluffed up a couple more branches at the top of the tree. The whole foyer was brighter and felt more inviting from the lights on the tree. "This should help to dispel some of the gloomy vibes in the house," I told him.

Still on the ladder, Bran faced me. "Let's banish the rest of that negativity out of here." His gaze met mine in a challenge, and he stretched out a hand to me from around the top of the tree.

He's offering to do magick with you. I realized with no small amount of surprise. "Okay, what sort of spell did you have in mind?" I said, reaching for his outstretched hand with my right.

Bran didn't take his eyes from mine. "Lend me some energy and follow along. I'll chant the spell, and you can do the closing," he said.

"Only the closing?" I raised an eyebrow at him.

"I've never worked magick one-on-one with you. I want to see how it goes this first time," Bran said reasonably.

"Okay." *Control freak.* I tried not to feel impatient that he didn't trust me more. *If he thought I was going to stand submissively by and watch, he had another thing coming...* I shook off my internal monologue and took a deep breath to ground myself. I visualized that I was steady and securely tethered to the earth, even though I was high on the staircase, and took a couple of nice even breaths. I let my own power flow from my center, down my arm, and to my hand. I flexed my fingers in Bran's and let him know I was ready.

"Two stand as one, in this time and hour," he said, maintaining eye contact with me. "With our combined magick we dispel all gloom and energy that—"

"Is sour!" I adlibbed, and fluttered my eyelashes at

him when he gave me a disapproving frown. "Hey, it rhymes— hour and sour," I pointed out.

"Yes it did. May I continue?"

"Sure, I just was in the moment." I managed a serious expression, but it was so damn easy to yank his chain.

"In reverence and joy," Bran began again. "With mind and heart; all energies not in alignment with us must now..."

"Depart!" I chimed in cheerfully.

"Autumn," Bran sighed, managing to be condescending even while he was several feet up in the air on a ladder, "you're breaking the energetic flow, I'll tell you when to do the closing."

"I'm sorry," I said, "I remembered that verse from when I saw Gwen do a banishing at the shop." I squared my shoulders. "Besides, it was Gwen who taught me that laughter can help banish gloomy vibes quicker than anything else."

He frowned over that, then his expression cleared. "Good point."

I gave his hand a friendly squeeze. "Let's start over and do the spell *together*."

Bran cleared his throat. "Say it with me then?"

All around us a dark, colder energy bore down. It unnerved me a bit, but I nodded at him to begin the spell verse in unison. "Two stand as one, in this time and hour; with our combined magick we dispel all gloom and energy that is sour."

As if we had done it so many times before, our voices fell in perfect time, and our magickal energies wove together from my hand to his— and his hand back to mine as we finished up the verse. "In reverence and joy, with mind and heart; all energies not in alignment with us must now depart."

The new, lighter and brighter energy was building up between us. It was warmer and stronger than what I'd imagined. I told myself to stay calm as I felt the pressure of the combating darker energy push against my back. I knew Bran was feeling it as well. I had a second of fear for him being up on the ladder and, all of a sudden, I wasn't so sure of what to do next.

"If you will allow me to add the next verse?" Bran asked smoothly.

With a nod, I silently gave him the go ahead.

"By the elements four, may light and happiness return to this place," Bran's voice sounded strong and sure. "Joy, protection and peace surround us now in a sacred space." As he finished, it felt like the entire house was holding its breath. "*Now* you can close the spell up," he told me.

Normally the smug expression on his face would have goaded me into some sort of verbal retaliation. But right now, his easy control of the battling energies of dark and light, and our combined magick, simply impressed the hell out of me. I raised my chin, determined to do my best and said, "By the powers of earth, air, fire and sea; as we will it..." I waited for him to join me.

"Then so must it be," we said as one, and the energy between us spiraled up and out.

The front door to the manor opened up all by itself, and the holiday music from the stereo became louder. I felt a rush of sour energy shooting down the steps towards the open door. I gripped Bran's hand tighter, as it seemed that the energy Bran and I had released was chasing the old negativity around and out.

Then I felt it all sweep past us and out of the house. The manor door closed smartly behind the departing energy, all on its own. I watched amazed as the lights on the tree seemed to pulse, and the chandelier in the foyer brightened as if it were turned up from an unseen switch. I took a breath, and the atmosphere felt noticeably lighter.

"Well *damn*, Sparky," I managed.

"That came out well." Bran gave my hand a friendly squeeze before releasing it. "Don't forget to ground and center your energy," he said, casually climbing down the step ladder. Once he reached the bottom, he called for Aunt Faye to come see the tree.

Aunt Faye came out from the kitchen, wiping her hands on a dish towel. She and Bran discussed the tree, and I reminded myself to reconnect to the earth. I came down the main staircase to join them, making the supreme effort to not show any reaction to Bran's easy handling of the battling energies of light and dark magick.

CHAPTER TWO

Having finished the assembly of the main tree in the foyer, Bran and I started working on a second, smaller artificial tree. We finally agreed to set it up in the family room off to one side of the fireplace. I regarded all of the bins of decorations, feeling overwhelmed, and started to wonder if decorating the manor *before* the girls got home was going to be too big of a job for the three of us to handle.

I heard a knock on the front door and went to the foyer. Before I could put my hand on the door knob the door blew open, and Marie Rousseau strolled into the manor, carrying several bags. "What's this I hear about a decorating party?" she said, unwrapping her striped scarf from her bright red coat.

"Hey Marie." I grinned at her as she gave the door a push with her foot to close it.

"Hey yourself. I ran into your great aunt at the market," she said, setting the bags aside. "Faye told me you could use a hand. Something about adding sparkle and magick?" Marie tossed her coat onto a bench in the foyer.

"We wanted to cheer up the girls," Bran said from the family room.

"Well then, it's a good thing the troops are on their way," Marie announced.

A moment later the door reopened, and Cora and Violet O'Connell from the flower shop marched in carrying boxes filled with red and white poinsettias. "Good Yule!" they cried as they came in.

On their heels were Theo and Zach with large open boxes filled with fresh branches of evergreens, and then came Lexie and Duncan carrying bags in from a local sandwich shop. "Happy Holidays, we brought lunch!" Lexie announced.

I went to Duncan to give him a kiss. To my surprise, he dodged me.

"Let me put down these bags," he said and walked stiffly into the family room. I waited for him to return, but as I watched, he dumped the food bags on the coffee table, took off his coat and gloves and sat down, alone.

Theo stuck his head into the family room. "Faye, love of my life, where are you?"

I heard Aunt Faye let loose a laugh. She came in the main foyer a moment later. She kissed Theo's handsome cheek. "You're only calling me that because I'm baking!"

I rolled my eyes at their silly flirting, knowing full

well that Theo was devoted to Zach. Zach only laughed at them. I stared at Duncan hard for a moment, and he returned my look with a bland stare. *Problem?* I sent the word from my mind to his.

No. I'm here, aren't I? He sent the thought back.

Trying a smile, I tipped my head in acknowledgement. Duncan didn't smile back. Instead, he turned to the fireplace. I wasn't sure what to make of him, but I went to give each of the coven members a welcoming hug. When I got to Marie, I added a squeeze. Over the past month, she and I had become a little closer and I considered her a friend. "I should have known you'd be here. Oh artsy crafty goddess."

Marie handed me a large shopping bag. "I have a little something new that might add that sparkle Faye said you were wanting."

"Oh?" I said, reaching in the bag and pulling out a box of metallic gold star shaped ornaments. Looking at the ornaments, I got the weirdest sensation of déjà vu. Without warning, I flashed back to a vision about Bran that I'd had months ago when I first came to live with Gwen.

Bran, all dapper and handsome in a tuxedo, was standing, beaming, by an evergreen tree that was lit up with white sparkling lights, and covered in gold star shaped ornaments. A woman wearing a long white dress walked down the manor stairs towards him. Her face was hidden by a veil, so I couldn't see her, or who she was.

With a snap, the vision ended. I shook my head, and the room gave a sickly little spin. Sights and sounds returned around me as the vision faded away. I shook my head again and realized that Marie was gripping my arm, speaking sharply to me.

"Autumn," she repeated.

"I'm okay," I said, even though I felt a little punch drunk.

Marie guided me straight towards the couch in the family room. "Sit down for a minute, you're pale."

"Are you alright?" Duncan asked as I sat next to him.

"Must have overdone it with the run this morning," I fibbed smoothly so everyone would stop staring at me. "No worries." I smiled at him, but he stood up, frowning at me.

Lexie passed out the food. Duncan brought me a sandwich and a bottle of water. "Here you go, put some food in your system." He handed them over and then Marie plopped down next to me.

"I'm fine. You don't have to hover. Either of you," I said.

Marie gave me a withering look, then smiled up at Duncan. "You go on, I've got your girl."

Duncan did not smile in return. He ran a finger down my cheek. I felt a trickle of his personal energy, but it felt *off.* "Eat something," he suggested brusquely and walked to the other side of the room.

While I puzzled over Duncan's behavior, the noise

increased exponentially as Violet, Cora and Aunt Faye began to debate the best places for the poinsettias to be arranged. Theo took Faye's side that the family room's mantle should be covered in the fresh greenery with the poinsettias being arranged strategically around the house. Zach argued that they should mix things up, and Violet sided with him.

Lexie took a few small logs from the basket beside the hearth and added them to the fire. I hid a grin as I listened to her argue, good naturedly, with Bran about the best way to stack logs. She seemed to enjoy yanking his chain almost as much as I did. I had to admit she was good for him. They were seriously adorable as they sat side-by-side on the hearth grinning at each other. The tough, loyal police officer and my too formal, serious academic brother.

"So, what did you *see*?" Marie asked, quietly. With the various conversations going on around us, it allowed for some privacy.

"Just a little replay of a precognitive vision I'd had months ago." I tried to brush it off.

"Spill it," Marie popped the top on her soda and drank.

I leaned in closer. "It was about Bran, I think he's going to get married. Soon," I said, and took a bite of my sandwich.

"How did seeing a box of ornaments kick that off?" Marie tilted her head. Her hair was braided in a myriad of micro braids and then bundled together in a thick mass at the nape of her neck.

I explained the vision to Marie, "The happy expression on his face, the woman in white walking to him... that was enough for me to know. Bran *is* going to be married. By the end of the year, judging by the decorated tree in the vision," I said.

"And the tree you saw was covered in gold stars?" Marie asked for clarification.

"Exactly like the star ornaments you bought today."

Marie grinned at me. "That boy, getting married without a heap of planning? He would *never* be spontaneous, it's not in his nature."

"We'll see," I said, thinking about the spur-of-the-moment spell we had performed a short while ago. I knew for a fact Bran could be spontaneous. *I really needed to forget what I'd walked in on in October when he and Lexie were...* Nope, unless I wanted to end up in therapy, it would be best to put that out of my mind. Forever.

The sandwiches were scarfed down, and then jobs were assigned. Cora and Violet would decorate the mantle and the four foot tree in the family room. Faye would oversee Theo's placement of various decorations from the family's totes around the lower level of the house. Duncan and Lexie would decorate the main staircase, and Zach, Marie, Bran, and I would trim out the main tree in the foyer.

Marie checked her watch. "We have three hours before the girls get home. Let's get to work."

I'd never decorated so much in such a short amount of time. But with the coven lending a hand, it was outrageously fun. We decided to decorate the main tree simply by using the bright red metallic and plain white glass ornaments the family already owned and adding the boxes of gold stars. The mood was so refreshingly cheerful now that I wondered if it *was* because Bran and I had done that big banishing spell earlier in the day.

As she handed out the star ornaments, Marie smiled. "These will really add that sparkle you talked about. Now I know why I felt compelled to buy eight boxes of these."

"A little Yuletide magick, no doubt." I wiggled my eyebrows at her as we placed the stars strategically to add impact to the tree.

Zach worked his way around the big tree tucking in branches of silk holly, singing along with the holiday music from the stereo. Cora pulled several spools of holiday ribbon out of one of her boxes and proceeded to tie up a massive tree topper ribbon. I had to appreciate her quick work of attaching the white and gold bow and then artfully arranging the streamers to cascade down the tree. In less than five minutes, she was done and back to work in the family room.

I jogged down the steps and stood by the front door to check our work. This holiday tree was very different compared to how heavily the Halloween tree had been decorated. But it was elegant in its simplicity, and those red and white glass balls popped against the green branches. The white lights sparkled, while the new golden star shaped ornaments gleamed. Seeing an aspect of my vision manifested in physical reality made my stomach feel all jittery, but the holiday tree was very festive, cheerful and pretty.

Bran had insisted that the family's traditional Yuletide garland go in its typical spot on the main staircase. It made sense, as it was ready to go with white lights and pre-decorated with silk sprays of holly, ivy and mistletoe. The massive twenty foot garland needed to be fluffed up after being stored, but Duncan and Lexie had stretched out the garland on the second floor landing and had gotten to work. With a minimum of fuss they attached it to the handrail with zip ties, and then plugged it into an outlet on the second floor landing.

"I have the outdoor lights set aside." Lexie walked over to stand with me and admire our work. "I bet the girls would like to decorate the front porch themselves tonight."

"Good idea," I said, watching Cora arrange a big crystal bowl of multi colored glass ornaments in the formal living room. She added a few poinsettias on tables, while Theo tucked fresh evergreen branches behind the ornate gilded mirror in the living room, creating a simple frame of greenery. I was seriously impressed with Cora as she worked methodically from room to room. By adding simple, natural touches here and there, the impact she created was huge.

"It's beautiful, Cora," I said to her.

She smiled at me as she walked past. "Give a floral designer a box of decorations, a little fresh greenery, and step back."

Violet, wearing a blue sweater with a snowman on it, carried a huge fresh evergreen wreath past us. She took an over-the-door metal hanger, slipped it over the front door and hung the decorated wreath on the inside of the door. "After the girls get home, then put the wreath on the *outside*."

I tugged on the white and red striped bow. "This is great."

"Before I forget," Violet said, blowing her purple streaked bangs out of her eyes, "Mom and I went ahead and placed the memorial wreaths at the cemetery ourselves, before we came over."

"Thank you," I said, quietly. "I would have done it myself in the morning."

"Do you mind that we did?" Violet asked.

"No," I said, "you were friends with Gwen, I appreciate you taking care of it for me."

Violet gave my hand a squeeze. "You need anything, anything at all, you call. Okay?"

"Thanks Violet," I said, appreciating her kindness.

After we finished the decorating, Duncan and Bran hauled the empty storage totes back up to the attic, while Zach swept the foyer. Marie, Lexie and I wandered into the family room, and I stood frozen as I saw all of the festive touches that had been added to the dining room, family room and finally over into the kitchen. The various holiday lights sparkled, making the manor seem magickal again. "Wow, the girls are going to love this!" I slung my arms around Lexie and Marie laughing with delight.

***

By the time three o'clock rolled around, I was a nervous wreck. Duncan, Violet, Cora, Theo and Zach had all gone back to work or home. Lexie was in the kitchen helping Faye with a batch of gingerbread cookies. Bran was lighting red and white candles in the living room and dining room, while Marie and I peeked out the front window, keeping watch for the girls.

I fidgeted nervously, my mind bouncing back and forth. *How would the girls react? According to Bran, the décor was very different from what Gwen had typically done. Maybe that was a good thing, or would that cause tears and sadness?* I nudged the curtain farther back to see better. *Why had Duncan left without kissing me goodbye? Perhaps he was tired… or was he frustrated because we hadn't spent any time alone since Gwen's death? Maybe I should—*

Marie poked me in the ribs. "You are projecting your worry."

"I'm a little anxious," I admitted, trying to relax as soft instrumental music of traditional carols played on the stereo.

Marie slung an arm around my shoulders. "You did a good thing here."

"What if they don't like it?" I bit my lip and wondered.

"Too late to worry now," Marie whispered. "They're walking up the driveway."

"Oh shit," I said. Marie grabbed my arm, and we scrambled to the foyer to stand by the big tree.

Bran let out a low whistle, and the rest of the family gathered in next to us and waited to see the girls' reactions.

I could hear Cypress Rousseau keeping up a bright chatter as she walked up the front porch steps. "...so I said to the choir director, he needed to add songs to the Winter Concert that were Pagan friendly too," she said.

"You did?" Ivy's voice carried into the house.

I squeezed Marie's hand while we waited for the girls to open the door. Ivy stepped in first, with Holly behind her. They both stopped and stared.

"Oh look at that!" Ivy said, sounding awestruck.

The twins stood gaping at the star covered eight foot tree. Cypress shut the door quietly behind the girls. She gave a thumbs up sign to us and moved off to the side.

Holly set her backpack down and peeked into the living room. "That's pretty," she said of the simple touches Cora O'Connell had done. She walked to the other side of the foyer and checked the family room. "Ivy, come and see," Holly said.

I tried to see the decorations through the twin's eyes. Red and white lights strung throughout the array of fresh evergreen branches on the family room mantle. A trio of hand-carved deer were tucked in the greenery as well. The small primitive tree was off to the side of the fireplace, where a fire burned merrily in the grate. The rustic tree was covered with white lights, vintage ornaments, and strings of wooden red beads that resembled cranberries. A bright red and white quilt served as a tree skirt.

I couldn't take the suspense and followed the girls as they looked around. I tried not to wring my hands as they took in the candles and red and white poinsettias grouped together on the dining room table.

"It's different from what mom usually did," Holly said, quietly. Her expression was so neutral I couldn't tell if she was angry, surprised or upset.

Ivy bounced into the kitchen. "Ooh, it smells great in here!" She snatched a cookie off a cooling rack and bit the head off a gingerbread man. "Hey, I love that fresh evergreen roping with the red bows for the kitchen windows!" she said with her mouth full.

"Autumn thought that the manor deserved a little bit of holiday cheer," Bran announced as he came into the room behind me. "She... I mean *we*— we all wanted to surprise you." He dropped a hand on my shoulder and stood with me.

"Bran and I set up the trees, and then the coven came over to help decorate," I explained.

"I did the baking," Aunt Faye said.

"It's *awesome,* you guys," Ivy said, her eyes brimming with tears.

She spun and rushed at Bran and me. I managed to not get knocked over when she threw her arms around us both— only because Bran steadied me. Bran ran a hand down Ivy's hair, and I heard her give a hiccupping sort of teary laugh.

Aunt Faye studied Holly as she walked into the kitchen to check out the decorations. "Well Holly, what do you have to say?" she asked her.

"It's not the same... but it feels like Yuletide." Holly smiled a little, running a hand over a green pottery bowl that was centered on the kitchen table. Little sprigs of fresh holly leaves were artfully arranged in with the bright red apples.

The rest of the gang strolled into the kitchen. Holly stood, staring at the group, until Aunt Faye held out her arms to her. Then Holly went to our great aunt and laid her head on her shoulder. Holly let out a shuddering sigh. "It's beautiful. Thanks everyone."

***

For the first time, I celebrated the sabbat of Yuletide on the morning of the winter solstice. The family, including Lexie who'd spent the night, all came downstairs together in robes, pajamas, or sweat pants. We gathered in front of the fireplace in the family room and exchanged simple gifts. Lexie built a fire, and she and Bran sat on the hearth. Aunt Faye held court in her favorite chair, while the twins and I sat on the floor. Merlin attacked his new cat toys with glee while we took turns unwrapping our presents.

Holly and Ivy surprised us all with framed photos. The photography was Ivy's, and Holly had them framed. I got misty when I unwrapped my present from the twins, a photo of me and Gwen together, that Ivy had taken at the Homecoming game. I decided immediately to add it to my framed photo collection on the mantle in my bedroom. It was also bittersweet when we realized that there were several gifts from Gwen.

"How?" I asked Bran as I studied the beautiful leather journal embossed with my initials.

"Mom usually starting her shopping early, and then stashed the gifts in the same place every year," Bran explained.

"I've wanted this book on herbs forever." Holly held a massive hard-back book on herbalism in her lap. As she flipped through it I could see photographs and descriptions of the herbs.

Ivy held a new camera lens, a gift from her mother. "It's almost like having her here."

"There was one gift for each of us, and a few more — but I couldn't figure out who those would have been for," Bran said. "Nevertheless, I wrapped up the gifts and put them under the tree for everyone."

"What did she get you?" I asked him, impressed at

the thoughtfulness of his gesture.

"A first edition of a book that I've been wanting for years." He held up the present that he'd unwrapped earlier. The one I'd assumed had been from Lexie.

Lexie slung an arm around him and lent him support. "What did you get, Aunt Faye?" she asked the older woman.

"Let's see..." Aunt Faye's voice sounded a little shaky. She smiled as she opened a package that contained a gorgeous plum colored fringed shawl.

Wow," Holly said, "that looks like silk."

"It is," Aunt Faye said. She gently folded the shawl back into the box and then cleared her throat briskly. "Let's get breakfast going." She stood up and Holly joined her.

"I already preheated the oven for the rolls," Holly said as they started towards the kitchen.

"Cinnamon rolls!" Ivy cheered and jumped up to help.

I stayed on the floor and started to gather up the discarded wrapping paper. Lexie handed me a garbage bag and then stood up to move her gifts off to the side of the hearth.

"Autumn, thanks for the insulated gloves. I really can use them when I..." Lexie's voice trailed off.

I glanced up at her. "Hey, are you okay? You're awfully pale."

"Yeah," Lexie shook her head slightly, then clutched her stomach. "I felt light headed for a second."

Bran shot to his feet and guided Lexie over to the big comfy chair Aunt Faye preferred. "You said your stomach was bothering you." He frowned and then crouched down next to her.

"I hope I'm not catching that flu that was going around." Lexie leaned back in her chair and blew out a breath. "I've been feeling off for a couple of weeks now."

"I'll get you some ginger ale," I volunteered. "That should help your stomach." I came back with a chilled can a moment later and tried not to smile at how Bran stayed by her side.

"Here you go." I handed Lexie the can. When she reached out for it, our fingers brushed. The room fell away— to be replaced by a vision.

Lexie sat in the same big comfy chair in the family room. The fireplace was unlit, and the mantle was decorated with an arrangement of sunflowers, ferns, and yellow and white candles. Lexie's dark blonde hair hung down her back, and she sang quietly to a baby that she held in her arms. The baby was wrapped in a light blanket, and it waved a small fist in the air. Lexie smiled, and pressed a kiss to the baby's thick red hair. Bran crouched down next to the chair and handed Lexie a bright yellow baby rattle.

I blinked a couple of times in reaction to what I had just *seen*. The vision faded away, and for once I didn't feel that slightly sick feeling that accompanied my visions. I saw the worried expressions on both Bran and

Lexie's faces, and my heart lifted.

"You've had a vision." Bran pointed at me.

"Yeah, I did." I worked hard to sound calm and as blasé as possible.

"Was it about *me*?" Lexie asked.

"Yes, of your future," I admitted.

"What? What did you see?" Lexie asked, looking a little green around the gills.

Neither of them knew, I realized. I couldn't help it, I stood there grinning at the two of them. *This was the best possible news, ever.*

"What's going on?" Aunt Faye came back into the family room, frowning at the three of us. Holly and Ivy trailed along behind her.

"So tell me. What did you see?" Lexie asked, taking a sip of the ginger ale.

I rubbed at my forehead and stalled. *Was there a guideline for telling a woman that she was pregnant— before she knew herself— because of a vision?* I wondered how to politely break the news.

I chose my words carefully. "Lexie, I don't think you have the flu. In the vision I had— you were sitting in that chair, singing to a baby."

"*What?*" Lexie and Bran said, in unison.

"There were sunflowers on the mantle. It felt like summertime, come to think of it..." I grinned at my brother as his face went paler than Lexie's.

"Oh my Goddess," Lexie whispered. She turned to Bran. "I skipped my period last month... but I thought that was because of the stress and everything that happened."

Aunt Faye patted Lexie's shoulder. "My dear, you need to make a doctors appointment."

While Holly and Ivy did identical happy little squeals, Lexie pressed her hand to her mouth, laughing and crying at the same time.

Bran took the ginger ale away from Lexie and set it aside. Then he drew her to her feet and pulled Lexie close.

Well, I don't have to wonder how Bran felt about the prospect of becoming a father. I felt myself tearing up a little as I watched them as they swayed back and forth, sort of dancing around the family room. After a moment they let go of each other, and Bran and Lexie sat down on the couch together.

"This is wonderful!" Aunt Faye said to the pair. "Congratulations to you both!"

"We should have the pregnancy confirmed by a doctor," Bran pointed out, but he was still smiling.

"You go right ahead," Aunt Faye told Bran. "But I am backing up Autumn's prediction."

Lexie sniffled, smiling up at me. "Were there any other pertinent details in your vision?" she asked.

Ivy sat down on Lexie's other side and gave her a hug. "You sounded very cop-like just now."

"Well?" Lexie asked me, sounding a little anxious.

"The baby was wrapped in a light blanket, and it had *red* hair," I said.

"Hair the same color red as Bran's?" Lexie laughed in wonder.

"Yeah, it had a *lot* of hair, oh and Bran, I saw you in the vision too." I focused on him. "You were kneeling next to Lexie and the baby, and you handed Lexie a yellow baby rattle."

Bran jumped to his feet. "A *yellow* baby rattle?" He repeated his eyes wide.

"Yes," I replied slowly, genuinely confused at his reaction to the rattle, of all things.

"Wait a second." Bran bolted out of the family room and dashed up the main stairs.

"What the hell?" Ivy said.

"Lexie, can I get you anything?" Holly asked her.

"Yeah, that ginger ale." Lexie pointed to her open can.

Holly went to fetch it and handed it to Lexie who took a quick shot of ginger ale as Bran jogged back down into the family room with a shopping bag.

Bran went directly to Lexie. "Remember how I said there were a few gifts that my Mom had bought that I couldn't figure out who they belonged to?"

"Yes," Lexie said.

"*This* was one of the gifts." Bran reached in the bag and pulled out a bright yellow baby rattle.

CHAPTER THREE

The next week passed in a blur of activity and excitement. Lexie was indeed pregnant, and the twin's eighteenth birthday came and went with a small party that they seem to enjoy. To add to the chaos, Bran announced to the family that he and Lexie were going to get married right away. In a handfasting—an old school wedding ceremony— on New Year's Eve at the manor.

Lexie seemed to be doing pretty well besides some dizziness and a bit of nausea. But bedsides our family, she was keeping her pregnancy quiet. She hadn't even told her parents, as she and Bran had decided to announce the big news at their wedding reception. Now, Aunt Faye and Lexie's mother, Nancy, were thick as thieves, planning the wedding and driving the caterer crazy with menu ideas. The twins were excited, and as the maid of honor, I got suckered into going shopping with Marie and Lexie for the wedding gown. While I was not a big fan of shopping, at least it got me away from the menu craziness.

"I don't want white. No matter what my mother says," Lexie warned Marie as we hit yet another department store. The after-the-holidays sales were in full swing, and I wondered how we'd find anything remotely bridal. My dress had been easy. Marie had found a tea length deep blue dress, and I had fallen in love with the 1950's retro vibe it had. The neckline was simple, and the dress had cap sleeves. The skirt poofed a little and had a bit of sparkly trim at the hemline.

Marie continued to work her shopping mojo and pulled various formal and cocktail type dresses for Lexie to try on. Meanwhile, the bride sat in the fitting room, flushed and overwhelmed, fanning herself.

I stood outside the open door of the fitting room and checked my cell phone, smiling over a text that Duncan, the Best Man, had sent. "Duncan says the groom has ordered the tuxedos."

"What color did they get?" Lexie snapped.

"Easy there, Lexie," I told her.

"Sorry." Lexie blew out a breath, and made a face. "I sounded like a brat, but I'm starving, cranky and tired."

"I was thinking of another B word— Bridezilla." I fluttered my lashes at my future sister-in-law.

"Watch it," Lexie warned me.

"You're not armed, are you?" I studied her as she sat in her bra and underwear, as if checking for her service pistol.

Lexie snickered. "Would you *please* text Duncan

back and ask what color tux Bran chose for himself, my dad and Duncan?"

"Sure, since you asked me nicely. Just keep your hands where I can see them," I ordered.

Lexie let loose a loud bawdy laugh at my snarkiness. Marie brought in a few more dresses for Lexie to consider. "By the gods, I'm *not* wearing pink to my handfasting." Lexie waved off the pale pink gown. She pressed a hand to her stomach as it growled loudly.

Marie dug in her purse and produced a protein bar. "Here, girlfriend, gnaw on this." She held out the bar, and Lexie pounced on it.

I leaned back against the doorframe and felt a little tingle. While Lexie considered and rejected dress after dress, I followed a little tug at my solar plexus and went back to the sales floor. I walked around the large circular rack where I felt a strong pull.

The sales rack was a mish-mash of sizes and colors. I trailed my fingers above the cocktail dresses, and when they brushed against a gold dress I felt a stronger tug from my midsection. I pushed the dresses apart and discovered a simple cap sleeved gown. It was long, and fluid. The top was a pretty nude color, and sequins shimmered against it in soft champagne gold. It was a size 12, and Lexie wore a size 10, but I pulled it out anyway. I held it out and considered. It was pretty, elegant and sparkly. It was marked down seventy percent too. My intuition had led me to this dress, and it felt like it was giving me a high-five over the find.

I took a deep breath and went back to the fitting rooms. "How about champagne gold?" I asked Lexie as I held it up.

Lexie tossed a silver and blue gown at Marie. "Oh *wow*. Bring that over here!"

As I walked to hand her the long gown I watched Lexie's entire expression change.

"Let's get this on you." Marie hustled Lexie into the gown, and I went to stand out by the three way mirror and waited.

A few moments later Lexie made her way out to the big mirror, and I held my breath. Marie followed her, wisely staying silent as the bride decided on the gown.

Lexie stood, shimmering in the champagne gold gown. It fit her well, and as Marie and I watched, Lexie began to run her hands down the skirt almost as if she were petting it. "This is it," Lexie stated.

"It's beautiful," Marie said.

"Is the top a little too big?" Lexie lifted her long hair up, twisted, and studied her reflection.

Marie moved in quickly to adjust the gown. "I can take this up a bit.' She reached behind and pulled the shoulder seams up a little. "See?" she said to the bride. "It would look more like this after I take it in."

"It's fabulous," I told her honestly. My cell phone chimed and I checked the incoming message. "Duncan says the groom's tux will be black with a white shirt and black tie." I watched while Lexie pursed her lips and considered.

"Can he get a champagne gold colored tie instead of black?" Lexie asked.

"That would be very nice with your dress," Marie said, "especially if he got a gold pocket square."

"Yes, let's do it!" Lexie agreed. Then she threw her arms around Marie and I. "Thanks so much for helping me!"

I struggled to hug her back and text Duncan at the same time. "It's a great color on you. Perfect for New Year's Eve too," I told her and then sent the text about the tie.

"Let's go pay for this and get you some lunch," Marie suggested.

"Hooray! Lunch!" Lexie cried, and dashed into a fitting room to change.

"Then, after lunch we have to go visit Violet and get your bridal flowers and bouquet ordered." Marie reminded her.

"Right," Lexie called out.

"Duncan texted me back. Bran has changed the tie and pocket square to a gold color." I told Lexie as she walked out with the gown draped over her arm.

Lexie's smile lit up the store. "Do you suppose Violet can get champagne colored roses for my bouquet?"

"Anything is possible," Marie said.

***

I had seen plenty of magick since moving to William's Ford. But seeing the family pull off a wedding in a week was pretty impressive. Twenty rented chairs were lined up in the foyer, and the holiday decorations added plenty of sparkle. I stood in my new dark blue dress and peered over the landing of the second floor. I watched a tuxedoed Bran stand and talk to Duncan. Duncan was Best Man today and was as polished and sophisticated as I'd ever seen him in his black tux. I lifted a hand to my own hair that Violet had worked into a pretty up-do.

Lexie's mother stood and talked with Aunt Faye, Violet and Cora O'Connell. Cypress chatted with Holly and Ivy, who looked great in their re-worn homecoming dresses. Kyle and Shannon Jacobs were in attendance as well. As it ended up, Shannon was Lexie's first cousin. They had left Sophia and Chloe, aka. Sleeping Beauty and Cinderella, at home with a sitter.

I checked the time on the hall clock. It was five minutes before 8:00 pm. I saw Lexie's father give me the nod. I smiled at him as he started up the stairs to escort his daughter to the ceremony. I ducked back in my bedroom where Marie was putting the finishing touches on the bride.

Lexie stood shimmering in the long champagne gold gown. The sequins caught the lamplight and quietly sparkled. Her hair was curled in loose waves, and they spilled down her back. A floral crown rested on her head with tiny baby roses in ivory and dainty sprays of gilded baby's breath. Lexie had kept her jewelry to a minimum with a pair of sparkly, champagne colored drop earrings. The dress didn't need anything else.

"Your father's on his way up." I said, and picked up my small bouquet of peach carnations and ivory roses.

Lexie seemed absolutely calm as Marie handed her the bouquet of ivory and pale peach colored roses. Marie pressed her cheek against Lexie's. "Blessed be," Marie said, and left to go downstairs.

A moment later, the music began for the bridal procession, and I glanced back at the bride. "You're beautiful, Lexie." I smiled at her.

"I'm not showing, am I?" she whispered to me before her father joined us

"No, don't worry, you'll be able to surprise the guests the way you wanted."

Lexie let out a breath and then held out her arm to her father as he arrived. "Hi, Dad."

John Proctor kissed his daughter's brow. "Love you, Lexie," he said.

I started forward and tried not to think how my father wouldn't be able to give me away at my wedding someday. I shook that sad thought off and slowly went down the stairs in my new black pumps. When I made my way around the curve in the staircase, I saw Duncan and Bran standing, waiting with the officiant.

I beamed at Great Aunt Faye, Holly and Ivy who sat in the front row on the right side. Marie and Cypress were in the row behind with Violet and Cora

O'Connell. Zach and Theo were behind them. I observed a few people from the university also sitting on the groom's side.

As I took my place past the officiant, I saw that Mrs. Proctor was already crying even before Lexie and her father came down the main staircase of the manor. Every one stood up, and I watched my brother turn to watch for his bride as she appeared around the curve of the staircase. It gave me an intense feeling of déjà vu.

The vision I'd had months ago had shown me Bran standing by a tree covered in gold stars as a bride walked towards him. While the bride wasn't wearing white as I'd seen, I realized as John prepared to give his daughter away that the white had been a symbol. A way for me to understand it was a *wedding* that I was seeing. At the time I hadn't known Bran was actually my half brother, but I was delighted that his bride, and my soon-to-be sister in law, was Lexie Proctor.

I took Lexie's bouquet, and the bride and groom joined hands, standing before their officiant. My eyes met Duncan's, and I had a hard time paying attention to anything else.

***

The ceremony had been lovely, and the photography session blessedly brief. The guests demolished the fancy catered food and were dancing to a combination of holiday songs and popular music. Duncan and I danced and mingled with the guests, but I had the funniest feeling that something was off with him even though he was perfectly polite, and a picture perfect Best Man— he appeared so stylish. *Not at all like my Duncan with his jeans and tool belt.* I laughed to myself recalling when I'd first met him; I'd figured he'd learned his smooth moves at some exclusive boarding school.

Now that I was witnessing him at a formal social event, I wondered if it was simply the elegant manners that were throwing me off. His etiquette was flawless as he politely danced with the bride, the twins, and even Great Aunt Faye; but every time I looked at him he felt more and more of a stranger. After the cake had been cut, and people started to dance again, I was finally able to move into a nice slow dance with Duncan.

I put my arms around him and lay my head on his shoulder. I reached out for him with my magick, as I always did when we were together, and I felt Duncan stiffen up. He pulled away from me a little and I was surprised at his snub. "What's wrong?" I asked. "You've been acting a little distant all night."

"I'm fulfilling my duties as Best Man." He held me away from him in a more formal slow dance type of pose.

I felt the familiar mingling of our magickal energies. They flowed from where our hands held, then down and around the two of us, wrapping us together in our own little magickal cocoon. My shoulders dropped and I relaxed a little. I smiled at him and tried again. "Things have been crazy lately with the wedding and the holidays. I've missed you," I said.

"That's alright... we needed to take a break for a while."

I stopped dancing and stared at him, shocked. "*What did you say?*"

"I think that maybe we moved a little too fast, too soon." Duncan gave my fingers a warning squeeze.

I noticed people staring at us, so I stepped back into the dance. Bran and Lexie swayed by us and we both gave them a smile. Mine was sincere, but Duncan's seemed false. "I'm afraid I'm not following you," I said to Duncan as calmly as possible as soon as the bride and groom moved out of earshot.

You probably didn't know that shared magick and psychic abilities can give a false illusion of intimacy between people. Duncan's voice sounded in my mind even as we danced in a room full of guests.

False illusion of intimacy? I sent the words back to him. That cocoon of energy was still snug around the two of us, and confused, I tripped a little.

Duncan righted me, but he blew out an impatient breath. I opened my mouth to speak, but Bran and Lexie were dancing right next to us again. Duncan pulled me a tiny bit closer as the luminous bride and groom danced past us. *Let's not make a scene.* I heard his thoughts clearly. He squeezed my hand. "Come with me." He led me away from the party and out onto the front porch. Once we were outside he dropped my hand immediately, turning away from me. The magickal energy that we'd shared ended abruptly.

I shuddered in reaction. "What the hell is going on? What's the matter with you?" I asked him.

"Oh, Autumn." He let out a long suffering sigh and shook his head. "What am I going to do with you?"

My stomach dropped and all of my instincts went on full alert. The man I thought I'd known seemed a stranger as he raked me with his gaze. His tone of voice had been insulting and dismissive at the same time, reminding me all too much of his twisted cousin Julian.

It also *really* pissed me off.

"Since your Aunt passed away, we haven't had much time together," Duncan said. "This imposed time apart has given me time to think things over."

I marched over and got up in his face. "Did you get hit in the head recently? 'Imposed time apart?' What the hell is wrong with you?"

He stepped back from me. "I simply think it's best for everyone if we take a break for a while."

My mind reeled. The callous brush off, his formal dialogue, and his mannerisms... Duncan wasn't even acting like himself. *He's trying to hide something.*

"Tell me what's going on with you, or I'll look for myself," I warned him. I didn't always have to touch someone to read them — not if there was enough juice in the atmosphere. The confusion, and yes, the *anger* I felt at Duncan's behavior was giving me plenty of power... So, I chucked my ethics, rifled through his memories, and I hit on one.

A big one.

My mouth dropped open in shock. "You have the bindings for the Blood Moon Grimoire?"

"Stay out of my memories, Autumn," Duncan snapped. "I was going to tell you... eventually." He turned away from me and stared out into the night. "They were a peace offering."

"A peace offering? Are you *crazy*?" I grabbed his jacket sleeve shaking it to get his attention while he stared off into space.

"I knew you'd react badly," Duncan sighed, and brushed my fingers away.

"You guessed right, you idiot!" I tried to keep my voice low, but I was starting to lose what was left of my temper. "Please tell me that you put the leather cover in a lead box, or at least surrounded the bindings with salt to protect yourself from their negativity."

"No, it wasn't necessary. I've got it under control, and I'm fine," Duncan shot back.

"You aren't acting *fine*," I argued.

"Don't bitch at me. You don't have the answers to everything. You're still a novice, Autumn. And unlike your family— I am perfectly capable of taking care of this."

I sucked a breath in at his insult to my family. *What the hell was with him?*

Duncan spun and surveyed me from the railing. "The

last few months have been pretty intense. But, I don't think you are experienced enough to handle things as they are now."

I felt my heart crack at his careless words. "Are you saying that I'm not *Witch* enough to be with you anymore?" I asked him quietly.

"Maybe...That depends on a couple of things," he said, making the hair rise up on the back of my neck.

My heart started to beat faster, from fear or confusion I wasn't sure. Standing there in that beautiful tux he seemed cultured and sophisticated in a way that I would never be. He moved slowly forward and leaned in close to my face. The multi-colored holiday lights on the front porch made his eyes seem almost orange. My heart dropped to my stomach. "Duncan," I began, reaching out to him.

"I was attracted to you— even before I knew who you were." His voice was low, almost a purr, as he ran his hands over my shoulders, tugging me closer and tucking my head under his chin.

Fascinated, I let him take charge.

"We come from very different types of magickal traditions," he said. "Two different worlds, actually." His grip became painful, even as he rubbed his cheek gently over the top of my hair.

"That's true." I managed, thinking of all the times I'd wondered what a magician of his caliber was doing with a new Witch like me.

He pulled back a bit to meet my eyes. "And in many

ways we are too far apart."

I slowly reached up to pry his fingers loose from where they dug in my arms. "You once told me that you walked your own path. Was that a lie?" I willed myself not to cry.

"No, it wasn't." Duncan suddenly let go of my arms, only to clamp his hands on both sides of my face. He lowered his mouth to hover above my own. "But the cost to both of our families has been very high." He brushed his lips over mine. "I don't want to see anyone else suffer."

I tried to stay calm. However, that soft kiss was at odds with the too tight grip on my face. My heart was galloping in my chest as I covered his hands. "You're hurting me," I told him as calmly as I could.

He brushed another devastating kiss over my lips even as he spoke, "I don't want you to *be* hurt again. Don't you understand?"

My body was sending me mixed signals. Part of me registered that he was digging his fingers too harshly into my skin. My intuition was screaming at me that I should get away from him; while another part of me was straining towards his mouth that he held just out of reach. "So you're breaking up with me for my own good?" I managed to get the words out.

"I have to. I want you to be safe." He took a quick nip at my bottom lip, then he eased the sting with another soft kiss.

My mouth dried up from fear, and crazily, desire.

"Duncan," I said trying to get through to him. I saw that his eyes were a burning orange... *and it wasn't from the holiday lights on the front porch.*

"Autumn," he whispered before crushing his mouth down on mine.

This was different from any other way he'd touched me before. Desperate, intense and a little frightening. I wasn't sure whether I should hang on and enjoy the ride — or be afraid of him. He lifted his mouth from mine, yanked my head back by my hair, and latched on to my neck like a vampire.

Despite myself I gasped, shivered, and held on.

"You've always been eager to learn more magick..." Duncan muttered as he nipped his way up the side of my throat towards my mouth. "Maybe I could..." He kissed my mouth hard, cutting off his own words.

He forced his tongue into my mouth, and I started to struggle against him— considered biting him to get him to stop. Maybe he read my intention, because he yanked his mouth away in the nick of time. He pushed his lower body into mine, backing me up, and pinning me to the wall. "Hey, take it easy," I said trying to get control of the situation. "We are on the front porch, *anybody* can see us out here."

"I bet you would enjoy it, the darker side of magick." His mouth twisted up into a cruel parody of his usual charming grin.

I measured this stranger who was treating me so roughly. This wasn't the Duncan I had come to know.

"Duncan *stop*," I said firmly and pushed away from the house. He shoved me back so hard, my head cracked against the siding.

I saw stars for a second. But the sharp pain of the assault cleared my thoughts. *The bindings of the grimoire...* Thomas had told me that the bindings of the Blood Moon Grimoire had sent Julian into madness. Trapped against the side of the manor, while Duncan ground his mouth down on mine, I realized that Duncan's exposure to the book's bindings had turned him violent.

"Duncan Drake Quinn, take your hands off me," I said, when he came up for air. There was *power* in names. Great Aunt Faye had taught me that. "Duncan Drake Quinn, stop—" He silenced me with another rough kiss. I tried reaching out to him from my mind to his. *Duncan, stop this! You're hurting me, damn it!*

Maybe I like it. His careless response echoed in my mind.

While his mouth smothered mine, a foul energy snaked around our bodies, and I could sense my own magick building up, and reaching out blindly to his... the way it always had. I felt his magick connect to mine, and for the first time it felt twisted, and wrong.

Stop! I pushed the word at him, fighting back in anger and fear. I tried to shout, but the sound was muffled by his mouth. As I strained to break free from his embrace, the magickal energy, always between us, snapped and flared to life. It ignited the surrounding air in an ugly, neon red color as I struggled against him.

Suddenly, I smelled roses. On that freezing cold porch the scent pulsed around me strong and true. *I wasn't alone tonight.* That realization helped to clear my head and reminded me who and what I was. Reaching deep inside myself, I pulled up my magick with the full intention of putting Duncan on his ass. With a growl of anger, I yanked my hands free and slapped both of them flat against his chest—striking out at him with every bit of magick that I had.

Duncan was knocked back a good five feet.

"Damn it!" He bent over placing his hands on his knees, panting and as he shook off my magickal attack.

Through my tears I saw a pink mist encircling me. It wafted around as I sagged against the wall of the manor trying to catch my breath. I glanced around, but there was no sign of my grandmother's ghost. Only her trademark scent. *Thank you, Grandma Rose!*

"Shit," I whispered. The palms of my hands felt like they were on fire, and I felt sick to my stomach. The after effects of his rough treatment and from me slapping out with magick to get him off me. I tested my raw bottom lip with my tongue and tasted blood.

Duncan lifted his head. "Why did you do that?" he asked, and seemed genuinely confused.

"Duncan, you are not yourself." My voice shook as I wiped the blood away from my lip, easing farther away from him. "The man I know would *never* treat me that way."

His gaze settled on my mouth and he licked his own lips, tasting my blood. Seeing him do that made my stomach lurch.

"The bindings of the grimoire *have* affected you," I said. "Do you even realize that?" As I watched, the circle of pink mist grew to enfold him as well.

He glanced down at the mist and shuddered. His eyes began to slowly change, almost to their normal shade of blue. "Autumn, what happened?" he said.

"Try and remember," I suggested, and stayed where I was.

Duncan reached out to me, I backed away, and he froze. His eyes going huge. "Oh shit! Did I hurt you?" he asked, obviously realizing what he'd done.

"Yes, you did." I wiped a few tears from my face.

"I don't know what the hell just happened to me." He walked over to the front porch railing and leaned over it. Duncan took in great gulps of air and I stayed away from him in case he acted out again. Slowly, the pink mist and the fragrance of roses faded away.

"Duncan, you have to get rid of the grimoire's bindings. They are affecting you—changing you, like they did to Julian," I said.

"I can't. I have an obligation to see this quest through," Duncan said, sounding tired. "This is why I thought we should take a break for a while... I had no idea that my reaction would be this severe."

I stayed where I was and watched him.

"I'm sorry that I hurt you... I won't let that happen

again," he said.

He sounded sincere, but as I studied him I could *see* all too clearly that if we were to stay together, this *would* happen again. Another fabulous perk of my being a Seer. My heart sank at the glimpse of our future together.

I squared my shoulders. "I won't change my mind on the danger of the grimoire's bindings," I said, shaking both from what had happened and from the cold. "If you intend to keep those bindings, then we are over."

"Let's not be overly dramatic," Duncan said, turning to face me, and it was still there— a bit of an odd light in his eyes.

He started towards me, and I took an instinctive step back. "You stay the hell away from me."

Duncan froze and then shook himself. As I watched, his eyes flickered orange, and back to blue again. "I'll go," he agreed. "Again, I am sorry things got... out of hand. I hope you can believe that." His soulful expression almost made me cry again.

"Go." I pressed my hands against my stomach that had started to pitch.

Duncan nodded and then moved so quickly away that he blurred. I shivered in reaction from his disappearance. I heard his car start up and I waited, watching him pull away from the manor.

Only after I was sure that he was gone did I let myself back in the front door. I ducked back inside, thankful that no one was in the foyer. I stepped out of my heels and dashed upstairs to the hall bathroom. I barely made it. After a hideous few minutes of heaving, I managed to get up and splash cool water on my face, then used some mouthwash and tidied up the bathroom. I checked my reflection in the mirror and my breath caught in my throat.

Little red marks from his fingers ran along my temples and jaw bone. My bottom lip was swollen and looked raw. The pretty up-do I'd had for the wedding was falling apart. While I stared at the forming bruises, tears rolled down my face again. I dashed at them angrily. *Stay strong, hold your head up!*

I grabbed a tissue, wiped away my tears and bumped my lip. I hissed in pain and figured my best bet would be to take my hair down to help cover up the marks. I quickly went to my room to repair the damage. I searched through the back of my hair for the pins and found a nice knot had formed where my head had bounced off the siding of the manor.

"Damn it!" I yelped when I brushed my fingers over it, and discovered it was damp. I checked my fingers and found a smear of blood. *Scraped but not cut,* I figured, because there was no other blood in my hair. I forced myself to take a steadying breath and pulled out my cosmetics bag. I gently applied lipstick to camouflage my lip and dabbed some cover-up over the purpling bruises on the sides of my face. I reapplied my foundation and had to pat more over the marks, finally adding powder to set it all.

I swore when I spotted the nasty love bite he'd left on the side of my neck— so I tried to hide that with makeup too. When I remembered that I was wearing the amethyst earrings he'd given me for my birthday, I practically tore them out of my ears. I dropped them inside my dresser drawer and saw that my hands were shaking. I stopped and braced myself on the dresser and let the shakes pass.

After a few moments, it was better. I took down the up-do, arranging my hair to cover as much of the bruises as possible. I smoothed out my dress, applied some lotion on my sore palms, and put on a happy face, determined to let *nothing* ruin the night for the bride and groom. I went back downstairs to re-join the party.

I got as far as the foyer when Shannon Proctor-Jacobs stopped me. "You still have my card, don't you?" she asked so cheerfully that it threw me a little. The guidance counsellor from the girls' school brushed at my hair, and tugged on one of my cap sleeves. "You missed covering up these."

"Damn." I glanced down and saw that there were marks on my upper arms too.

"The Proctors are protectors and guardians." Shannon informed me quietly. "Lexie and her father chose the police force; but there are other ways to protect and to serve." *Call me when you are ready to talk.* Her voice sounded so clearly in my mind that I jumped.

I studied her quiet hazel eyes. Here was someone, a

fellow Witch, that I could confide in. Someone who could be impartial. I followed my gut and nodded to her. "Next week good for you?"

Shannon smiled. "Of course." She gave my elbow a gentle squeeze and let me go.

I dove back into the party and performed my maid-of-honor duties. I scooped up Aunt Faye's discarded silk shawl from a chair and draped it around my arms to hide the marks Duncan had left. I accepted a glass of sparkling wine from Marie, then I eased into the background.

A little before midnight, Bran raised his glass to address their wedding guests. "Lexie and I wanted to thank all of you for joining us tonight," he said with one arm around his bride. "In the final moments of this year we remember all of our loved ones who couldn't be here this evening. We honor our past, enjoy the present, and look forward to our future."

"Cheers!" Everyone lifted their glass in salute to the bride and groom and drank.

Ivy held up her phone. "It's ten seconds till midnight!"

Bran and Lexie exchanged a brilliant smile. Lexie raised her water glass. "The new year is going to be exciting." Then she focused on her parents. "Bran and I are expecting a baby in late July!"

The clock struck midnight and everyone cheered and kissed.

John and Nancy Proctor were jumping up and down

in excitement. "A baby? A baby!" Nancy cried, holding onto Lexie. John hugged Bran and slapped him exuberantly on the back.

I stood back and watched as everyone congratulated the bride and groom and celebrated around me. Shannon grabbed Lexie in a quick hug, the twins and Cypress tossed streamers and confetti, and I reminded myself to smile.

I slipped into the living room to sit on the couch alone, while everyone partied around me. I sipped at my glass of sparkling wine and thought about the vision I'd had on the morning of the winter solstice. That precognition had led to this beautiful wedding celebration. To comfort myself, I shut my eyes and recalled the image of a red-haired baby swaddled in Lexie's arms— and as everyone else celebrated the beginning of a new year, I realized something else.

That baby blanket had been pale blue.

CHAPTER FOUR

The winter months were long, dark and bitter, and as they rolled by I tried not to become bitter myself by dwelling on what had happened between Duncan and I. The hardest part was realizing that I wouldn't be seeing or talking to him again. I missed him— the kind, funny and down-to-earth Duncan I had fallen for.

Maybe I'd been naïve about being involved with a member of the Drake family. Or perhaps I'd been overly romantic, but I was still standing. I reminded myself that I *had* successfully used my magick to zap him hard enough to get him off me. And a 'novice' couldn't have pulled that off. So, that had to count for something.

I had gone to speak to Shannon Proctor-Jacobs the week after the wedding. I suppose it was like Witch therapy, and while I was honest with Shannon, I did *not* share with the rest of my family the details of what had happened between me and Duncan. It was too humiliating, and besides, Lexie and Bran deserved their happiness.

When anyone asked, I simply said that Duncan and I had argued, and then decided to spend some time apart. I hid the bruises he'd inadvertently given me, and they'd taken a couple of weeks to fade. I'd left my long hair down, worn scarves, and used a lot of cover up to hide the marks on my face, arms and neck. Those weeks of having to hide the bruises left me angry and resentful, but determined to never be vulnerable to someone emotionally— not ever again.

When you trusted people, they let you down. If you were foolish enough to open your heart to them— they would leave you— one way or another. First there was my father: He'd lied to me my whole life, bound my powers and hidden the legacy of magick from me. Next, my mother had turned her back on me completely in fear and anger when I'd embraced the Craft. Aunt Gwen had opened her home and shared her family with me. I'd gotten past her omission about Bran, and we'd started to work our way back to being family. She'd been my first formal witchcraft teacher... However, she too had been taken away. Her death, yet another casualty in the search for the Blood Moon Grimoire.

Finally, there was Duncan. He'd opened a door into love and a beautiful world of magick, only to slam it in my face for reasons of his own. Reasons that he claimed were for my own good, yet somehow became twisted in the end. So yeah, I could admit to being afraid to love anyone else, and I knew I was becoming resentful at having love taken from me, in one form or another, again and again.

Shannon was working with me on my resentment and fear. Originally, I'd thought to talk to her casually one time, get her insights, and call it a day. But she was either a sneaky Witch or a damn good counsellor because I'd been seeing her once a week at her home since early January. It was a hell of a jolt to have her point out to me that I had abandonment issues. That was humbling, and I still found myself shying away from even casual friendships with most men. Well, except for Bran. We'd actually been getting along very well.

The irony of that— did not escape me.

To take my mind off everything, I threw myself back into my studies and focused on achieving my degree. When my schedule permitted, I studied the Craft with Ivy, Holly and Great Aunt Faye. I helped the girls fill out their paperwork for college and dorm living in the fall. I jogged outdoors with Lexie whenever the weather allowed. I worked part-time at the family's shop and stayed as busy as humanly possible.

Finally, winter gave way to the spring equinox, and the sabbat of Ostara came. I was relieved to see the leaves on the trees bud, and the earliest of the flowers beginning to bloom. By late March the daffodils were waving in the chilly spring breeze, the newlyweds were happy, and Lexie had a cute baby bump. Aunt Faye ran the manor and oversaw the business side of Gwen's store. The twins had moved into Gwen's former bedroom suite. Their previous room right across the hall from Bran's—was going to become the nursery. Life went on, and I tried to focus on happy things.

I sat in Shannon Proctor-Jacob's cozy red kitchen and listened as her little girls, Sophia and Chloe, ran screaming through the house. There was a chilly rain falling so they were not allowed to play outside this afternoon. Which disappointed their mother more than it did the girls.

"So, how are you doing with physical contact these days?" Shannon asked me.

"Better. Not great, but better," I sighed. "At least I didn't jump out of my chair in class when my professor handed me a paper from over my shoulder."

"I see." Shannon sat and sipped tea out of a mug while the girls ran around.

"He was standing behind me. I didn't see him coming," I explained. "I jumped pretty hard in class, and everyone laughed. I covered it up by making a joke out of it. Besides, I'm better than I was a few months ago."

"Can anyone make you react, or is it only men?"

I frowned as I thought about her question. "Mostly men, but I still flinch if someone surprises me. And that's really embarrassing." I blew out a breath. "I never used to be like this... but ever since that night with Duncan, I don't like people having their hands too close to my face."

Shannon got up to check on her dinner. "You seem very comfortable around Kyle and the girls."

"Yeah, I am. But Kyle's cool, he's so laid back," I explained. "Your husband has this relaxed Zen-like vibe. Maybe it's because he's a Yoga instructor?"

"You should take a Yoga class. It would help with your stress."

"No way," I said to Shannon. "I'm too big of a klutz, I'd probably take out half the class, and blow everyone's 'Namaste'."

Shannon chuckled at that. "You are very good with the girls, they adore you."

"I like your kids. They're fun. Even though they seem obsessed with trying to braid my hair all the time." The noise from the girls suddenly reached an earsplitting level. "Besides, your kids are *angels*," I said straight faced.

"Autumn!" Three and a half year old Chloe Jacobs ran into the kitchen and threw herself into my arms, holding on as if her life depended on it. "Save me!"

I saw that her five year old sister was running towards us with murder in her eye. "Ah, Shannon," I warned her. "You've got yourself a *situation* here."

Shannon turned from the crockpot stew she had going and moved to intercept her eldest daughter. She nabbed Sophia before she could get ahold of her little sister.

Sophia waved a broken, half dressed doll at her mother. "See what she did!"

After a few moments of intense negotiation Sophia was distracted from her vengeance by her mother, who snapped the doll back together and diverted her eldest with a few oatmeal cookies and a glass of milk.

Chloe stayed on my lap, her face buried in my chest. "You're safe now," I whispered to her after Sophia left the room a few moments later.

"I didn't mean to break it." She glanced up at me, and those big blue eyes would have melted an iceberg.

"Accidents happen, Cinderella," I told her and dropped a kiss on her head. I snuggled her closer on my lap and recognized that her mother was right. I didn't mind having kids physically close to me, or in my face. Not at all.

"Why do you call me Cinderella?" Chloe demanded.

"Because when I first met you on Halloween, I thought you *were* the real Cinderella," I answered.

"It's a nickname, Chloe," Shannon said as she handed her youngest a cookie and some juice in a toddler cup.

"What's a nickname?" Chloe wanted to know.

"It's sort of a special name between friends or family." I tapped my finger on the tip of her nose and made her giggle. "For example, I call my cousin Holly — Blondie."

Sophia popped back into the room and regarded me with curiosity. "Holly babysits for us. But Holly's hair is *red*," she corrected me.

I tried not to smile at her superior tone of voice.

"The color of hair that Holly has is called strawberry-blonde. I called her Blondie as a joke once, and the name sort of stuck."

Both girls seemed to think that over.

"Well, I didn't want to call her strawberry," I told them both in a serious tone of voice. "I'm allergic to those."

Chloe bounced on my lap, all bright eyes and cheer. "That's silly," she announced.

Sophia walked over and picked up my long French braid to play with it. "What do you call Ivy and Bran?" she wanted to know.

"I call Ivy *Shorty* because she's shorter than me." The girls seemed to think that was hilarious. And for the first time in a long time, I found myself chuckling.

"Dare I ask what you call Bran?" Shannon said.

"Sparky," I said with relish, and that had everyone laughing.

It felt good to laugh again. Making those cute little girls giggle had made me understand that I'd allowed what had happened with Duncan to steal most of the joy out of my life. That had to change. It *would* change, I decided. *I would change.* After leaving Shannon and the girls I sat at a stop light in town, while the truck's wipers swiped at the rain. I checked my rearview mirror and wondered how to kill an hour and a half before I met Marie Rousseau for dinner.

A somber face with sad green eyes stared back at me from the rear view mirror. My old faded red hoodie, while comfortable and comforting, did nothing for my washed out complexion. My glasses were cute, but I'd kept my long brown hair pulled back in a braid for weeks now. And since I'd had to wear makeup so carefully while my bruises healed— I'd gone the complete opposite direction and almost stopped wearing cosmetics altogether once I didn't have to hide the marks.

I was a little shocked at my own reflection. It was almost as if I was seeing myself clearly for the first time, in a long time. "Autumn Bishop, what the hell happened to you?" I asked myself.

The light changed, and it was then that I saw a hair salon directly across the intersection. Before I could change my mind, I hit my blinker light and pulled in to the parking lot. "Just do it. Start somewhere," I told myself as I parked the truck, grabbed my purse and ran through the light rain to the door.

"May I help you?" the receptionist asked me.

"Yes," I said. "I need a hair cut. Do you have anyone who can see me right now?"

A tall, muscular black man leaned out from around a partition wall. He had a neat, short boxed beard, which accented his cheekbones and sculpted face. His hair was cut in a buzz style, a bit longer on top, very short on the sides and halfway up his head. "I can see you now," he said.

My jaw dropped. I'd never seen such a beautiful man in all my life. "Okay." I walked over and had to look way up to meet his eyes. *He had to be at least six foot five.* "Hi, I'm Autumn," I said, willing myself not to be nervous.

He put his hand at my back and led me to his chair. I tried not to cringe away from his casual gesture. He noticed me stiffening up, and gave my shoulder a friendly pat "I'm Rene. Let's talk hair," he said and began to unfasten my French braid.

"Oh." I jumped a little in the chair at him undoing the braid, and then cursed myself, feeling like an idiot. *He's a hairdresser Autumn... he might be a big man, but he's obviously gay. He has to touch your hair if he's going to cut it.* I kept up a silent lecture, willing myself to relax as he worked his fingers impersonally through my hair. I tried not to, but I did flinch a few times when his fingers touched my scalp. *Breathe you idiot! He's not going to pin you to a wall... you're not his type...* I discovered that I was holding my breath, so I released the air I'd been holding, banishing the self-deprecating inner monologue.

"Relax, Autumn, I can feel the tension coming off of you. You're safe with me." Rene's deep voice rumbled, and somehow— I did manage to relax.

It was strange, but there was something almost familiar about him. I met his eyes in the mirror and saw that they were a startling shade of sage-green. I wasn't sure if they were more striking because of his caramel skin tone, or if it was because he was simply one of the most gorgeous men I had *ever* seen. "Rene, I need to do something different." I attempted a smile, but it came out more like a grimace.

Rene held my gaze, and I felt a little buzz as he continued to work his fingers through my hair. I let my eyes go unfocused and saw a bright purple aura all around him. He raised an eyebrow in challenge at me in the mirror, and I nodded my head in recognition. I smiled this time and meant it. *Rene was a magickal practitioner.*

"Is this an 'I'm over a man, and I need a change' haircut?" Rene snapped a cape out and fastened it round my neck.

I watched him in the mirror. "It sure the hell is."

"How much length do you want off?" he asked as he began to work a comb through my hair.

I shut my eyes. "Take it up to shoulder length," I said spontaneously.

"So about eight inches off, then." He lifted a section of my hair and considered. "There's plenty here to donate to Locks of Love."

"I like that idea," I told him, my stomach churning as I watched him in the mirror. *I hadn't had more than a trim to my hair in years. My long hair was a part of me...*

"Do you trust me?" Rene snipped his scissors above my head.

Even without my current issues, it was intimidating having a man with the size and build of an NFL player standing over my chair— with scissors. I offered up a prayer to the Goddess, and took my glasses off. "Let's do it."

***

I felt so much lighter. I sat in the salon chair gazing at my reflection, and a stranger stared back at me. Rene had added sassy bangs, and soft layers around my face. My hair now brushed the top of my shoulders and seemed to shimmer with whatever magickal concoction he'd used on it.

"It even looks good with my glasses," I said turning my head from side to side.

"You doubted me?" Rene tucked the blow dryer away in its holder at his station.

"You're a genius," I told him.

"Damn right." He unsnapped the cape, and I stood up.

"Thank you, Rene." I steeled myself and held out my hand.

"You're welcome *cher.*" He took my hand gently in his huge one. "You come back and see me in six weeks."

"I will." I smiled at him as he fussed with my hair a little more, congratulating myself on not panicking, as his hands were on either side of my face. *Go me!*

I purchased the products he'd used on my hair and settled the bill. Rene filled out a card with an appointment for me in May. I accepted the card and read his name. "Rene T. Rousseau?" It clicked. "Are you related to Marie?"

"Of course. She's my sister." His eyes seemed to be twinkling.

"Really?" I blinked at him. "I'm headed over to have dinner with her, right now."

Rene threw back his head and laughed. I found myself smiling over the deep booming laugh. "Maybe I'll see you later," he said.

"It was nice to meet you, Rene. Thanks for the haircut," I said walking to the door.

"I'll see you soon, *cher*."

I wondered about Rene as I made the ten minute trip across town to Marie's place. Marie never mentioned she had a brother. Then again, I'd been so focused on school and my own issues lately. Maybe she had, and I'd never paid attention. The rain had stopped, and I couldn't wait to see Marie's reaction to my new haircut. I parked behind her shop and headed for the back stairs to her second floor apartment.

Marie opened the door, and her mouth dropped open in surprise. "Damn girl! Look at you!" Never one to stand on ceremony, Marie yanked me inside.

"What do you think?" I asked and managed not to react to the good natured grabbing and yanking. While Marie exclaimed over my new hair style, I told her how I'd walked into a salon and met Rene.

"That boy's talented all right." Marie walked in a circle all around me. And I did okay— until she reached for the short layers around my face.

I cringed away from her and felt shame. "Sorry," I said quietly.

She froze and stared at me. "So, it's true then." Marie's voice lowered as she very slowly dropped her hand.

"What's true?"

"Rene called a bit ago asking me why I'd never mentioned that my friend was recovering from an abusive relationship."

"It wasn't an *abusive* relationship," I said and then wished I would've kept my mouth shut.

"No, of course not. A smart, sassy young Witch like you randomly flinches when someone gets too close to her face, *or* if a man touches her."

I felt my cheeks heat up and tried to focus on my breathing. Mortified that she knew, I dropped my eyes to the floor, not knowing what to say.

"I thought we were friends," Marie said, sounding hurt.

My head snapped up. "We *are*."

"Then talk to me, Autumn. I'll listen, and I won't judge."

Maybe it was time to take another step forward. "Can we sit down?" I asked, gesturing towards her sofa. Without a word Marie sat, and I joined her. I picked up a colorful throw pillow and hugged it over my middle, and considered. Marie was about ten years older than me and had been one of my aunt's best friends despite the fact that she was almost twenty years younger than Gwen. *You can trust her.* My intuition whispered to me, and I felt the tension in my stomach begin to lessen.

"Take your time," Marie invited.

"It happened the night of Bran and Lexie's wedding..." I stumbled for a moment over my own words. *What could I say to her about Duncan's problem that wouldn't break the promise I'd made to my grandmother to keep the information about the bindings of the grimoire a secret?* I took a deliberate breath, grounding myself. "The truth is that Duncan is no longer in control of his emotions or his actions," I told her. "He's become involved in some... darker magicks."

"What? When did *that* happen?" Marie asked.

"My best guess would be sometime after Gwen's accident and New Years Eve. I think his intentions were probably noble at first, but over time what he's working with has had a negative effect on his personality."

"Did you try to talk to him about it?"

"That was one of the things we fought over, that and him saying he wanted to take a break for a while, so I would be safe." I hugged the pillow closer to me.

"Safe? Safe from what?" Marie wanted to know.

"It's complicated."

Marie crossed her arms over her chest. "How bad was your fight?"

"Bad," I said quietly, studying her for a moment. "I'm going to show you something," I said. "But only if you swear that what we are discussing stays in this room. You don't talk about this with my family."

"Okay, it stays here in this room. I promise," Marie said.

I retrieved my purse and pulled my phone out. Taking a deep breath, I sat down next to her again. "The only other person who has seen these photos is Shannon Proctor-Jacobs." I pulled up the saved pictures.

"Your hands are shaking," Marie pointed out.

"This is hard for me," I confessed and handed her my phone.

Marie gasped as the first picture came up. It was a selfie of me with my hair pulled back. The marks from where Duncan had gripped my face stood out stark and purple. Fingertip shaped bruises ran along my hairline from my temples and down around my jawbones. I swiped over to the second picture. The second photo was of me standing in a camisole, my head turned to the side and all of the bruises along my face and jaw, the hickey on my neck, and the small discolorations around my upper arms stood out.

Marie narrowed her eyes as she studied the pictures. "What in the hell could make Duncan change so fucking much— that he would be capable of *this*?"

"There's an item he's been working with," I said. "And it seems to adversely affect anyone who has contact with it. Duncan *thinks* he's in control of this dark magickal object— but he's not. And it *has* affected him."

Marie silently handed me back the phone and released a breath as if to steady herself.

I closed down the file and set the phone on her coffee table. "I had to zap him pretty hard to get him to stop. It knocked him back a good five feet and left me feeling wiped out for days after expending all that energy."

"Tell me... please tell me you burned his ass," Marie demanded.

"I know I did. My hands were bright red for a few days afterwards... almost like a sunburn."

"Good. Then you *did* hit him hard with your magick. I hope it left marks on him!" Marie hissed.

I thought about it for a moment. "Marie, I don't think he meant to leave bruises on me." Before she could yell at me over that I added, "But honestly, I fully intended to kick his ass. That makes us even then, I suppose..."

"Self-defense is *not* the same as assault!" Marie said firing up.

"Oh I agree with you, which is why I told him we were over *and* to stay the hell away from me."

Marie folded her arms across her chest. "So you've been seeing Shannon for help?"

"Yes, I've been going to her for counselling regularly, since the week after the wedding."

"Autumn, you should have come to me, right away." Marie's brown eyes were intense, and I gulped at the serious expression on her face.

"Yeah that would have been bad; nothing like pissing off the Voodoo woman," I said— half serious.

"Hoodoo," Marie corrected me.

"What's the difference?" I asked.

"Voodoo is a religion. Hoodoo is a magickal mix of shamanism, Voodoo, Santeria, Roman Catholicism, folk magick, and European witchcraft. It's a melting pot that originated in New Orleans..." Marie narrowed her eyes at me. "Don't you change the subject."

"It was an honest question." I gulped nervously, as she tapped a finger on her lips. "Marie, what are you plotting?"

"I'm thinking about how I'm gonna lay the roots *hard* on that boy."

"Well, shit!" I squeezed the pillow for comfort. "Ask me again why I didn't come to you earlier." When Marie threw back her head and laughed, I tried one more time. "Don't hex Duncan. He's not worth the karma," I said.

"Girl, you let me worry about that." Marie winked at me, leaving me torn between alarm and some very inappropriate laughter. She stood up and held out her hands.

Placing the pillow aside, I took her hands and stood up to face her. "Thank you for listening and for being my friend," I said as she pulled me close for a hug.

"You should go ahead and cry," she suggested. "It'll make you feel better."

My breath hitched as I fought against tears. "I'm not

crying over Duncan Drake Quinn. Not anymore."

"Good for you." Marie patted my back gently. "I'm right here if you need me. I'm not going anywhere."

My breath hitched as I worked hard not to cry at her kind words. *Oh how badly I wanted to believe her!* I dropped my head on her shoulder for comfort. It was the only time anyone, other than Ivy, or Shannon's little girls, had hugged or held me in three months.

"You have any more troubles from that boy, you come directly to me," she said firmly.

"Yes Ma'am." I sniffled.

"Don't you 'Ma'am' me! I'm not *that* much older than you are!" Marie said, sounding insulted.

I gave a watery laugh and allowed myself to take comfort from a friend. As we stood there I felt a weight slide off my shoulders.

"Are you up for some dinner?" she asked after a little while.

"Sure," I said, feeling relieved that we had cleared the air between us, and that I didn't have to carry the burden all alone.

"You want a margarita?" she asked me.

"God, yes!" I breathed.

"Coming right up." She shooed me to the kitchen barstools, and I watched as she mixed up a big pitcher.

A couple hours later, we sat out on her little veranda in bistro chairs, sipping margaritas at a pretty glass topped table. Despite the cool spring weather, gorgeous and lush ferns dangled above our heads from hanging baskets. Marie had attached oversized plantation shutters on either side of the windows and had painted them a bright green. The verdigris stood out from the old red brick façade of the building. Her balcony railing was an ornate wrought iron painted in shiny black.

"This balcony makes me think of New Orleans."

"Have you been?" Marie refilled our drinks and added fresh slices of lime.

"No, I hope to someday, but I've seen pictures of the French Quarter," I said, propping my feet up on the empty chair between us.

"Sometimes I miss home, but when I saw this building, I knew it was my own little piece of NOLA right here in William's Ford."

"Do you still have family there?"

"After Katrina, most of us left. I was drawn here, and your Aunt Gwen was one of the first friends I made." Marie sighed over her memories.

"What about Rene? I don't remember you talking about him before."

"He's only lived in William's Ford since January." Marie paused, sipping at her drink. "He asked me about you today... after you left the salon."

"Who asked about me?" I was having a hard time following her, maybe it was the three... or was it *four* margaritas I'd had?

"Rene asked about you, you idiot." Marie chuckled at me.

"Rene, why would he? I'm clearly not his type."

"Why, because you are white?" Marie sounded offended.

I snorted out a laugh. "No, because I'm not a *dude*— you idiot."

"What?" Marie burst out laughing.

"Any man who is that gorgeous, *and* a stylist— has to be gay." I tried to be reasonable.

Marie set her glass down and wiped away her tears of laughter. "Honey, I assure you. My brother is *not* gay."

"What?" I spilled some of my margarita on the table. I righted the glass and frowned at Marie.

"He's simply a beautiful, *heterosexual* man who happens to be a stylist." She passed me a few napkins to mop up the spill.

My mouth worked, but nothing came out. "Good grief, he's like ripped and everything... He could be a model in a magazine."

"He was a model. It's how he paid his way through cosmetology school and bought the building the salon is in. That was *his* salon you were in." Marie pointed out.

I stared at Marie. "Well, holy hotness, Batman," I managed after a moment.

Marie cackled at that, and topped off my drink. "He doesn't take many clients any more, he's focused on the business side of things now— and the expansion. He's turning the salon into a day spa."

"Hello?" A deep male voice called out.

"We're out on the balcony!" Marie said back.

I swung my head towards the door, and Rene stepped out to join us.

"Hey," Rene said, staring right at me. His gray sweater accented the silvery green of his eyes and clung nicely to a very broad, muscled chest.

"Hello, gorgeous." The words popped out of my mouth before I thought better of them. Rene grinned at me, and Marie threw back her head and laughed. I held up my fourth— fifth margarita and frowned at it. "Marie what the hell do you put in these things?"

"Magick," she said.

"In that case," Rene said pulling up a chair between us. "*Laissez les bons temps rouler.*"

"Huh?" I said.

"Let the good times roll," Rene translated.

CHAPTER FIVE

I woke up early the next morning, still fully dressed, with a blanket tucked around me. The half-light of dawn seemed overly bright, and I shut my eyes in defense, rolling over to bury my head in the pillow, remembering a second too late that I was on Marie's couch— not my full size bed. I fell off the couch hitting the hardwood floor with a thump that jolted me completely awake. "Sonofabitch!" I swore from my sprawl on the floor.

"Good morning," said a deep male voice.

I looked up to regard an out-of-focus man standing across the living room. I pushed up to my knees and watched as a pair of blue jean covered legs walked towards me. I dragged a hand through my hair, surprised at how much less of it there was, and jerked when I noticed that my glasses were being held out in front of my face. I pushed them on, grabbed the offered hand, and was hauled to my feet.

The quick motion did not make my stomach happy.

"Oh god, I am *never* drinking that many margaritas again ..." My mouth tasted terrible, and it took me a second to realize that it was Rene who had helped me up. I focused on him, and then jerked hard as I saw that he was standing in front of me wearing a smile, a pair of jeans, and nothing else.

"You're cute when you're hung over," Rene said.

I worked very hard not to gape at the incredible sight of him— *shirtless*.

I failed.

My mouth was literally hanging open. I snapped it shut and relied on my super power of sarcasm to get me through. "Yeah, I'm sure I look *devastating* this morning," I said, turning away to the bathroom.

Five minutes later I emerged having washed my face, brushed out my hair, and with fresher breath by means of rubbing toothpaste on my teeth with a washcloth. I sincerely hoped Rene would have a shirt on by the time I came out, but alas, my hopes were dashed. He leaned against the counter in the kitchen sipping from a cup of coffee, while Marie cooked something at the stove. His incredible eyes followed me as I made my way over to the breakfast bar. I sat down and Marie placed a bottle of ibuprofen and a glass of water in front of me.

"Thank you,' I said sincerely. I took three pills and chugged the water.

"Feel up to eating something?" Marie asked.

Oddly enough, I did. "Yeah, but you don't have to

cook for me."

"I like to cook. Do you have classes today?" Marie asked.

"Ah, no. Not on Fridays." I glanced up at the clock on the brick wall of her kitchen, being careful to keep my gaze averted from Mr. Hotness. "It's my turn to work at the shop today, but I don't have to be in for a couple of hours."

"I'll make you some tea, I know how you drink it." Marie selected a K cup from a carrousel of varieties and tucked a big mug in place. A moment later the machine gurgled to life.

Cypress slammed out of her room, and I cringed at the loud noise. "Morning!" she said brightly. She bopped over to the kitchen, grabbed an apple out of a bowl, a granola bar, and scooped up her backpack. "I gotta go. We have an early cheer practice this morning." She gave both her aunt and uncle a noisy kiss goodbye, waved at me, and then slammed the front door behind her on her way out.

I dropped my head in my hands and prayed it wouldn't fall off my shoulders. "Oh god, today is going to suck." I thought about everything I had to do today and shuddered. "The last time I had a hangover was when I was an undergrad."

I heard Rene and Marie chuckle at my statement, and when Marie handed me the mug of hot tea, I grabbed it like a lifeline. I sipped, willing the shot of caffeine to clear my head. I tried not to react when Rene came over and sat down next to me.

"Do I make you uncomfortable?" he asked so only I could hear.

"No," I lied, doing my best not to stare at all of the rippling muscle and defined abs that were on display. I took too big of a sip of the hot tea, and choked. When he grinned at me, I ignored him.

Marie brought plates to the breakfast bar. Before Rene could reach for his, she gave a playful swat to his shoulder. "Go put a shirt on before you eat at my table."

Yes, please go put a shirt on. That's too much beefcake for a girl to face early in the morning. Especially with a hangover. I let my breath out quietly as he went to comply.

I nibbled on some toast and waited to see how it sat on my stomach. "Thanks for letting me crash here," I said to Marie.

"That's what friends do." She nudged my plate towards me. "Try some eggs."

Rene came back and sat next to me. He had put a shirt on— sort of— a tight, white ribbed tank. *Oh god.* It was sexy as hell too. *This was clearly my karmic punishment for drinking too much.* I stoically focused on Marie.

After we ate breakfast, I helped Marie clean up and thanked her again for allowing me to spend the night. I managed a polite goodbye to Rene and drove back to the manor to hit the showers.

I'd styled my new haircut like Rene had shown me

in the salon. Standing before the mirror in my room, wearing my bra and jeans, I took a critical study of my reflection... I hadn't done too badly with my hair, but there was no way I was getting my contacts in today.

Time to rejoin the world. I pulled off my glasses, squinted at my reflection and hauled out my little used bag of cosmetics. I stepped up as closely as possible to the mirror and got to work. I applied foundation to cover up the circles under my eyes, brushed on some powder and blush, and added black mascara. I managed to draw a neat line with black liquid eyeliner above my eyelashes. I thickened the line, going for the 'cat eye' style, like Ivy always wore, and somehow I pulled it off. Hanging around my gothic cousin had its perks.

I added a touch of eye shadow in bronze, and put my glasses back on and checked my reflection. *Nope, you couldn't even see the eye shadow.* I pulled the glasses down my nose, deepened the lid color dramatically, added pale gold highlight under my brows and blended.

I pushed the glasses back in place to check the results. "Hello, new me," I said to my reflection. I tilted my head a bit, added a bit more blush. Pleased with my work, I pulled a peacock blue cami cautiously over my hair and added a thin black cardigan sweater. I zipped up the brown boots Aunt Faye had bought me, snagged my purse and made it to *Enchantments* at a quarter to ten to open the shop, right on time.

Today was going to be a better day, I decided, as I opened up the store. "Bring on the customers," I announced as I unlocked the front door.

By two o'clock in the afternoon the ibuprofen had worn off. I'd located the first aid kit behind the counter and managed to take a couple of aspirin. The shop had been so busy it surprised me. *Was everyone and their brother out shopping today? Perhaps it was post-Ostara sales?* I had not a clue.

I slid some sandalwood incense and a decorative incense burner into a bag for the latest customer. "Thank you for shopping at *Enchantments*." I smiled but didn't mean it. The customer left, and I sipped my ginger ale; seriously considering ripping the bells off the front door of the store. They made my head throb. The damn things sounded shrill and discordant every time the door opened and someone came or went.

It suddenly dawned on me that for the first time all day, no one was in the store. I set the soda can on the counter, eyeballed the area rug beneath my feet, and lay right down on the floor behind the counter. I shut my eyes for a moment and took a deep breath. My head was *killing* me. It seemed the universe was not impressed with my new hair cut, cleverly applied cosmetics, or by me showing up to work on time...

Clearly my punishment for last night would be—death by margaritas.

I had managed about five minutes of blissful solitude when I heard the bells chime from over the door. I groaned. "Be right with you," I called out. I popped one eye open and listened while the customer walked around the store. Maybe they'd leave, or maybe they'd rob us blind— while I lay miserable on my back behind the counter. I was psyching myself to get up when a face appeared over the counter, grinning down at me.

"Hello *cher*," Rene said.

"Hey," I crossed my arms over my chest, answering him as if nothing unusual were happening.

"Rough day?" Rene asked.

"No, why do you ask?" I said casually.

He was so tall that I could see him smiling at me, even as he walked around the counter. Of course, he looked amazing. "Do you always lie on the floor behind the counter?"

"Only on Fridays, and during very specific cycles of the moon," I said completely straight faced.

He laughed at that, and I found myself smiling in response. "Come on," he held out a hand. "I'll help you up."

I leaned up on my elbows. "What are you doing here?" I asked.

"Checking on you."

"I'm perfectly fine," I said.

"Yeah, I can see that." Rene rolled his eyes at me, and before I could come up with another clever come back— he stepped in, bent over, and hooked me under my arms, pulling me up to my feet like I weighed nothing.

I hadn't even had time to panic at him touching me, as he'd picked me up, let go and stepped back immediately all in one smooth motion. I felt the oddest little tingle of energy from his hands. "Holy shit, you're strong," I said without thinking about it. *And gentle.*

Rene didn't preen at my compliment. He simply stood waiting, wearing a worn bomber jacket and those same faded jeans he'd had on this morning. Part of me, a part of me that I'd thought had gone dormant after what had happened with Duncan, stirred to life. At five foot nine, I was tall, and not built like a waif either. But Rene made me feel incredibly feminine. To cover my reaction, I made a show out of straightening the flyers for an upcoming food drive that were on the counter.

"I was wondering if you'd like to have dinner with me tonight," Rene asked casually.

"Wait, what?" The papers went everywhere. "Did you just ask me out?"

"We can keep it friendly if that makes you feel better." He sounded cheerful. "No pressure."

I frowned at him. "I'll be honest, Rene. I don't know if I'm in a good place to start seeing anyone. I'm trying to deal with some things... and I don't always react well to people getting close to me."

"I noticed yesterday at the salon." He bent and picked up some of the fallen papers.

"I suppose you and Marie talked." I tried not to feel embarrassed.

"We did, but only so I would know what might trigger your panic."

"Oh." I felt a little flutter that he'd been considerate

enough to ask about that. I straightened up the flyers and thought about it. "Actually I already have plans to go to the movies tonight— but I can't imagine you'd want to go along."

"Try me."

"I'm taking two little girls to go see the new *Cinderella* movie."

"Oh yeah, I saw the trailers. That could be fun." He sounded serious.

"Sophia and Chloe are five and three and a half years old. They're my cousins. Second cousins, really, and I thought their parents could use an evening off."

"What time is the movie?" Rene asked.

"The movie starts at 5:45."

"The big multiplex theatre out on the highway?"

"Yeah. Their mom is picking me up at closing time. Then I'll drop her at home and use her car." When Rene tilted his head at that I added. "Because of the girl's car seats."

"I can meet you at the theatre." Rene nodded like it was all set.

"Seriously? I'm having a hard time imagining that you'd want to see this particular film."

"Do you know how many clients are going to come in my salon wanting us to copy that *Cinderella* hair style for prom, or their wedding?"

I couldn't help it, I giggled. Here stood this big guy, all buff, handsome and he wanted to see the movie for *research*. "Might even be a tax write off."

"There you go." He smiled back at me. "I'll see you around 5:30." He checked his watch.

"Okay. We'll see you there," I said. "If you're sure."

"I'm sure." He winked at me and turned to go.

I didn't dawn on me until after Rene had left that my headache had completely disappeared.

True to his word, Rene met us at the theater and he bought the girls a big tub of popcorn. The four of us settled in with Chloe and Sophia between us, and I had to wonder at his ease of being with the girls. They knew Rene from the salon and chattered away. I tried to think how many single men I knew who would voluntarily go to the movies with little girls.

Halfway through the movie Chloe had abandoned her seat and was sitting in my lap. I didn't mind at all. Once the movie was over, Sophia had snagged Rene's hand, and I ended up carrying Chloe in a piggyback ride out of the crowded theater.

The girls were talking a mile a minute about the movie, and Sophia was already asking Rene if he could do her long blonde hair up like Cinderella's at the ball.

"Please Rene, *please!*" Sophia swung Rene's hand back and forth.

"Told you." Rene winked at me.

I eased Chloe down and firmly took her hand. "Stay right by me," I warned before we could step off the sidewalk and out into the parking lot. I glanced left, right, and left again and stepped down. "Let's go, girls," I said.

"Rene's not a girl!" Sophia corrected.

I glanced over my shoulder, "No, he certainly is not." I made eye contact with him when I spoke, and he gave me an intense look in return. The four of us strolled out to the car together. I was so distracted by Chloe's happy chatter *and* keeping an eye out for the other cars that were coming and going; that I didn't see the couple until I almost bumped into them.

"Sorry," I said automatically. The happy mood that had followed us out of the theater plummeted. My stomach dropped, and I felt a rush of energy run down my arms. Without thinking, I pulled Chloe closer to my side.

Duncan stood right in front of me with a sleek platinum blonde on his arm. "Hello, Autumn."

God he'd changed! That was all I could think. His hair was longer, and he'd grown out his facial hair into a medium stubble mustache and beard. *It was like he'd aged five years since I had seen him last.* His eyes seemed tired as he stared at me.

"Duncan," I managed, as my heart started to trip in my chest. In seconds, I summed his date up. "Hello Angela," I said politely to Bran's former girlfriend.

"Autumn." Her nod was perfectly civil but the raised eyebrows and slight sneer in the general direction of the girls and Rene put my back up.

The air seemed thicker and my chest got tight. I felt Duncan's familiar magickal energy wrapping around me. I shuddered and then felt Chloe tremble beside me.

My protective instincts kicked in and I mentally pushed back at the energy, refusing to allow it any closer. I scooped the little girl up and set her on my hip. Perhaps she was picking up on the energy because Chloe hung on tight.

"Go away," Chloe said, frowning at Duncan and Angela.

Before anything else happened, Rene placed an arm around my shoulders. "If you'll excuse us."

"Of course," Duncan inclined his head and he and Angela walked past, but then he swung his head back to stare at us as he walked away.

His gaze hit me— almost like a physical blow to the gut. I winced and tried to shake it off.

Sophia make a face at the couple. The little girl muttered something, making a gesture as Duncan and Angela walked away.

"What did you say, Sophia?" I asked the five year old.

"Nothing." She smirked at me and walked innocently to her side of the car.

Rene bit back a laugh, "That girl threw a banishing at them."

"Sophia!" I tried to make my voice sound stern.

"What?" She gave me a look far too mature for a five year old. "He has bad energy, he pushed it at you, so I banished him."

"Where'd you learn that?" I said, helping Chloe into her car seat.

"From my grandpa," Sophia grinned at me as she got in the backseat to sit next to her sister. "Want me to teach you?"

I bit down hard on my lip so I wouldn't laugh. After Rene and I got the girls settled in their car seats, he walked over and took my hand.

"Wait for me. I'll follow you home." Rene's voice was soft, but the tone was serious.

I looked up into those incredible eyes. "I promised the girls burgers after the movies," I managed to say.

"Chicken nuggets!" Chloe hollered happily from her car seat.

"That's fine. We'll all go together," Rene said. His gaze held mine, and I realized that I *would* enjoy his company, not only because seeing Duncan had shaken me... but because I wanted to spend some time with him.

***

I let myself in the manor and found Lexie, Bran and Aunt Faye gathered around the breakfast bar comparing paint swatches for the nursery. In a mellow mood, I started to pull up a barstool to join them.

"Oh wow! Look at you!" Lexie jumped up.

I'd forgotten they hadn't seen me since I'd had my hair cut. "Thanks, I got it cut yesterday afternoon." I stood and waited while Lexie inspected my hair.

"That's wonderful. *You* look wonderful." Aunt Faye

nodded.

Bran blinked at me. "That hairstyle makes you seem more polished and older."

"Was that a compliment?" I pressed a hand to my chest. "Quick, somebody go note the date and time on the calendar!"

"Your hair is great." Lexie gave my arm a squeeze. "Now come here, I want your opinion." She tugged me towards the paint swatches.

"We have a little disagreement going on," Aunt Faye explained.

"I want neutral tones for the nursery." Lexie waved a paint swatch at me.

"But I like this sunny yellow." Bran held up another paint swatch.

"That's too bright," Lexie argued, and they were off. A debate on wall color was now in full swing.

I sat down and scanned all the different color samples they had on the counter top. "Hmmm..." was the best I could manage.

"How was the movie, dear?" Aunt Faye smiled at me over the good natured bickering between the newlyweds.

"It was fun. Sophia and Chloe enjoyed it."

"And did you enjoy spending some time with Rene?" Aunt Faye asked innocently.

I didn't even bother asking how she'd known. "We're getting to know each other— as *friends*."

"Rene's a nice guy." Lexie grinned. "*And* he's pretty

hot."

"I only just met him," I said.

"So?" Lexie wiggled her eyebrows at me.

Bran gave his wife a frown. "The only man you should be thinking is hot— is your husband."

Lexie snorted out a laugh, poked Bran in the ribs and made him smile.

Hoping to change the topic, I picked up Lexie's favorite paint swatch. "What color is this, khaki?"

"It's called 'pale buff'," Lexie said.

"It's a little bland," Bran said completely seriously— and the irony of that statement had me biting my lip, so as not to laugh.

"Since we aren't going to find out the gender of the baby until he or she is born, I think we should do a soft, neutral nursery," Lexie explained.

"Bran wants yellow..." Aunt Faye held up a picture that Lexie had printed out from a website. "However, Lexie wants this soft buff color on the walls with white trim,"

I studied the picture with all of the tone on tone printed fabrics and paint. "Oh I see, creamy white, buff and tan. That is pretty *and* relaxing, I suppose."

"Exactly!" Lexie pounced on my comment. "See? I told you." She nudged Bran.

As I grinned at them, I was reminded of the vision I'd had of he and Lexie and their red-haired baby. I'd made up my mind on the night of their wedding to not tell *anyone* what color that baby blanket had been. "So this color swatch is more of a vintage teddy bear tan... not khaki."

Bran's face softened. "Vintage teddy bear. I like the sound of that a lot more than 'pale buff'."

"Maybe you could add a few old teddy bears to the room?" I suggested. And the parents-to-be were now searching for vintage teddy bear theme accessories on Lexie's tablet.

Satisfied that the subject was changed for now, I said goodnight and headed up to my room. I made the top landing before Ivy and Holly both got me.

"Whoa!" Ivy said jumping out in front of me, her arms splayed wide. "You're hair is so much shorter!"

"It's pretty. I like the bangs and the layers around your face," Holly chimed in. She'd been acting more like her old self for the past few weeks.

I sighed, wondering how long I'd have to go through the 'shock and awe' phase of a different hairstyle. "I had about eight inches cut off. I needed a change."

"Because of he-who-shall-not-be-named?" Ivy raised her eyebrows.

"Yes, my haircut is because of Voldemort," I said, deadpan.

"Ha! Nice pop-culture reference. But actually I meant Duncan." Ivy trailed along behind me to my room with Holly bringing up the rear.

I set my purse down deliberately and considered them. Ivy sat on the edge of my bed, swinging her feet, and Holly perched quietly on the bench at the foot of the bed. "I cut my hair because I wanted a change. It had *nothing* to do with Duncan Quinn."

Ivy patted the bed next to her. "Come over here."

I went and sat beside her. "I told you before, Ivy, I'm not going to talk about why Duncan and I broke up."

Ivy focused on my bedroom door. She raised an eyebrow, tilted her head— and the door swung shut and locked. "Okay it's only us now." She flipped her choppy brown hair over her shoulder. "Autumn, you don't have to talk about what happened, because we talked to Duncan ourselves."

I narrowed my eyes at her. "When?"

"We went to see Duncan a couple weeks after the wedding," Ivy admitted.

My heart jumped to my throat. *My god, they'd put themselves at risk and hadn't even known it.*

"It surprised me a little at how angry he was," Holly said. "He told us to mind our own business, then he booted us out of his house and told the both of us to stay off his property."

Shaken, I laid a hand on Ivy's knee. As soon as I'd made the physical link— I got a postcognitive flash of insight. "He also grabbed your arm and yelled at you." I heard myself say.

Ivy blinked at me. "Yeah, it did hurt my feelings a little. How did you know that anyway?"

"I saw what happened when I touched you." I lifted my hand and dropped it into my own lap. "Stay away from him, girls. He's not the person we knew. Not anymore."

"What happened to him?" Ivy and Holly asked at the same time.

I sighed. "There's an object he's been working with," I said, "and it seems to badly affect anyone who has contact with it..."

Holly jumped to her feet. "Well then why doesn't he get rid of it?"

"Because he thinks if he has possession of it— that he can keep everyone safe," I said.

Holly went to study my collection of framed family photos on the mantle. "Duncan once told me that if *I* learned from my magickal mistakes, I would be a better, stronger Witch," she announced in her quiet voice.

Ivy nodded at her sister's statement. "And we've all seen that you took what happened last year after the Halloween Ball seriously."

I walked over to Holly. "Hey, there is a difference between immediately working to heal the damage you caused—"

"I *hurt* Leilah with magick." Holly cut me off, tears welling up in her eyes. "I'm still so ashamed of what I did."

"Hold up," I said. "I was there. The second you came back to yourself, you rushed to her side and began sending her healing energy."

"But I did make her choke again..." Holly pointed out.

"Yeah, but you *stopped*," I said. "And as far as I know you've been behaving yourself magickally for the past five months or so."

Ivy went to her twin. "You've been studying your ass off to gain better control of your temper and your powers. I know, because I've been watching you."

"Holly," I set my hands gently on both her shoulders, waiting for her to meet my eyes. "Making amends and studying to have better control of your magick is a hell of a lot different than knowingly exposing yourself to negative energy, realizing you're being affected... and then still choosing to continue on that destructive course."

"So that's the *real* reason you two broke up," Ivy said.

"Yeah," I said.

Holly studied me. "You hid what he did to you for a few weeks, didn't you?"

I gazed into my cousin's aqua-blue colored eyes and recognized that she'd sensed through her empathy what had happened. *Damn! I thought I'd kept that to myself... I should've known better... living in a house with an empath.*

Ivy hooked her arm around her twin. "He hurt you," she said. Being linked with her sister, I guessed she was picking up on that information through their bond as twins. Ivy's eyes seemed sharper, and more green, as she studied my face. "I'm so sorry."

"You had marks, here." Holly reached up and trailed

her fingers in the exact places I'd had the little fingertip bruises. From around my jaw, down the sides of my neck and to my shoulders. "They've long since faded, but they've left an energetic imprint behind." When she brushed her fingers across my skin, I felt a little tingling warmth all over. Finally, she trailed her fingers down my arms and across my palms. "I removed the imprint. You are free of them. Do you feel better?" she asked after a moment.

I didn't question how she'd known where the bruises had been, or her comment about energetic imprints. I believed her. "Thanks. I do feel better, a little lighter," I said.

"If you would have come to me then I could have helped you heal— faster." Holly's voice was soft, but firm. She stepped back, and Ivy dropped her hand from around her sister's waist.

"I was humiliated by what happened. I didn't want the family to know... Bran and Lexie had just gotten married. They deserved their happiness," I admitted to them.

Holly met my eyes. "I understand feeling that way... After mom died, I thought it was somehow my karmic punishment..."

Speechless, I could only gape at my cousin.

"For a long time I carried that guilt," Holly's voice shook.

"You are *not* responsible for your mother's death," I said firmly.

"You absolutely are not!" Ivy agreed.

"But *someone* was," Holly announced. "I knew when we saw her body at the funeral home. I could *feel* the residue from a spell that had been cast against her."

Clearly, I had underestimated my young cousins. Here I'd thought to protect them, and they'd known and understood more than I'd thought all along... "Aunt Faye told Bran and I that she detected something like that as well," I confided to the girls.

Ivy took her twin's hand, and then reach for mine. "We need to all stop being focused on ourselves and our own issues and start working together."

I took Holly's hand, linking the three of us together in a circle. As soon as I did, I felt a slight tremor beneath my feet. I saw Ivy's eyes go wide as she looked at something over my shoulder.

The scent of roses bloomed in the air, and Holly gasped. I knew before I could turn around what they were reacting to.

"Hello, my girls," our grandmother's ghost said.

CHAPTER SIX

I glanced over my right shoulder. Yup, there she was. Resplendent in her worn out denim overalls, bright pink sweater and goofy gardening hat. "Hi Grandma Rose," I said.

"Hey, Grandma!" Ivy was practically bouncing up and down in her sneakers.

"I..." Holly's eyes popped wide and her mouth moved a few times before she managed to get any other sound out. "Hello Grandmother."

Our grandmother's ghost grinned at us, a few feet from where the three of us stood hand in hand. I gave the twins hands a little warning squeeze. "Don't break the bond," I warned.

"You've all been through so much." Grandma Rose seemed to drift a little closer. "And you've stayed strong. I'm very proud of you all."

After the past few months of ghostly visits, I knew the routine. Grandma Rose wouldn't stay for long... "What did you come to tell us?" I prompted her.

She nodded to me. "Three are found and there is but one left to find; Listen to the message of the crow to enlighten your mind."

Oh god, the bindings of the grimoire. Three were found. Two sections and the cover. I'd kept that a secret as she'd asked me... maybe the time to keep that secret was at an end?

"Is she working a spell or something?" Holly asked.

"Shh!" Ivy flared her eyes at her sister. "She rhymes. It's her thing," Ivy said to Holly—as I'd explained it to her, last November.

"Oh, okay," Holly said, her eyes still huge in her face.

"Go ahead Grandma." I nodded at her to continue.

Her voice echoed in the room as her ghost moved in a slow circle around the three of us. "To expose what was concealed, all lies must be brought to light: Only then will the good overtake evil in this fight."

To expose what was concealed, bring all lies to light, I thought, trying to memorize her words. *All lies.* My stomach turned over. I tried to focus on her image, but she had begun to swoop around us unbelievably fast. I saw Holly and Ivy's hair rippling from the circling movement. I tossed my own hair out of my face as the wind whipped higher. Which shouldn't have been possible— as we were indoors.

"Holy crap!" I'd never been afraid of my grandmother's ghost before, but it took a lot of effort to stay standing in the maelstrom her ghost was creating. I could see the twins were also fighting to stay upright.

"Oh my Goddess..." Holly gasped.

"Awesome!" Ivy shouted as a gale seemed to howl through my bedroom.

My door burst open, and Great Aunt Faye, Bran and Lexie spilled into the room. "What's happening?" Bran demanded.

"Join the circle!" I said, as the wind intensified. Lexie, Bran, and Aunt Faye all reached out, laying their hands on top of where Ivy, Holly and I were linked. Smoothly, we all expanded the circle, keeping physical contact with one another.

Now standing as a circle of six, the wind slowed, and quieted. The newlywed's mouths dropped open as they saw, for the first time, our resident ghost.

"Hello again, Rose," Aunt Faye said, cool as a cucumber.

"Grandma Rose!" Bran said, sounding shocked, but he was smiling.

"Wow," Lexie managed, laughing a bit.

Rose now stood still and serene, in the center of the circle. She appeared to be very real as the combined energy of six Witches, or maybe seven (if you counted the unborn baby) held her safely in place. "Three Witches are needed to finish what was once begun; A Maiden, Mother and a Crone will bind what was undone."

"Of course," Holly whispered. "The three aspects of the Goddess and three different Witches to bind the magick of the grimoire... a Maiden, a Mother, and finally a Crone."

Rose's image began to waver. "You have until the fourth blood moon to finish this quest; If you are successful then many will find their rest."

"Thank you Rose," our great aunt said. "We release you." Aunt Faye deliberately dropped Lexie and Ivy's hand, and Rose's image began to fade away.

I opened my mouth to protest, but Aunt Faye silenced me with a scowl. As I watched, my grandmother's ghost reached out to Bran and Lexie. She appeared to lean into them and I could hear her speaking, but could not make out the words. She blew us all a kiss—and was gone.

We all stood there staring at each other for a few moments. Belatedly, the rest of us released hands, and the impromptu circle moved apart.

Lexie let her breath out slowly and perched on the edge of my bed. "That was intense!"

Aunt Faye smoothed her long silvery hair back from her face. "How very interesting..." she said.

"Why did you break the circle?" I asked Aunt Faye. "She might have stayed longer, told us more, if you hadn't have done that."

She sent me a serious look, and her pale eyes seemed to be lit from within. "The fact that Rose's ghost can affect physical reality to this extent tells me that she is getting desperate to have us finish the quest for the Blood Moon Grimoire." Aunt Faye went and lowered herself slowly down on the padded bench, and that made me wonder. *Had this ghostly encounter drained the old girl of some of her powers? Or was she simply tired?*

Ivy leaned against my desk, folding her arms. "She's given me and Autumn clues about the BMG before," Ivy said.

Bran frowned at Ivy. "BMG?"

"Yeah, 'BMG'— short for Blood Moon Grimoire." Ivy rolled her eyes. "Duh."

Holly picked up a notebook and ink pen from my desk. Pulling out my desk chair, she made herself at home and began to take notes. "Help me remember everything she said to us." She pointed at Ivy and me.

"Yes, we should document this latest visitation," Bran agreed.

Ivy and I went back over what our grandmother's ghost had said before the rest of the family had burst in. Holly wrote quickly, and then Bran dictated word for word what Grandma Rose had told the entire family.

"I have it all here," Holly said a moment later. She pushed her long red-gold curls behind her back. "Do you want me to read it out loud to everyone?"

"Yeah, go ahead," I said.

Holly swiveled in her chair and read, "First she told the three of us that she was proud of us. Then she began the charm: '*Three are found and there is but one left to find; Listen to the message of the crow to enlighten your mind. To expose what was concealed, all lies must be brought to light; Only then will the good overtake evil in this fight. Three Witches are needed to finish what was once begun; A Maiden, Mother and a Crone will bind what was undone. You have until the fourth blood moon to finish this quest; If you are successful then many will find their rest'.*"

"So is that a spell, or a prophecy?" I wanted to know.

Holly tapped the pen against the notepad as she mulled it over. "It's more like a spell, a prophecy *and* directions all rolled into one."

"Well, she did leave Bran and I with a prophecy," Lexie said quietly as she and Bran exchanged smiles.

"What?" I demanded. "What did she say to you two?"

"Well, if your grandmother's ghost is to be believed, then the doctor got the due date wrong." Lexie sighed. "Damn it."

Bran gave Lexie's shoulders a supportive squeeze. "She said, '*The child will be born on Lughnasadh eve; Under a blue moon their birth will blessed be'.*"

"A blue moon?" I asked, while Holly grinned and wrote that information down as well.

Bran turned to me. "The second full moon of any calendar month is traditionally called a blue moon. And there *are* two full moons in July this year,"

Ivy reached past Holly and riffled through the little desk calendar I had sitting out by my laptop. "The date for this year's blue moon is July 31."

Aunt Faye smiled at Lexie and Bran. "Lughnasadh,

the first of the harvest festivals, is often celebrated at sundown on August the first. That makes July thirty-first Lughnasadh eve."

Lexie winced. "Which means that the baby will be almost *a week overdue*."

I pointed at my sister-in-law. "But you have to admit, a Witch baby born on a blue moon, that's pretty cool."

"Remind me of that when I'm a week past my due date," Lexie suggested.

***

Over the next few days I considered what my grandmother had said about *all lies coming to light*. I'd hated carrying this secret for so long... and it was, when you got right down to it, lying by omission. Explaining about the existence of the grimoire's bindings— and what they did to people— was all twisted up with how Duncan and I had broken up. And that only made it harder for me to explain to my family.

After mulling it over, I made the decision to share it with them. I waited until after dinner was finished. I took a deep breath. "I have something I need to talk to you all about," I said.

Slowly, I told them what Thomas Drake had confided to me at the cemetery, the day of Gwen's burial. I admitted everything I knew about the bindings of the Blood Moon Grimoire, what Thomas had claimed they had done to Julian, and that Duncan had possession of them now. After I'd made my little confession, the dining room rung with silence.

"So you've known about this for over six months but didn't feel the need to share it?" Bran's voice rose as he glared at me.

"Grandma Rose made me promise not to tell anyone about the bindings last October." I scowled right back at him. "When she appeared to us the other day and spoke about how *three parts were found, but one was left to find*, I knew it was time to share this with the family."

Lexie studied me from across the dining room table. "So the old man wants us to work together, eh? I find that hard to believe, especially since Duncan now has the bindings of the grimoire. The bindings that Thomas Drake claims sent Julian over the edge— and into a locked psych ward."

I nodded. "Duncan stupidly believes he can keep everyone safe if *he* has possession of the bindings."

Holly laid a hand gently on my shoulder. "*That's* what you meant when you told Ivy and me there was an object Duncan had been working with."

From my other side, Ivy took my hand in support. "An item that negatively affects anyone who comes into contact with it."

"Yeah." I nodded to the twins, then shifted my attention to the rest of the family. "Having the bindings in his possession... it changed him." I searched for the right words to explain to everyone. "Duncan is darker, and not in complete control of his actions— or of himself. Not anymore."

"He hurt her," Ivy said to the family, and my face turned red in mortification.

When Bran started to shout, Lexie cut him off by simply raising her hand. "Is that why you two broke up?" Lexie asked.

"We argued, and it got physical," I said, feeling extremely uncomfortable at her appraisal of me.

"Did he leave marks on you?" Lexie's tone was bland and impersonal. I had a hunch she was using her "cop" voice.

"He did," I answered her as calmly as I could.

"Do you want to file charges against him for battery?" Lexie asked me so casually that I recoiled at the word *battery*.

"No, I don't want to file charges..." I said, wondering if it was possible to die from the shame of speaking about this in front of my entire family.

"Damn it, Autumn!" Bran exploded, jumping to his feet. "I can't believe that he abused you, and you took it, then covered it up!"

"The hell I did!" I snapped back. "The truth is I zapped Duncan so hard to get him off of me that it knocked him back a few feet and left my hands red and sore from *my* magickal attack against *him* for a week afterwards."

Bran gave me an approving nod. "Well good. That's more in line with the sort of behavior I *would* have expected out of you."

"Still," I hesitated for a moment, "I used my magick to cause harm. And I did it on purpose."

"Hey," Lexie said, "self-defense is not the same thing as assault."

Aunt Faye leaned across the table, her expression intense. "I also happen to agree with Lexie about magickal self-defense. However, you should've told us right away. You should never have faced this alone."

"I was humiliated by what happened," I admitted.

"That's a common reaction with the victims of physical abuse," Lexie rested her hands on her pregnant belly. "I wish you would have come to me for help, Autumn."

"I *have* been getting help." I met Lexie's steady gaze. "I've been seeing your cousin Shannon for private counselling for the past few months."

Bran made a growling noise that had me eyeballing him warily. He stalked around the table and stood over my chair. "Besides Shannon Proctor-Jacobs, who *else* knows about this?"

I wasn't comfortable with him standing over me, so I stood too. "I've confided in Marie Rousseau, about what happened between me and Duncan, only recently. And Rene, well, he sort of figured it out for himself."

"Have you seen Duncan at all, or had any chance encounters with him since this occurred?" Lexie wanted to know.

"The other day when I took Sophia and Chloe to the

movies. I bumped into him and his date in the movie theatre parking lot."

"Other than that?" Lexie asked.

"No." I faced her from across the table. "He's stayed away from me."

"You're my sister the same as Holly and Ivy are," Bran said. "Nobody hurts my family and walks away from that."

It took everything I had not to cry when he'd said, *my sister.* I cleared my throat instead, and we both stood there glaring at each other. "You going to go all masked motorcycle hero on me again?" I asked.

"I might," Bran said, and to my complete and utter shock, he put his arms around me, giving me a hug.

I let out a ragged sigh and laid my head on his shoulder. "Thanks," I said, my voice muffled.

He patted my back. "You don't always have to prove how strong you are by facing everything alone."

I found myself surrounded a moment later as Holly and Ivy joined in the hug, making similar comments. Lexie came over, nudged Bran aside and wrapped her arms around me. Her belly bumped against me and I sensed a light *thump.* "I think I felt the baby kick," I said.

"You probably did." Lexie laughed giving me a squeeze.

"The Bishops stick together," Ivy said, placing her hand on Lexie's belly.

"All right, everyone." Aunt Faye broke up the group

hug.

We turned to her as she sat at the head of the table. She seemed to be in complete control of her emotions as she tapped her manicured fingers on the mahogany surface, and I had the craziest thought: *She looks like some ancient Monarch preparing to do battle.*

"Taking everything that has happened into consideration," she said, "I have decided our best course of action is to call a gathering of the leaders from the current magickal families."

"You're going to call the council and assemble a Grand Coven?" Bran asked her.

"Yes," Aunt Faye nodded. "That's exactly what I'm going to do."

"Wait, we have a council?" I struggled to keep up, feeling way out of my league.

"Of course, dear," Aunt Faye said.

"The assembly will be here at the manor?" Holly asked.

Aunt Faye leaned back in her chair. "Yes indeed."

I looked around at my family. *Council? Grand Coven? Holy crap this sounded serious.*

"What about our coven members?" Ivy said. "Zach and Theo aren't part of the founding families, but they should still be here."

"I agree," Bran stated.

"Certainly we will extend the invitation to our coven brothers." Aunt Faye said. "I'm terribly fond of those two."

Holly put a hand on her hip. "When do you plan to have the gathering?"

Aunt Faye pursed her lips as she considered, "I think this coming Sunday afternoon, the day after the third lunar eclipse in the cycle."

"We don't have to wear robes or anything, do we?" I tried to make a joke.

Lexie nudged me with an elbow. "When the council convenes, they actually *do* wear ceremonial robes."

"Oh." I took the hint. This wasn't the time to make snarky comments.

"Aunt Faye, as the head of the family, *will* wear a ceremonial robe," Lexie explained.

Bran patted my arm in sympathy. "The rest of us are not required to wear robes to attend the council gathering. We simply have to dress appropriately for the event."

"Define 'appropriately'." I used air quotes.

Ivy grinned at me, "We dress formally, but in classic, witchy black." She was obviously enjoying the prospect.

Aunt Faye stood. "Naturally we wear black." She seemed a little scandalized at the thought of anything else.

"Well," I said trying to match her serious tone, "as one would expect."

***

The month of April arrived, and the weather turned cold again, just for spite. Even though the new tree leaves were green and the daffodils and early tulips paraded cheerful colors, the temperatures hovered in the mid forties with enough rain and wind to make it feel cold.

Saturday morning, in the dark pre-dawn hours before the lunar eclipse, Ivy and I bundled up in deference to the weather. I layered a sweatshirt over the cami I had slept in, grabbed a scarf and my heavy winter coat. Like me, Ivy had tugged on jeans and thrown a hoodie over her pajama top. I tugged my red cap over my new haircut, and I was able to witness a rare sight, indeed. Ivy went out of the house without her makeup on. I simply wanted to witness the event, but Ivy wanted to photograph the eclipse.

Unlike the eclipse we had seen last fall, this one was occurring an hour or so before sunrise. When I looked up into the sky, I was surprised to see that instead of the bright red shadow that had slid over the full moon last fall, this moon seemed to be slowly disappearing. By the time we jumped in my old truck and headed west, the bright full disc had changed to a waning half moon in the western sky.

At Ivy's directions, we turned onto the highway and headed west. After a moment, we took a side road off the highway, and now, bare farmer's fields were on our right. At a railroad crossing, instead of taking a sharp left to continue on the road, I pulled into a little turn-around area. I pointed the nose of my truck towards the west.

While Ivy set up her tripod and snapped pictures of the lunar eclipse as the moon set, I leaned against the front bumper of my truck, shivering in the cold. We watched for fifteen minutes as the dark gray shadow of the earth took the brightness of the moon down to a dramatic and slim red crescent, low in the western sky.

"Damn, it's cold this morning," I said as my breath puffed out in the air. "Maybe Holly was the smart one to stay in bed."

Ivy pulled her black knit cap lower. "It does feels like fall out here instead of spring. This is a good viewing spot, though." She clicked away at the eclipse with her fancy digital camera. After a few moments she put the lens cap back on the camera and stuck her hands in her coat pockets.

I felt a rumble and then heard the warning bells. The guards were lowering at the railroad crossing. The train rumbled around the bend, and any other comment we would have made to each other was lost in the noise of the passing train. I pushed my glasses back up my nose and huddled deeper into my scarf and coat, while Ivy uncovered her camera lens and took more photos. The train rolled past us and, eventually, it became quiet again. While we watched the sliver of crescent disappear in the sky, a trio of crows flew low over the field and then past where we stood.

"I don't see the moon anymore," I said.

Ivy checked her phone. "The eclipse hit totality."

On cue, the sky behind us began to brighten. I looked to the east. The sun was rising. "I was hoping for the big blood moon show that we had last October."

"Not all lunar eclipses are the same," Ivy pointed out.

I tipped my head towards the truck. "I'm getting back in." I started the engine and cranked up the heater.

Ivy shivered dramatically, packed up her tripod and camera and then joined me.

"Feel like grabbing breakfast?" I asked Ivy.

"Doughnuts?" Ivy suggested, making me laugh.

"That sound's good."

"Great!" Ivy put her seatbelt on. "I know the perfect place!"

Every time I thought I had William's Ford all figured out, it threw me a curve ball. I followed Ivy's directions across town, and we pulled up in front of a little brick strip mall, which must have been built in the 1970's. It boasted an accountant's office, a dance studio for the university, and on the far end— a bakery.

As I walked up to the door, I noted the name of the business. 'Blue Moon Bakery' was painted on the front windows in old fashioned, almost gothic-style letters. I slanted my eyes over at my cousin. "Interesting name," I said.

"You betcha." Ivy wiggled her eyebrows.

The smells that greeted me when I opened the door were fabulous. While we waited our turn in the line, I checked out the space. Soft blue walls were decorated with several large, vintage signs that advertised milk, butter and fresh eggs, lending an old fashioned inviting atmosphere to the bakery. A little coffee station was set off to the side, and four tiny two-top tables with metal ice cream chairs were arranged against the front windows. As I watched, the last empty table was snagged by a college-age couple.

While the customer area was small, the glass display cases offered an amazing array of pastries and doughnuts. More breads and pastries were on wire racks behind the counter as well. The place was packed, and I noted people of all ages standing in line.

A short, stocky man and a brawny teenager hustled behind the front counter. They both wore white ball caps and had navy blue aprons tied around their clothes. They seemed, at first glance, to be ordinary people. Nevertheless, I cast my senses out in curiosity and wondered what I'd find.

Ivy bellied up to the counter, all smiles. "Morning, Mr. Jacobs!"

"Ivy," Mr. Jacobs flashed a grin. "And this must be your cousin, Autumn."

"Good morning." I nodded to the man and wondered if he was a relative of Kyle Jacobs, Shannon's husband.

"I've heard a lot about you, young lady." Mr. Jacobs tilted his head to one side. "Were you two out watching the eclipse?"

He'd asked about the eclipse. Bingo.

"Yeah," Ivy said. "I took lots of pictures."

Mr. Jacobs nodded at that. "Well, what can I get you?"

"We'll take a dozen doughnuts. Surprise me on the varieties," Ivy announced.

Mr. Jacobs tugged a pre-folded white box off the shelf and began to fill it. "Done."

Ivy and I shuffled over to the register, and I pulled my wallet out to pay. Mr. Jacobs rang us up. He casually handed me back my debit card, and our fingers touched. When they did, I sensed a little buzz of power from the shorter man.

The older man's blue eyes seemed to twinkle, and he grinned at me, confirming my hunch that though he might be a baker— that wasn't all he was. "I'll see you girls tomorrow night at the manor," Mr. Jacobs said.

Ivy took the box that bore a blue crescent moon logo on the lid. "See you then!"

"Nice to meet you," I said to him. We stepped out of line and made our way to the door. I said nothing else until we were back in the truck and headed towards the manor. "What a *charming* doughnut shop," I finally said.

Ivy laughed at my double entendre. "Yeah, they have the *best* doughnuts in town." She pried up the lid on the box and took a dramatically long sniff of the contents.

"The gentleman who waited on us, is he a relative of Kyle Jacobs?"

"Sure, that's his dad, Oliver," Ivy said.

"And Oliver is a member of the council?"

"He's the head of the Jacobs' family line now."

"So, he's Sophia and Chloe's grandfather," I said. *That's the man that taught Sophia the banishing spell.*

"Uh huh." Ivy snuck a hand inside the doughnut box. She broke off a piece of a cake doughnut and offered it to me.

"Oh-my-god!" I mumbled around a mouth full of food heaven.

"Yeah, he has the magick touch with doughnuts," Ivy joked.

"I'll say."

We shared a laugh as I pulled back into the manor's driveway. The tall, black, decorative metal gates swung closed slowly behind us as we drove past.

CHAPTER SEVEN

The High Council had officially gathered at the manor. Five other families had been invited, and four had accepted the invitation. The fifth of the magickal families, the Sutherlands, had announced they preferred to stay neutral— and obviously the Drakes, and their connections such as Leilah Martin and her mother, had not been invited at all.

The current heads of the magickal families; John Proctor, Great Aunt Faye, Oliver Jacobs, Marie Rousseau, and Cora O'Connell had convened in the living room to privately discuss the Blood Moon Grimoire and the current situation. Seeing the serious expression on Aunt Faye's face when she had slid the pocket doors closed behind her had made me very uneasy.

Not sure of what my role was for the event, I stayed behind the kitchen island in my one and only black dress and played hostess. As everyone else calmly visited and enjoyed the evening, I fell back on my

Bachelor's degree in anthropology and indulged in a little participant observation...

In other words, I people watched— or I suppose that would be 'Witch watched', and I had to admit, it was very interesting observing the by-play and connections between the various families and coven members. Not to mention seeing everyone wearing a different version of formal black clothes and lots of magickal silver jewelry.

Ivy was chatting animatedly with Violet O'Connell. Violet wore skinny black trousers, killer high heels, and a chic black tunic that shimmered in shades of her trademark purple. Ivy laughed at something Violet said and was rocking a short black dress with long sleeves that featured cut-outs over her shoulders. My cousin's mini-dress could have passed for Club wear. A long pendant featuring a triskele dangled almost to Ivy's waist.

Cypress and Holly stood together by the family room hearth. Cypress wore a trendy black and grey striped dress with a large dark, teardrop shaped crystal hanging from a silver chain. Holly's witchy dress, oddly enough, reminded me a lot of Wednesday Addams. Her classic black short dress had cap sleeves and a white rounded collar. She had worn it with ebony tights and black ankle boots. At first, I thought I'd been the only one to notice, but, shortly before the guests had arrived, Ivy had taken one look at her twin and asked why she hadn't put her hair in two braided pigtails. For effect,

Ivy did the whole 'ba-dah-dah-dum, *snap, snap*' from the Addams Family.

And Holly had *snapped* back. While Holly may have been working on control for the past few months— her temper was surprisingly closer to the surface than we'd all thought. She hadn't gone into "Dark-Magick Holly" mode, but she had taken a swing at her twin.

I'd never seen Holly strike out at someone— physically. Ivy had laughed and easily dodged the punch, but she retaliated by playfully yanking her sister's long curly hair, which only made Holly dive after Ivy. It had taken both Bran and Aunt Faye to separate the twins. They'd probably still be fighting if Lexie hadn't walked in and started barking orders at the twins like the cop she was.

The good news was that Holly had only thrown a punch and not any bad magick... so I guess that counted for something. The twins were staying away from each other tonight, and that was probably for the best.

At the moment, Kyle and Shannon Jacobs were chatting up Bran and Lexie. The Jacobs were dressed sophisticatedly tonight. Shannon in her maxi length, midnight-hued dress and Kyle in a dark colored sweater and black pants. Bran stood very formal in a black suit — he had opted out of wearing a tie and had left the top two buttons of his dress shirt open.

Lexie was pretty in a simple black maternity dress with her honey blonde hair loose over her shoulders. She too wore a silver pendant, a tree that was overlaid with an upright pentagram. On closer inspection, I realized that the entire Proctor family; John, his wife Nancy, Lexie and Shannon, were all wearing the same design of pendant.

Zach and Theo were present even though they had no links to the original founding families. They were present as members of our coven, allies and honored guests. From where I stood they appeared to be discussing the pros and cons of various local colleges with Cypress and Holly.

An hour later, the High Council was still in the living room, shut away from the rest of the crowd for their meeting. I couldn't help it, but I was getting more and more anxious from the waiting.

Holly walked over to the kitchen island and helped herself to some lemonade out of a glass pitcher. "Hey," she said.

"How much longer do you think this will take?" I asked her.

"Hard to say." Holly sipped at her drink, and her white, crescent-shaped pendant gleamed in the light. "Don't worry. After the council members have their conference, they will gather everyone together and announce their decision."

"Oh," I managed, trying not to focus on the fact that now all of the council members would know exactly what had transpired between me and Duncan. It made me embarrassed, but I told myself to ignore it. "I've never seen this before." I picked up the enameled moon from the bodice of her dress. "Is it new?"

"It belonged to Mom," Holly said. "I found it in her jewelry box the other day. It almost seemed like it was waiting for me."

The crescent hung from a silver chain and was slightly larger than a quarter. I flipped it over and saw that the front of the moon was white, while the back was black. "Oh hey, it's reversible. That's cool."

"It's the waxing and waning moon," Holly explained.

"And the family crest," I said.

"It also shows the duality of the moon and of magick," Holly said.

I studied the glossy enameled crescent and thought about it. "So increase and decrease, light and dark, positive and negative energies, constructive magick and baneful..." I met my cousin's eyes and felt a little chill roll over my skin.

"Everyone is a moon and has a dark side which he never shows to anybody," Holly quoted.

"Didn't Mark Twain say that?" I asked, setting the pendant back in place.

The corner of Holly's mouth quirked up. "Yes, he did." She helped herself to a cookie and strolled off.

As I served lemonade, coffee and tea to the guests, I thought about what Holly and I had discussed about the dualism of the moon and magick. I focused on the rest of the crowd. To my surprise, Violet's young teenage brothers, Eddie and Kevin, were present tonight, as were Sophia and Chloe Jacobs. The boys were sitting in the family room, talking animatedly to Lexie's mom Nancy about video games. Sophia, dressed in a black and white polka dot dress, was curled up in Aunt Faye's favorite chair, playing a game on her mother's smart phone.

I turned in time to catch Chloe, who had launched herself at me. "Autumn!"

"Hey there, Cinderella." I swung her up and settled her on my hip, accepting a sloppy kiss on the cheek from my favorite little Witch.

"Where's the kitty?" she demanded. She was adorable in her black velvet toddler dress, white lacy socks, and shiny patent leather Mary Jane shoes.

"Merlin's around here somewhere," I said, offering her a cookie from a tray on the counter.

"Did my grandpa make these cookies?" Chloe asked.

"Nope. I did."

"Oh, okay," she said taking a huge bite. "They're good," she announced a moment later, making yummy sounds.

I had to laugh at Chloe's enthusiasm.

"Sorry I'm late," said a deep rumbling voice from behind me.

"Hi Rene!" Chloe called over my shoulder, bouncing happily on my hip.

I shifted and saw Rene coming in through the potting room door. *Good god.* Was my one clear thought.

For such a large man he was somehow graceful and

masculine at the same time. Like a model— which he'd been, or maybe he reminded me more of a dancer or a professional athlete. Tonight he wore a dark silky dress shirt tucked into black pants. As I watched him stroll in, his sleeves billowed a bit, making me think of dashing rogues and sexy pirates.

Dashing rogues and sexy pirates? Flabbergasted at my inner monologue and raging hormones, I struggled against my reaction to him. I desperately tried to act casual, but it didn't help that I knew exactly what the man looked like without a shirt on.

Nope, that didn't help me at all.

"Hello *cher*," he said walking straight to me. I tried not to act surprised when he pressed a friendly kiss to my cheek.

The grin on his face confirmed that he was well aware of my reaction to him. "Nice shirt," I said.

"Kiss me! Kiss *me*!" Chloe demanded, reaching for him.

"That's what all the girls say," Rene joked.

"I'll bet they do," I said dryly as Rene took Chloe. He tossed her high in the air making her squeal.

"You look wonderful," Rene said to me, while Chloe tried to force feed him her cookie.

I glanced down at my own basic black dress. The jersey fabric stopped a couple inches above my knees. With a scalloped neckline and elbow length sleeves, it was hardly the fanciest dress in the room. "Um, thanks," I said after a moment.

Rene laughed. "You sounded so suspicious." He set Chloe down and she scampered off in search of the cat.

In desperation, I held up a tray of cookies between us. "Would you like a cookie?" I took a deep breath and tried a smile.

He ignored the tray, stared straight down into my eyes and moved closer. "You should smile more often."

I knew when a man was flirting, and this wasn't a casual flirtation. As Rene stood there grinning down at me, I realized this was more like a friendly declaration of interest or, maybe, pursuit. While a part of me want to jump up and cheer that such a gorgeous man found me attractive, another part of me wondered if this was a good idea considering everything that had happened.

Suddenly, Merlin darted across my feet, running away from the attentions of Chloe who'd spotted him and decided to give chase. I jumped and simultaneously backed up into the kitchen island with a solid thump. Glassware rattled behind me and the big tray bobbled.

"Easy there, darlin'." Rene reached out and steadied the tray with one hand.

Merlin leaped up to the kitchen sink and then jumped up to the space between the top of the ivory kitchen cabinet and the ceiling.

Chloe barreled in after Merlin. "There's the kitty!" She hopped up and down and pointed.

Merlin leaned over the cabinet edge and hissed. "Merlin!" I scolded him. "Stop that." I put the tray down before I could spill any cookies on the floor.

"He doesn't like me." Chloe wrapped an arm around my legs. She sounded close to tears.

"That's because you chased him," I explained, patting her on the head.

"But the chase is half the fun," Rene said to Chloe, or maybe to me.

Determined not to react to the double entendre, I braced myself and glanced up at him. When I did, I found that Rene had moved nearer still. Trapped between the kitchen island, a clingy three year old and Rene, I had nowhere to go. My heart beat hard in my chest, but not out of fear. I knew he wasn't a threat to me. I felt like I was in a sort of trance as I stared up into those silver-green eyes. It had to be a trance... because my super power of sarcasm abandoned me as he leaned in closer.

"Hey, move you guys," Eddie O'Connell said. "You're blocking the cookies."

Snapped out of whatever stupor I'd been in, I stepped neatly aside so Eddie, Kevin and Sophia could help themselves. Chloe went off in search of her mother, and I resumed my hostess duties.

"Sorry," Rene grinned at the kids. "I distracted her."

Before I could manage a snappy come back, Aunt Faye stepped into the kitchen. "The council has adjourned. If we could have everyone join us please?"

The families all gathered together in the main foyer of the manor. For the sake of space, the council members had assembled up on the steps. I did a quick head count— seventeen people as well as the five council members were present. I ended up sandwiched between Ivy and Rene while we waited to hear what they had to say. Rene gently tugged me closer to him by putting an arm lightly around my waist, allowing Bran and Lexie some room.

Ivy, standing right next to me, obviously noticed. She grinned and wiggled her eyebrows suggestively.

I rolled my eyes at her and shifted my stance somewhat, testing the waters, so to speak— I gently leaned my left shoulder against Rene's broad chest.

Rene tightened his grip slightly, and the movement snugged my left side up against his chest. *Wow...* He was solid as a rock and *warm*. I waited, but there was no panic. I felt safe and completely comfortable standing there with him. *Well, go me!*

Aunt Faye cleared her throat and everyone fell silent. "The council has met to discuss the recent events affecting us all..."

I tried to listen to Aunt Faye as she outlined the council's plans. But I was too distracted by Rene. I closed my eyes and tried to concentrate on her words, but it felt like I was drifting. That scared me a little, so without thinking, I reached for Rene's strength. I connected with him, making him an energetic anchor, spontaneously linking my energy in with his.

I felt him react with a slight start when the connection was made. But as soon as I did it, I felt stronger and more grounded than ever before. I opened my eyes and gazed up at my great aunt, but instead of seeing her standing on the stairs, a different scene seemed to be overlaid onto present time.

Once long ago, the high council had gathered deep in the forest around a bonfire. An old, white haired woman in Colonial fashion stepped up to speak to those gathered around the fire, and everyone fell silent. I couldn't make out her words, but her expression was serious and her voice was strong.

As Aunt Faye began to address the group in the manor, the vision faded away. I felt myself return from a clearing in the woods to the manor. I blinked as the old woman's and my great aunt's faces melded together. Past and present had just interconnected.

I shuddered, returning back fully to the here and now, and felt the room give a slow tilt. I gripped ahold of Rene's forearm with both hands and waited for the room to become completely still again.

"You alright, *cher*?" Rene whispered into my ear.

I blew out a quiet and slow breath. "Yup, I took a little side trip. I need to ground and I'll be fine," I whispered back.

"Here," Rene said, pulling me closer so that now my back was flat against his chest.

That snapped me back quicker than anything else he could have done— for a couple of reasons. Number one: the earthy, grounding energy I soaked up from that much body contact was not only impressive, it was eye opening. And number two: My backside was firmly tucked against his hips— which presented a whole other set of realizations. *Oh my.*

I gave his arm a friendly squeeze, released my energetic connection to him, and as discreetly as possible I eased slightly away.

Fortunately, no one seemed to be paying attention to Rene and I, as they were all focused on Aunt Faye as she addressed the group. I struggled to turn my attention to her as well. After a few minutes I felt more like I had gained some semblance of magickal control.

The council members took turns speaking, explaining that now all of the families had one goal: To pool their magickal resources and to search for the rest of the Blood Moon Grimoire. They were determined to put a stop to any more deaths caused by either the grimoire's— or the Drake family's dark magick.

Once again the Bishops and the other families were at odds with the Drakes. As it was in Colonial times, the magickal lines had been drawn. A Witch war had begun.

***

An hour later, everyone had left except for the Rousseaus. Marie was having a conversation with Bran, Rene, Lexie and Aunt Faye at the dining room table, while the twins and Cypress were talking in the family room.

Overwhelmed by what I had seen during the

council's conference with the group, and more than a little distracted by my experience with Rene, I quietly gathered up the kitchen trash and slipped out the back door.

The spring night was chilly, but the skies were clear. After dumping the garbage in the cans, I strolled around to the back patio and stared up at the stars. The moon was slightly less than full as it cast shadows on the ground, and I took a few deep breaths trying to reconnect to my favorite element, the earth. I pulled up stabilizing energy and came to grips with the fact that I hadn't even asked permission to work with Rene as a psychic anchor. I had pretty much, just *used* him.

"Shit," I breathed the word out and wondered what to do next. I imagined Gwen was frowning down on me from the other side. "Gwen, if you were still around," I said, "I bet you'd rip me a new one." I sighed up at the moon, wishing that she was here for me to confide in and to talk to.

I stayed where I was, gazing up at the sky. I felt Rene approaching— more than I heard him. "Where's your coat?" he said.

I didn't want to meet his eyes, so I continued to study the moon. "I'm not cold," I said, wondering how to apologize.

"We should talk about what happened in there." His deep voice sounded stern.

Time to face the music. I turned to him. "I'm sorry," I said quickly. "I shouldn't have linked in energetically with you like that without your permission. It was rude and manipulative." I hugged my own elbows for comfort.

Rene's brows lowered to a straight line. "Was your *linking in* with me accidental or planned?"

"No! I didn't plan that ahead of time..." I reached out and placed a hand on his arm in apology. "I'm sorry you'd even think that," I said softly, searching his eyes. As he didn't appear to be too happy with me at the moment, I removed my hand from his arm.

"So, what made you do that?" he asked.

How can I explain?" I huffed out a breath and tried to anyway. "When Aunt Faye started to speak, I felt myself drift. Like I was shifting to another time, and it caught me off guard. My first instinct was to anchor myself, and once I was linked into your energy, I got hit with a vision of the past."

Rene stood, calmly regarding me with his arms crossed over his chest. "That's what you meant when you said 'side trip'... I see."

"When I leaned against you, all I could feel was warmth and strength..." I trailed off and tossed up my hands. "Okay, big guy, I'll be honest. You make me really nervous because I'm attracted to you. My linking in with you wasn't calculated. I sort of responded and reached out to the strongest, safest energy in the room."

"Next time you should ask before you help yourself to another person's energy," Rene said, with no vocal inflection at all.

I'd basically stolen energy from him, I thought with no small amount of shame. *Like some uninvited psychic vampire, I'd taken his energy without permission.* "Did I hurt you?" I asked quietly.

Rene shot me a look, very offended, very male. "Don't be ridiculous."

"Still, I apologize, *again*," I said.

"So to be clear, you linked into me since you needed my strength, *and* because you're attracted to me?" His deep voice rumbled, and I could suddenly see that he was trying not to smile.

"That's what I said." I narrowed my eyes at him.

"I feel so used, so cheap," he said, and then he started to laugh.

"Jerk." I glared at him. "Are you seriously going to joke about this?"

Rene tossed back his head and laughed harder.

"Damn it!" I swore. "I'm standing here, feeling like an ass because I vamped you. I'm trying to give a sincere apology, and all you can do is—"

He cut off my tirade by scooping me up straight off the ground.

"Eep!" I squeaked as my feet dangled. I grabbed onto his arms for balance, and my hands didn't even wrap half way around his biceps. Once again, I was reminded of the sheer size of him.

"I figured that would shut you up." Rene stood holding me easily around the waist. "So, what are you going to do now?" His voice had deepened, and his intense expression had my heart galloping in my chest.

"Well I'm not going to vamp you again, that's for damn sure."

He didn't laugh. "You don't scare me, darlin'."

"I scare myself, sometimes," I said as our eyes locked on each other's.

Rene moved deliberately in, giving me time to evade. I didn't. It never even crossed my mind. Instead, I stayed still, held my breath and waited. I kept my eyes open and on his as he slowly lowered his mouth... and kissed me.

I don't think I'd ever kept my eyes open while kissing someone. It was strangely more intimate. His kiss was gentle but very thorough, and he seemed to take his time. I gripped his arms tighter and held on. I'd never been kissed that way before. Not ever... almost as if he were savoring the moment.

When he shifted to kiss my cheek and then pressed a kiss to my bangs I started to tremble. My head felt like it was spinning, and I began to recognize the symptoms of losing control of my powers. "Rene," my voice shook as he rubbed his lips over my hair. "I should probably tell you... that I'm finding it difficult not to reach out energetically when there is this much body contact."

"Fair enough," he said, lowering my feet to the ground.

I stood within his arms and belatedly slid my hands away from him. "Sorry," I said no longer touching him.

"Hey," he tipped my chin up with one finger. "I appreciate the warning this time. Now I know to be careful with you."

I met his eyes and searched his expression. He didn't seem angry, but I knew he was thinking about something else. "What?" I asked.

"I was wondering if this was something that Duncan taught you?" Rene asked easily, but having my ex's name brought up in the conversation kind of put a damper on the moment.

We both stepped apart at the same time. "I never thought about it like that..." I said dragging a hand through my hair. "I suppose in a way, he did."

I had a sudden flashback to the day I'd passed out in the family room. The day I had recognized the photo of Duncan's father as the ghost I'd been communicating with. When I came to, I'd been loopy, and Duncan hadn't asked permission, he'd simply clamped a hand on my shoulder and pushed hot, vibrant energy into me so hard that my back had arched in pleasure. It had been an amazing experience, and his energy hadn't been strictly healing.

As a matter of fact, the more I thought about it... Every time Duncan and I ever had sex, there had been a sort of magickal energetic exchange as well. Our first time, the energy had been so chaotic that our combined magick had blown out light bulbs *and* fried the bedside clock... *Oh shit. Had that all been a type of dark magick? Or chaos magick maybe?* My stomach churned at the thought.

"Your face is giving your thoughts away," Rene said.

"I was thinking back... and I realized..." I paused and searched for the right words. "Well, let's say I'm suddenly seeing my last relationship with very different eyes."

"That type of intimate energy exchange without full knowledge of what is happening, or consent from your partner, is manipulation, plain and simple." Rene frowned.

And that was the end of that. I thought. *Rene would probably avoid me now...*

He simply held out a hand to me, and I took it. "Walk me to my car," he said.

I nodded silently and let him lead me as we walked around to the front of the manor. It was dark along the side of the house, and I walked behind him, feeling miserable. *Now that he knew what I had learned from Duncan, I supposed that made me sort of damaged, or tainted goods?* I slowed down, looking intently at the ground, trying to pay attention. *Odds were I'd put an even bigger humiliating cap on the evening and trip on something, a pebble, or even an air pocket...*

"Come on." Rene gave my hand a friendly tug.

I was confused by Rene's calm acceptance of everything. He didn't seem angry. *Maybe Rene was only concerned as a friend?* It was time to find out. "Rene," I asked cautiously as I stepped around a bag of potting soil that leaned against the house, "we can still be friends, right?"

Rene came to a sudden stop, and I smacked right into his broad back. "You want to be *friends*?" he asked.

God! Leave it to me! Of course I had to run into him. I rubbed my head where it had bounced off him. "Well, I figured you probably weren't interested in me that way anymore, considering— you know— everything."

"Is that what you figured?" he said tilting his head to one side.

"Well, yeah," I said honestly.

"Allow me to clear things up for you," he said. That was all the warning I got before he smoothly pulled me to him— and kissed me.

His tongue teased my mouth open, and my mind went to mush. Rene kept his eyes on mine as he nudged me back step-by-step, easing me against the side of the manor. He kept his hands at my waist, and I reached out to place a hand on the center of his chest.

Our kiss became more intense, and he did allow me to touch him briefly in return. But when he gently caught my hand and placed it back at my side, I understood in my one single moment of lucid thought that he was trying to keep my magick, as well as other things, under control by avoiding too much body contact.

I pressed my hands back against the siding of the house, as his hands roamed down to my hips. I'm not sure how long we stayed out there against the side of the manor kissing each other, but I was pretty sure that my brains had begun to leak right out of my ears. At some point, though, we both realized we could only go so far. He eased back from me and leaned his forearm against the manor. For a moment he pressed his head against it and seemed to be composing himself.

As for me, I prayed the house would hold me up as I fought to catch my breath. "So, okay. I guess you don't want to be 'just friends'?" I said.

Rene's shoulders began to shake with laughter.

"I haven't had a make-out session like that since high school." I pressed my hand to my chest, working on evening out my breathing.

Rene whipped his head up and raised his eyebrows in question.

"Oh, no worries, big guy." I smiled at him. "This was definitely hotter." We weren't touching each other now, and I so wanted to reach out to him. Instead, I pressed one finger to his bottom lip. I gave his lip a soft caress and then I lowered my hand.

"Girl, don't tempt me..." His voice was a low sort of rumbling growl.

Something about that low bass growl made everything in me tighten. "Oh god," I whispered, "do me a favor, and *don't* do that low growl thing again."

"What?" Rene leaned above me, his face close to mine.

"That deep growl. It's hot." I shuddered. "I'm trying to be sensible here, and that's not helping when I'm trying to cool down and pull myself together."

Rene burst out laughing. "Come on, walk me to my car." He took my hand again, and we walked around to the front yard. He escorted me to the front porch, catching me off guard when he lifted our joined hands and pressed a kiss to the back of mine.

"I want to see you again," Rene said. "I'd like to get to know you better."

"I'd like that," I said, and then remembered. "Next month there is a fund raiser at the museum. It's a big fancy event and all the grad students have to be there to help out. I've got two tickets, would you like to go with me?" I'd never asked a guy out before. It was a little different.

"Marie told me you were getting your Masters degree. I'd like to see what you do." Rene said.

"It's a formal event, so you'll have to wear a suit."

"I think I have something," Rene said.

"I'll bet you do, Mr. Former Model." I tried not to react when he seemed abashed. "I'll call you tomorrow after class and we can talk more about it."

"Fine we can talk tomorrow. But I want to see you before the fund raiser." Rene's voice rumbled in that low bass, and I felt my insides do a happy quiver.

"Stop that," I said trying to keep a serious face. "Goodnight Rene."

"Goodnight." He gave me a little smile, let go of my hand and walked to his car. I stayed where I was and watched as he drove away.

CHAPTER EIGHT

A month had passed since the High Council meeting, and the time seemed to fly by. May had arrived, and I'd celebrated the sabbat of Beltane with the coven at the O'Connell's house. We'd actually set up in the garden, and it had been filled with flowers, of course —they were florists after all. It had been a magickal and fun evening where we all created little hand-held bouquets out of magickal herbs and flowers. Tussie-mussies, they were called, and Violet talked about the language of flowers and faery magick.

Between my school schedule and Rene's expansion at his spa, we'd only been able to see each other twice. We were starting to get to know each other better, socially... However any hopes or ideas either one of us may have had for being alone, or for romance, had been sabotaged each time.

On our first official date, we'd tried the classic pizza and a movie. We'd only been seated at a cozy booth when Holly, Ivy and Cypress had also arrived at the local pizza place. They'd seen us, called out a cheerful *hello,* and had piled into our booth without asking. Later, they tagged along with us to the movies.

On our second attempt at a date, we'd decided to go to dinner in the downtown district. Rene had made a reservation at a quiet restaurant, and we'd enjoyed an interesting conversation about magick and a nice meal. We left the restaurant for a stroll through the riverfront park, and it seemed like every person I'd *ever* met since moving to William's Ford was also out and enjoying the pretty spring evening.

Everyone had wanted to talk, and by the time we'd made it back to Rene's car we discovered that he had not one— but two— suspiciously flat tires.

Rene had to call a tow truck, and we walked hand-in-hand over to the spacious apartment he shared with Marie. Which then lead to us visiting with Marie, who'd been home. While I'd enjoyed seeing my friend, it had felt a little weird as I was dating— or should I say *trying* to date her brother.

Rene had driven me home in Marie's car, and we didn't even get the opportunity for a goodnight kiss... since Bran and Lexie had been in full view, relaxing on the front porch in the swing as Rene had pulled up.

It was starting to feel like a conspiracy.

Now I considered my current wardrobe choices. I'd been busy with classes and my studies for the past few weeks, and before I knew it, the Museum event was here. I blew out a frustrated breath. *If I'd have been smarter I would have gone shopping last week...* However, even though my hair and makeup were done — I was now standing in my bra and best black dress pants in front of my open closet, and panic mode had set in.

I'd pulled my black blazer out and a nice gray button down top, but studying it now, I worried it wouldn't be dressy enough after all. My concession to the formal nature of the event was to wear the black heels I'd worn to Bran and Lexie's wedding.

I needed help, or at least another opinion. Before I could open my mouth to call out, my bedroom door popped open and Ivy strolled in. Her black t-shirt read, *The color black reflects my soul.* "You rang?" she said.

"How did you—"

"Cousin," Ivy rolled her eyes and sighed, "how many times do I gotta tell ya? You project your emotions loudly—"

"When I'm upset," I finished.

"Or frustrated." Ivy stepped to my side and surveyed my clothes. "Hmmm... you sure you want to wear a blazer and slacks?" She waved her hand and a section of clothes slid over all by themselves to one side.

"Show off." I elbowed her.

Ivy reached in and pulled out a familiar, sparkly dark blue dress. "How about this instead? This was pretty on you."

"No, that's the dress I had on the night Duncan and I broke up." I took it from her and stuck it back in.

"Besides, I have to *work* this event," I explained. "So nothing too fussy, but I still need to look slick."

"Gotcha." Ivy pushed her hands apart, and a few more dresses slid over on the rack. "The black one isn't dressy enough." She dismissed the dress I'd worn to the High Council gathering with a flick of her wrist. She considered my other shirts and frowned.

"I was thinking of the blazer with this," I said, and pulled out a dove gray blouse. "But the outfit needs something else. It needs a—"

"Really bad-ass top, and some statement jewelry," Ivy finished. "I think I know the perfect thing... Hang on a second," she said, and walked to the door. "Lexie!" she shouted at the top of her lungs.

"You know," I pointed out to Ivy, "hollering for a pregnant woman, who is also a cop, is probably not the smartest move on the planet."

A moment later a scowling, ponytailed Lexie appeared. "What's the problem?" Then she saw me, the open closet doors and figured it out. "Oh, fashion crisis."

"Sorry for the dramatics," I said, before she could bite my head off. Lexie was a touch grumpy these days. While her pregnancy had gone smoothly to date, she was in her third trimester now, and her baby belly strained against the red stretchy maternity top she wore. She was currently working in the department as a community relations officer. The desk job frustrated her, and she missed being out on patrol.

"Can Autumn borrow your bright green sleeveless top?" Ivy asked.

Lexie tipped her head to one side. "The emerald green with the ruching?"

"Yeah, that's the one." Ivy nodded.

"It's in my closet, you can go get it," Lexie said to Ivy.

Ivy bounded out of my room and off to Lexie and Bran's. "So, tonight is the big Museum fundraiser?" Lexie sat on the padded bench at the foot of my bed. "You're taking Rene to this, right?"

I eyeballed her, wondering where she was headed. "Yes. He's going to meet me there."

"You two seemed pretty cozy that night after the Council meeting," Lexie said with her tongue in her cheek.

"I'm not sure what you mean." I stalled for time and prayed Ivy would show up with the top.

I happened to step outside that night. I was looking for you," Lexie explained.

Oh god, what had she seen? I flashed back to the night I'd accidentally walked in on her and Bran. I struggled not to show my embarrassment.

Lexie rested her hands on her belly. "I heard something, walked around the side of the manor, and got a full view of the two of you making out."

I said nothing as Lexie sat there with her bland 'cop face' expression.

"Anyway, I wanted to say that I approve." Lexie

smiled at me.

"Well golly." I raised an eyebrow and shot her a withering look. "Thanks, Mom."

Lexie laughed. "I figured you might be having a hard time after everything that happened with Duncan. But I wanted to tell you that Rene Rousseau is a good man."

I was saved by further comment when Ivy brought me the emerald green top. I slipped it over my hair and adjusted it slightly. I slid my jacket on, and checked my reflection in the full mirror by my closet.

"Nice," Ivy decided. "You need to add some jewelry, though." She went and began to root around in my jewelry box. "Wear these earrings," she said, holding out a shiny silver pair. The Celtic knotwork boasted a tiny peridot stone and the green would coordinate with the top. I worked the wires through my ears as Ivy announced she had a silver cuff bracelet I could borrow.

"What you need," Lexie announced, "is a necklace or something to accent the draping neckline of the top."

As if Lexie's words had conjured her up, Great Aunt Faye appeared in the doorway carrying a small jewelry box. "I have something for you."

Aunt Faye lifted the lid, and I saw a silver crescent moon pendant nestled on a bed of blue velvet. She lifted out the pendant and held it in her hand for a few moments. "This pendant once belonged to my mother, your great grandmother, Esther."

I studied the heirloom piece. A single moonstone

was inlaid within the silver. "It's pretty."

"The pendant has been handed down in the family," Aunt Faye explained. "For a time it belonged to your father."

"It did? I never saw him wear it," I said.

"No, you wouldn't have," Aunt Faye said. "When Arthur abjured his Craft and left to go back east with you and your mother, he left this behind."

I stared at the silver crescent shaped pendant. The open Celtic knotwork design seemed to flow around the stone, and it was distinctive *and* familiar to me. It was very similar to the tattoo that Gwen had on her shoulder — and had been on my father's back. "This is the family crest," I said.

Lexie and Ivy had walked over to stand next to me. "That's beautiful," Lexie said.

I reached up and touched the pendant. When I did I felt a little current of energy from it. "Why are you giving this to me now?"

Aunt Faye's eyes seemed to glow in a pale translucent gray as she stood there. "Gwen had been saving this for you," she said, holding the pendant out. "As she was the eldest female in the immediate family, it was her duty to hold this for you until you could accept it and all that it entails. When she passed away that task fell to me."

"I see," was about all I could manage.

"Typically the family crest is bestowed upon a Witch who has turned twenty-one," Aunt Faye said.

"However, that isn't always the case. As you'd only returned to us, and had to accept this part of your heritage, it was understood that you would be given time."

"So Gwen had kept it safe for me?" I asked, feeling a little misty.

"Gwen loved you, Autumn. She'd hoped to give you all the time you would need... However, things changed. It wasn't until very recently that *I* felt you were ready," Aunt Faye explained.

Ivy had stood uncharacteristically quietly throughout this exchange. She touched my arm, drawing my attention to her. "Do you understand what she's really offering you, Autumn?"

"You've gone through a great deal in the past several months," Aunt Faye said. "Though you have suffered, you have also learned and grown as a Witch. You've embraced your Craft and have proven to me and to the rest of the family your worthiness to wear this, one of our most sacred and personal of symbols."

When understanding hit, it made me feel calm and grounded. Centered like I'd never been before. *By accepting the pendant I would accept it all.* I took a deep breath. I wanted to make sure when I spoke my voice was clear, and not shaky from emotions. I thought about what I should say, but then the words were simply there. "I happily accept my legacy."

"Blessed be," Aunt Faye said, holding up the pendant.

I bowed my head and bent down slightly so she could fasten the thin silver chain around my neck. Once she did, I lifted my head, and she pressed a kiss to my cheek.

The pendant nestled right above my cleavage. To my surprise, it felt warm against my skin. I automatically reached up to touch it.

Aunt Faye touched the pendant. "By wearing this in public it is a sort of announcement to other practitioners that you are now a recognized part of the Bishop family line, and our magickal traditions," she explained.

"The legacy of magick," I said.

"Yes, indeed." Aunt Faye nodded.

"Thank you Aunt Faye. I'm honored," I said, and meant it.

***

I quickly discovered that the 'help' they expected out of the grad students for the fund raiser consisted of standing around passing out programs and waiting to run errands for the director and the board members. We'd been informed right before the opening that we weren't supposed to interact with the attendees or to answer questions, as the museum staff were on hand to do that.

Basically, we were like minions for the museum.

I stood behind the front desk of the museum and handed out programs to the attendees of the event with my fellow grad-student Emily Parker. Emily and I had a casual friendship from taking classes together. She was as annoyed as I was at the discovery of our minion status, so at least I wasn't alone in my frustration.

Emily had her pretty blonde hair arranged in a sleek bun tonight. Her navy blue wrap dress was practical and simple with a deep V neck and knee-length hem. She stood comfortably in four inch navy pumps, and even though I was wearing low black heels, I was still taller.

"So," Emily said to me. "Did you bring a date tonight?"

"Yeah, he's on his way," I said quietly as I passed out programs to an affluent couple. The man gave us a careless nod as his brunette companion, who I recognized as Leilah Martin's mother, strutted past me and into the event. I sincerely hoped Ms. Martin's poppet making, hex-casting teenage daughter was home and behaving herself tonight.

I reached up and straightened out my pendant. As I did, I felt a little tingle of power— and felt steadier. I blew out a quiet breath and put my game face on.

At the next lull of conversation, I gave Emily a nudge. "Did *you* bring a date?" I asked her.

"Actually, I did." Emily's smug tone made my gut tighten, and I slanted a curious glance over at her.

"Oh?" I tried to sound casual. But all my instincts were warning me that something was about to happen.

"Here he is now." Emily's face lit up. I raised my eyes to regard a large group of people who had just stepped through the main doors.

Three men and two women walked into the museum together. The men were handsome and smooth in tailored suits, and the women appeared sophisticated and elegant in a way I could never hope to be. Both women were in little black dresses, and as they strolled in as a unit, I felt my stomach turn over.

The Drake family had made their grand entrance to the fund raiser. Thomas, Rebecca, and their sons Duncan and Julian. I'd never seen them all together before, and as they stepped into the lobby, everyone stopped talking at once. The Drakes were dressed to impress, and honestly, their *go to hell* attitude—impressed the hell out of me.

I raised a hand to my crescent pendant and felt a little steadier. I reminded myself to ground and to act casual as they all approached. Thomas led the way, and I noted that he appeared the same as he always did. Very GQ mature-man-about-town, in a charcoal colored suit, and dark tie. He confronted the crowds with a slight sneer, as if he were surveying the attendees and found them all lacking.

Julian, in a pearl gray suit, walked beside his father. He was, as ever, the classic tall, dark, and handsome young man. I struggled not to show my shock at his attendance to the fund raiser. Even though I knew he'd been released in January, I still hadn't seen him out in public before tonight.

Rebecca, Duncan's mother, held her brother's arm

and seemed lovely, elegant, and somehow fragile. Rebecca didn't even make eye contact when she took her program from me. She acted as though we had never met. After she moved past, I got an unobstructed look at Duncan.

Besides bumping into Duncan at the movies, I hadn't seen him since the night we'd broken up five months ago. I summed him up in seconds, keeping my own expression impersonal. He wore a tailored, spring gray suit and vest with a white shirt and patterned tie. He now sported a mustache and tight beard. His dark blonde hair had been cut shorter in a simple casual style. The sides of his hair were short, the top longer and slightly slicked back. Between the tasteful suit, the new hairstyle and hip beard, he was completely different from the man I had once known.

Which made me wonder: *Had I ever really known him at all?*

Duncan had stopped and was assisting his date with her wrap. I recognized the super-thin blonde. He was with Angela again. Bran's former girlfriend looked like a movie star in her glittering, little black dress. Duncan and Angela smiled at each other and began walking straight towards me.

Even though I had braced myself for their approach, I could feel his personal energy from where I stood behind the desk with Emily. I wasn't surprised that it felt darker and *wrong*. As he walked closer with Angela, I could almost see his energy reaching out. Like dark red energetic tentacles... searching and seeking to attach themselves to me whether I gave him permission or not.

Hello, Autumn. How's the new boyfriend? I heard his voice crystal clear in my mind. Flinching from what I would have sworn was his hand clamping down on my arm, I sucked in a stabilizing breath and prepared myself for an energetic battle.

I visualized flames coating my hand and deliberately brushed away the feeling of the attachment on my arm with a brisk downward motion. Still, I didn't take my eyes off of him as he strolled forward with Angela. After working with Aunt Faye and the twins all winter, now I knew better than to look away from a magickal opponent. *Back off.* I sent the warning out— from my mind to his.

Duncan smiled at me. It was unblinking, slow and devastating. It sent a chill down my back. *Challenge accepted,* he sent the message telepathically. It sounded louder this time as he was getting closer.

I saw out of my peripheral vision even more energetic tentacles coming my way. But this time Duncan Quinn wasn't dealing with a girl who was new in town, flustered over his attentions, *and* the discovery of Witchcraft in her family tree.

This time, he was dealing with a Witch who had been training her ass off for months. Using a psychic protection technique that Gwen had first taught me, and that Great Aunt Faye had been helping me to refine, I bore down, pushing his energy away while visualizing a sharp, jagged, quartz crystal-like shield surrounding me.

I actually heard the *snap* as the protection sealed around me, and I saw Duncan's eyes blink in surprise. Now protected from any unwanted energies, and telepathic communications, I felt safer and warmer. A little bead of sweat rolled down my back from the effort it took to hold the shields, yet I maintained my composure. *And* I retained my protective shields. I resisted the urge to smirk at him, when he shifted course and walked over to Emily's side of the desk instead.

"Welcome to the fund raiser, would you like a program?" Emily held out a program to Angela who was passing nearest to her.

"Thank you," Angela murmured. Duncan stared after me for a couple of seconds once she accepted the program, and then he turned his attention to the woman on his arm.

As soon as they were far enough away, and out of Duncan's telepathic range, I eased my protection. I was about to congratulate myself for my successful bit of witchery, when I noticed Emily was speaking animatedly to someone.

A handsome dark haired man wearing a pearl gray suit.

Julian stood in the lobby of the museum as confidently as if he'd never left, looking healthier than I'd ever seen him before. His dark hair was styled into a modern pompadour, and his hazel eyes were clear and focused. As he stood and spoke quietly with Emily, I realized that Julian was her *date*.

"You look wonderful," I heard him say as he gave Emily's cheek an air kiss. Julian whispered something to Emily that had her smiling. He ignored me completely and left to join the rest of his family.

Stupefied, I watched as Julian seemed to be greeted with affection and warmth by the museum staff and board members. Men were shaking his hand and women were flirting and smiling at him.

What the hell? I worked very, very hard to keep a bland expression as my mind whirled with what I was seeing. I hadn't seen him at the museum, or even heard his name mentioned for the past few months. Not once while I'd been taking classes. His office had always been closed, and I'd assumed he was no longer a board member. *Clearly, I'd been mistaken.*

I cleared my throat and nudged Emily. "So your date is Julian Drake?"

She nodded, beaming at me. "Enjoy the evening," she said, passing out programs to another couple.

I took a deep breath, making sure that when I did speak, I could manage a polite tone of voice. "Emily, are you aware that Julian Drake abducted and abused my teenage cousin last year?"

"Well, Autumn, he was hardly responsible for his actions," she replied casually.

Shocked at her dismissive tone, I had to check my

first instinct which was to put her on her ass for that comment. "I beg your pardon?" I said.

"Julian confided in me, about his past problems with addiction," Emily said reasonably. "He's gotten help and he's working hard to turn his life around."

It took me a few seconds to get socially acceptable words to form. "He told you he had an *addiction*?" I said.

"He did. He was very up front about it when we started seeing each other," Emily said. "Julian told me that he was at his lowest point, when he'd lost his grasp with reality last fall."

"Are you serious?" I said a little too loudly.

Emily pressed a hand to her throat, as if I'd insulted *her*. "He's been working very hard to prove that he is worthy of the second chance the judge has given him."

"Oh, that is such *bullshit*." I shot back.

The Education Director of our Masters Program appeared. "Is there a problem here, ladies?" she asked. By the expression on her face I knew the woman had overheard our conversation.

"No Ma'am," I said.

"I think you two are finished with the programs, why don't you both go mingle?" she suggested while giving me a death glare.

"Sure," I said, watching her slowly walk away. I stayed busy arranging the remaining programs on the front desk for any other attendees to pick up. When I glanced up a few moments later, I was unsurprised to see her chatting with Julian. *He'd told me himself once, that she was a friend of his...* Clearly no mention of Julian's past behavior would be tolerated at the museum. *I would have to really watch myself now.*

Emily put her hand on my arm. "Autumn," she began, and acted hurt by my reaction to Julian. "Maybe you should learn to be more tolerant."

I sucked in my breath at her statement, but stayed silent.

She continued to plead his case. "Did you know that as part of his community service Julian speaks about his experience with drug addiction to student groups?" Emily said. "Julian works with the suicide hotline too, and helps other young people at risk. I am so proud of him, and how he's changing his life."

My mind reeled. The slick son-of-a-bitch had spun his dark magickal obsession with the Blood Moon Grimoire, and his abduction of Ivy into a phony story about him loosing control of his actions, because of *substance abuse*?

I shifted to watch him, and sure enough, I overheard people congratulating him on his sobriety and hard work to turn his life around. There was Thomas looking proudly at his son, while Duncan and Rebecca stood by in support. My stomach heaved. The Drakes had actually conned the general public of William's Ford into thinking Julian had overcome a drug addiction!

"Excuse me," I managed to say, heading for the ladies room.

I went to the nearest restroom, and once there I was thrilled beyond words to find it empty. I stalked over to the nearest sink and leaned against it for a moment. I blew out a shaky breath and wished to hell Rene was here. I needed back-up with *all* of the Drakes in attendance.

I was on the verge of reaching for my cell phone in my blazer pocket when I felt it vibrate. I checked and saw a text from Rene: I'm here in the lobby. Where are you?

I sent back: Hiding in the ladies room. Be right out.

I checked my reflection in the mirror and nodded in approval at the way my new haircut made me seem polished and actually a bit more trendy. Nodding at my reflection, I centered my crescent pendant, psyched myself up, and left the restroom.

I had managed about five steps and was so busy watching for any possible Drake family close encounters— that I walked right into Rene. "Sorry," I said as I bounced off his chest.

"What's wrong?" Rene steadied me with one hand when I teetered on my heels.

I gazed sunnily up at him, and I suddenly felt many eyes upon us. "The entire Drake family is here," I said under my breath.

"Any problems?"

I reached up, acting as if I were brushing lint from his dark navy lapel. "Duncan tried a little energetic power play as soon as he walked in the museum," I said so only he could hear.

"Well, well..." His eyes narrowed even as he flashed a heart-stopping smile. "Is that a fact?" I watched him scan the crowd. "We do seem to have an audience."

"We do." I nodded as I saw Duncan and Angela moving into view.

Rene pressed a kiss to my cheek. "Why don't you show me around?" he asked with a casualness that belied the intense light in his eyes.

I took the arm he offered, admiring how his crisp white shirt and black tie set off the subtle pin stripe in his suit. "I'd be happy to," I said, ignoring Duncan and his date, and steered Rene towards one of the local history exhibits.

He pressed his hand on top of where mine laid in the crook of his arm. "Lead the way, *cher.*"

CHAPTER NINE

Rene handled the surrounding Drakes and any possible magickal threat with a quiet strength and awareness that made me reassess him as a magickal practitioner. The natural aura that rolled out from Rene was impressive. I held my breath for the first few moments, as I had almost expected some type of flashy magickal attack from Duncan after his energetic stunt in the lobby. But even though I spotted him and Angela several times— the museum wasn't that large, after all — he'd kept his distance from us.

Within a half hour, I had learned something *else* about Rene Rousseau; that women made fools of themselves around him. I think we'd managed a few moments of private conversation before female after female ambled their way over to introduce themselves to Rene. No matter what their age, background, or relationship status, women seemed to flock around him.

To his credit, he was polite but did not encourage a single one of them. He was business-like, and answered questions about his salon and future spa. He also never let go of my arm. Not for a second. My lips twitched as I wondered, *Just who was protecting who?* Taking pity on him, I steered us to a less crowded, and darker, part of the museum in the north wing by the offices. As soon as we were out of sight, Rene sighed.

"Well, I think you broke about a dozen hearts out there tonight." I grinned up at him.

Rene muttered under his breath and rolled his shoulders as if he were tense.

I tucked my tongue in my cheek. "I foresee that your salon will be *very* busy on Monday..."

"That reaction out there is one of the reasons I don't mingle with the society types that often," he admitted.

"Well big guy, we all have our little crosses to bear. You *were* a professional model after all." I fluttered up at him like another star struck fan. "You're sort of famous and everything..."

He chuckled at my silliness. "Like you ever cared about any of that."

I patted his arm sympathetically. "If it makes you feel better, when I first met you, I thought you were gay."

Rene did a double take.

"But, to be honest, I thought that more because you are a stylist than because of your looks," I said. "Sorry about that."

His mouth opened, then closed. He stared at me for a couple of seconds and then he started to laugh.

"Seriously? Well there goes my ego."

"Ha." I rolled my eyes at him. "I did a search on the internet, and it seems to me like your *ego* should be safe. Especially after posing with all those gorgeous female models." I pressed a friendly kiss to his cheek. "So, okay, you photograph well... I won't hold it against you."

Rene grinned at me and leaned down. "Come here," he said, playfully tugging me closer by the lapels on my jacket.

I lifted my mouth to his, anticipating his kiss. Before we could— I heard someone clearing their throat.

"Excuse me, Miss Bishop?" One of the professors from my grad classes stood a few feet away.

"Hello, Sir," I smiled fondly at the tall white-haired gentleman who nervously tugged on his bow tie. Dr. Hal Meyer was one of my favorite instructors. He oversaw the archives and was a quiet older man with a subtle, dry sense of humor. I'd been working with him for months.

"I was wondering if I could ask you to fetch the files on the future museum expansion from my office?" he asked quietly.

"Of course." I waited while he dug his key card from his pocket.

"I'm sorry to interrupt." He glanced up at Rene. "But I'll never find the files as quickly as she can."

I quickly introduced him to Rene, and the men shook hands. "I'll go up and be right back," I said to Rene.

"I'll wait here for you." Rene gave my hand a little squeeze as I left.

I nodded at him and started down the hall, I checked over my shoulder and saw that Professor Meyer was chatting to Rene easily.

When I hit the stairs, I stopped and slipped off my heels, scooped them up and jogged quickly up the stairs towards his second floor office. I swiped his card key and let myself in the office. I hit the lights and went to his desk. It was, as usual, a disaster. The man was meticulously neat when it came to the archives... yet when it came to his own desk— not so much.

I found the folder he wanted and tucked it under my arm. Because I was genuinely fond of Dr. Meyer I stopped and straightened his desk for him. A few moments later I was out of the office and about to turn around the corner of the stairs— when I came face to face with Julian Drake.

I stepped back immediately. I swung my gaze around and saw that we were alone. *Shit.* I didn't think twice, I dropped the file and tossed my shoes, I pulled up energy from the earth, and when I did I felt power burn across both of my open hands. My magick made a green glow in the dimly lit corridor.

Julian held up his hands in a surrendering type of gesture. "Hey, hey! Hold it! I only wanted to talk. To apologize to you!" He came slowly up the final step and stood a few feet away from me in the hall.

I narrowed my eyes at him. "I am not afraid of you."

My voice came out in a growl. "Come a little closer you son-of-a-bitch and see what happens." I raised up a hand, hoping he would give me a good reason to hit him with my magick.

"Easy, *easy...*" Julian's voice was coaxing and soft, the way you would try and talk down a snarling dog. "If you want to throw a punch, go ahead. I deserve it. But I am not here to make trouble, or to cause you any harm." He lowered his hands and stood still, leaving himself open to any sort of strike— physical or magickal.

His words and his actions— leaving himself wide open to an attack surprised me. So much that the power that had flared to life in my hands began to flicker and go out. I sized him up as he stood there. "What do you want?" I asked, shifting to the balls of my feet in case I needed to move quickly.

He met my eyes before he spoke. "First off, let me say how very sorry I am for my behavior last September." He hunched his shoulders and cleared his throat nervously. "What I did, abducting your cousin... it was inexcusable. All I can say in my defense is that I truly wasn't myself."

My temper snapped. "You're sorry? You think that makes this all better?" I walked right up to him and grabbed him by his fancy designer necktie. I yanked him down so we were eye to eye. "You *hurt* her! She had bruises, rope burns and a black eye from where you hit her."

Julian stood still, acting as if he was totally cowed. "You are absolutely right. There is *nothing* I can say that will ever make up for it." Julian's eyes searched my face, but he remained completely still. "Go ahead... hit me," he invited. "I deserve it."

I was so angry that it took me a moment to realize that while I was right up in Julian's face— *he wasn't fighting back.* He was waiting for me to hit him, *hoping* that I would use magick on him. "Fuck you, Julian." I let go of his fancy tie and then shoved him away from me. "I'm not going to give you any reason to have me thrown out of the Masters program, *or* for you to press charges against me."

With one gesture from Julian, the security cameras in the hall sizzled and popped out one after another while I watched. "There. I told you, I won't cause any trouble for you, or your family." Julian's voice was soft, almost pleading.

"So you fried the security cameras. Big deal."

"Duncan once told me that you can read people by touch."

"He did?" Thrown off, I stared at him in shock.

"Seer of the Bishop family, I invite you to read me." He held out his hand, palm up. "See for yourself that I'm telling you the truth." Julian visibly trembled. "Please."

I considered his formally worded request. By reading him I would know if he was lying to me. Most of all, I'd know if he was up to anything else. "If you make one wrong move— I'm going to kick your balls up to your throat," I said, and had the supreme satisfaction of watching his eyes go wide.

"I won't move," Julian said, his voice strained.

"There's no security cameras to protect you now," I reminded him. I took a step closer and waited. Then another. When he stayed still, I reached over and laid my fingertips against his open hand.

The hallway at the University fell away. *I saw Julian opening up a wrapped parcel and finding the red leather cover of the Blood Moon Grimoire. He looked at it curiously and set it aside.* The vision shifted. *Julian is holding his hands above the bindings and it seemed like he was pulling energy from the leather cover. Then it was a tumble of images one after another too fast to differentiate... but the feeling of dark power and confusion grew and grew.* I caught glimpses of my own face, Ivy's and then Duncan's. *A growing sense of panic. Fear.*

Another flash came of Julian shouting at his own reflection in an ornate mirror; he slammed his fists against it and the glass shattered. Then darkness. Pain, pleasure, and more fear combined until it felt like I was suffocating. There was an impression of slowly coming to consciousness, struggling to be free. Hearing someone call to Julian, over and over. Fighting to embrace the light. Awareness, sadness, regret.

Julian crying in someone's arms. Someone... but I can't see their face.

Gasping, I yanked my fingers away from his hand.

For a few seconds we stood there, both of us struggling for breath. "Holy shit," I managed. My eyes filled with tears, and my stomach roiled as I met his eyes, and I understood what he had endured *and* fought his way out of.

"You saw it all, then?" Julian gave me a sad smile, wiping his eyes.

"I saw enough." I repressed a shudder.

"Now do you understand? We need your help. It's Duncan. He's the one in trouble, and I don't think I can help him. Not alone."

I wanted away from him. Even after seeing what he'd been through. I wanted time to sort it out and process the information. I bent to retrieve the file for Dr. Meyer, careful to keep my eyes on him. "Duncan has made his choices. Now he has to live with them," I said, and tried to make myself believe that.

"I thought you two loved each other?" he asked and picked up my shoes.

I flashed back to the horrible night on the front porch, and his psychic attack tonight. "No. Not anymore," I whispered, my throat feeling tight.

"Hear me out. The Blood Moon Grimoire *ruined* my life. I was stupid and trusted the person who gave me that damn cover. They knew what would happen to me. I didn't understand what was happening until it was too late." Julian stepped closer and his eyes searched mine. "It took months to find the way back to myself. I wouldn't wish that on anyone. But now Duncan is the one being consumed by the dark magick."

I frowned at him. "Julian, I am not the one to help Duncan. Why don't you ask your father for help?"

"I have to go." He slowly handed me my shoes, then eased to the staircase. "Please know that I am telling the truth when I say that I am sincerely sorry for what happened with Ivy. I know I can never make up for it. But I have tried to balance the scales of karma out as best I can."

I felt slightly ashamed as I studied him, especially when I recalled my words to Holly about making amends and working to be a better practitioner. "What did you mean when you said 'balance the scales'?"

"I submitted Ivy's photographs anonymously for consideration. And made sure they were in the finals for the art scholarship at the University."

"What?" I said. "Why would you do that?"

Julian shrugged. "I only wanted to help her."

"That's not necessary," I said firmly.

Julian started to go down the steps. He paused to smile up at me. It was the first time I'd ever seen an open and honest smile from him. "Autumn, she won the scholarship *on her own*," he said softly and with conviction. "All I did was to make sure that the powers-that-be considered her work."

I didn't know what to say to him. I was shocked, and this altruistic act was the last thing I ever expected out of him.

"The letters went out this week," Julian said. "She will receive her scholarship notice in a few days. Ivy's very talented. She deserves a chance to chase her dreams. It's the least I could do." He gave me a slight bow, and vanished. Like Duncan and his mother could do. He cloaked his movements so smoothly he seemed to disappear.

"Julian, wait!" I called after him, "*Who* gave you the cover of the Blood Moon Grimoire?" My voice echoed in the empty stairwell. He was gone.

I shook my head at the unexpected revelations of the evening, and for the first time I wanted out of that museum, badly. I quickly slipped my heels back on and made my way back downstairs. I found Rene and Dr. Meyers right were I'd left them, and Rene flashed me a concerned look as I walked over to them on shaky legs. I handed the file to Dr. Meyer, he thanked me and left. Since no one else was standing nearby, I moved directly into Rene's arms.

"Hold me for a second," I said laying my head on his shoulder.

"What happened?" Rene said running a hand down my hair. "You were gone too long."

I made the supreme effort to simply enjoy the physical comfort of being held, and tamped down any desire I had to combine my magickal energy with his, or to leech strength from him. I let out a sigh. "I'd like to go now," I whispered. "I ran into Julian upstairs, and we talked."

"Are you okay?" Rene asked.

"Yeah, I'll tell you all about it after we are away from here."

"Too many eyes watching and ears listening, eh?" Rene tilted his head.

"Exactly."

"Done." Rene took my hand, and I pointed out the nearest exit.

"I'll show you the new gardens," I said brightly and loud enough for anyone who was eavesdropping— and I knew there was— to hear me.

We walked out the side door and made our way along the landscaped path in the brand new expanded gardens. It was dark outside, but there was some solar lighting along the garden pathways. As Rene and I slowly made our way through the landscaping, we nodded politely at other attendees who were also headed home. Rene gave my hand a supportive squeeze, and I forced myself to act casual.

We had only stepped around a corner of the building when I spotted Duncan and Angela tucked into a shadowy alcove of the museum gardens. Duncan stood, pinning Angela against the side of the building. Her arms were stretched out over her head and held in place with one of Duncan's hands. I imagine most folks wouldn't have detected them. It *was* a dark corner... and it wasn't so much that they stood out visually, as they stood out energetically.

Oddly, no one else was in the gardens now— only

the four of us. I sensed that a reluctance had been thrown over the area to give them some privacy. But it was either a hurried and sloppy reluctance, or it was a damn clever one. *No... it was in fact a clever one,* I understood. *The spell had been designed so a few very select few people would see past it.* As in Rene and me.

I think Rene recognized at the same time I had that we'd been set up for this little voyeuristic show. As we both stopped dead in shocked surprise, simultaneously.

I heard Angela whimper, and I flinched. She'd managed to rip her mouth away from his. She whispered something to him and he laughed low, boosting her up higher against the wall. I saw her feet draw up on either side of his hips and watched as her arms wrapped around his neck. Duncan began to reach for his belt, and I realized they were going to have a go, right there in the public gardens of the museum.

I had seen more than enough. Embarrassed, I turned my head away from the couple and started to run. How in the hell I managed to run and not break my neck in heels I had no idea, but run I did, until I got to Rene's car.

I opened the passenger door, threw myself in and covered my face with my hands. Bad memories, all the things I had tried to forget from New Year's Eve came flooding back. I tried to slow down my breathing, and I fought a short, nasty battle with a panic attack.

Rene let himself in, and pressed a hand in support to my arm. After a moment, he started the car. "Autumn, you need to put your seatbelt on," he said quietly.

I lowered my hands and clicked the seatbelt into place. I blew out a shaky breath. "I'm okay," I said. "I got it."

"Don't cry, *cher*." Rene covered my hand with one of his.

"Working on that," I gritted out.

"You know that was deliberate, don't you?" Rene released my hand and smoothly backed the car out of the space.

"Yes. I know." I gulped hard and pressed a hand to my stomach. "That was like a sick replay of what could have happened to me... if I hadn't fought back that last night Duncan and I were together."

Rene stopped at the exit of the parking lot and studied my face. "If I would have known that, I would have kicked his ass." His voice had gone into a low bass growl. "That was vindictive, plain and simple. He set you up back there."

"I'm pretty sure that was the point. Just a little emotional terrorism. Since he couldn't get to me earlier — he went for the kill shot later."

"Tell me what happened earlier tonight," Rene said, driving through town.

I tried to stay calm as I explained to Rene how I'd successfully fought off Duncan's energetic attack earlier, then I explained everything I'd learned from my weird talk with Julian. He'd tensed up while I spoke, but otherwise stayed silent as I filled him in.

Rene pulled the car over to the curb. "Basically, the Drake's came at you on all fronts tonight. Mentally from the psychic attack, emotionally through your connection to your family, and intimately with the little show Duncan arranged for us."

"You're absolutely right," I said, and noticed that he had parked along the road in front of the riverside park. I leaned my head against the head rest. "Bottom line? What Duncan was doing with Angela was the equivalent of a sucker punch to the gut for me."

"Let's take a walk, the moon is still in the sky," Rene said.

I toed my shoes off and hopped out of the car. I waited until Rene took off his suit coat and laid it over the front seat. He locked the car doors and we walked together towards the riverfront. I reached for his hand automatically, and we walked in silence towards the river. I let him lead the way, and I smiled when we ducked under a familiar willow tree. It had grown, and now most of its branches trailed along the ground.

"Ivy and I broke an old binding spell that was on me last year, right in this spot." Wiggling my bare toes in the grass, I reached up and ran my hands through the draping branches. Immediately, I felt better.

"Really?" Rene watched me intensely as I walked around under the tree, letting my hands run through the little green willow leaves.

"Then I was so excited that I'd broken free, that my magick got away from me. I called a cold front in.

Made it rain," I said. "It knocked me on my ass."

Rene slipped an arm around me. "What happened then?"

"I got dizzy so Ivy made me lay down in the grass, then Aunt Gwen appeared and..." My voice broke as I recalled Gwen glowering down at us with her big black umbrella. "And then she chewed us out for playing with weather magick." That was it. I'd reached my breaking point.

Rene pulled me close when I began to cry.

"Damn, even though I was only with her for a short time, I miss her so much," I said, trying to wipe away my tears.

"Of course you do. She was your first Craft teacher, and you loved her." Rene nudged me down to sit on the soft spring grass with him.

I leaned my head on his arm and let the tears come. After a little while I pulled myself together. "Sorry," I apologized.

"What for?" Rene asked.

"Tonight pretty much sucked. I'm a terrible date," I admitted.

"Not even close." Rene pulled me closer. I felt much smaller and very feminine sitting like that. I tried to smile up at him, and he softly wiped my tears away with his thumb.

"Thanks," I said.

"I have something for you," he said. Rene reached into his slacks pocket and handed me a small red bag. "I meant to give this to you earlier, but tonight was a little crazy." He dropped it in my hand and I observed that it was made from red leather.

"What's this?" I asked him.

"A gris-gris bag for protection," Rene said. "I made it for you."

"*Gree-gree*?" I tried to sound it out. "What's in it?"

"This gris-gris is a bag filled with stones, herbs, metal charms and sigils for protection. I conjured this for you with items I felt would be in alignment with your personal energies."

I looked at the little bag in the palm of my hand and it gave off a sort of low energetic hum. When I closed my fingers around it, a feeling of warmth washed over my body. It definitely had herbs in it, and I when I pressed my fingers to it I could feel some small stones. I'd never felt anything like it before... This was a new magick for me, earthy and strong. "Can I open the little bag?"

Rene's eyes met mine. "You should keep it tied shut, and on your person at all times."

"Okay." I tucked the gris-gris in my jacket pocket. "How's that?" I grinned at him.

"Promise me you'll keep it on you."

"I will." I leaned back against his arm. A movement in the branches above had us both glancing up. A crow peered down, and seemed content to stay on the branch. He tucked his wings under him and held still.

Rene gave my arm a gentle squeeze. "Autumn, if I

would have known the details of what happened with Duncan..."

"Yeah?"

"I wouldn't have done what I did the night of the High Council meeting."

"What do you mean?" I blinked up at him.

"I held you against the house, that must have brought back some bad memories."

"You didn't at all! You had me so worked up that when you nudged me back against the house I couldn't even think straight. You were very gentle with me... you never *pinned* me, or trapped me anywhere."

"Marie told me that he left bruises on your jaw and arms... If I knew exactly what had happened with Duncan, I could have made sure not to put you in that situation again." Rene was staring into my eyes, and his sage green eyes were intense. "When we are together, *whenever* we get to that point— I don't want to bring back any memories of him or what violence happened between you."

My mouth dried up. "Alright," I said. *Maybe if I simply got it over with...* I tried to speak as calmly as possible. "He grabbed my face and dug his fingers in. Here," I said, and with the barest of touches, showed him on his own face. I lowered my hands and tried to psych myself up to finish.

"Go on." Rene stayed still and waited.

"He bit me. On my bottom lip, making it bleed, and he left a nasty hickey on my neck." I blew out a breath, determined to be done with it. "Finally, when I fought back, he shoved me against the house so hard he cracked my head against the siding, and then held me in place against the side of the house by my upper arms."

"Show me," Rene said, quietly.

I demonstrated again on Rene's arms where exactly, but it felt slightly ridiculous, as my hands could not even wrap around his shoulders.

"Which explains why you've been skittish about people touching your face, or making any sudden moves." Rene nodded as he thought it over.

"I've gotten better about the 'hands near my face' thing." I pointed out.

"Darlin' we are really going to have to take things slow." Rene's deep voice rumbled, and as I was practically sitting in his lap I could feel the vibration in his chest.

I smiled up at him. *How did I get so lucky as to find a man like this?* Deliberately, I snuggled closer. I tucked my head under his chin and wrapped one arm around his back. "Hey, Rene ..." I said as if I were thinking things over.

Rene seemed to enjoy having my arm around him. "Um hmm?" he said, and it felt like a big purr.

"I was wondering..." I asked him, and pulled back to check his expression. "If you were dizzy, that is."

Rene chuckled softly.

"Because if you were..." I kissed his jaw softly. "I was going to suggest that you lie down in the grass with me."

With one smooth motion from Rene, we were both on our sides in the soft grass. I wrapped my arms around his neck when he pulled me close. I closed my eyes with a sigh when he kissed me. Then he stopped.

"What?" I asked, opening my eyes with a frown.

"Look at me." Rene's voice was that delicious bass growl, and I shivered. "Look at me, Autumn," he urged.

I couldn't resist yanking his chain. "Why?" I fluttered at him. "Because you're so pretty?"

His lips twitched. "I want you to remember who you're with," he said.

I touched my nose to his. "Big guy, there's not much chance I'm gonna forget."

A breeze rolled out from the river, it sent the long draping willow branches to swaying. It seemed as if they had rearranged themselves, providing more privacy.

"Did you do that?" we asked each other.

"No," we said in unison, and then laughed.

"This is a magickal place," I whispered.

He cupped the back of my head, encouraging me to meet his gaze. "Look at me now," Rene murmured as he lowered his mouth to mine.

There are many kinds of magick... I thought, staring straight into his eyes. And Rene Rousseau was turning out to be one of the best.

CHAPTER TEN

I stared up at the ceiling, churned up and unable to sleep. Merlin snuggled on my stomach, and I rubbed his silky kitty ears while he happily purred. Usually that was comforting to me, but not tonight. I was all churned up and unable to relax.

Rene and I had stayed under the willow tree for a long time. I'd laid in his arms, in the grass and we'd gazed up at the sky through the draping branches, talking for hours. There was plenty of kissing and touching too, and I wasn't sure if I was impressed by the thoughtfulness of his restraint... or if I was cranky because things hadn't gone beyond kissing and touching. It's not that I was in a rush to start another serious relationship, it was just that the man certainly knew how to wind a girl up and leave her wanting... more.

But I was learning a lot by being involved with Rene — romance with another magician did not have to be intense or overwhelming. It could, in fact, be slow, fun, *and* sexy. I couldn't wait to see him again, we were supposed to meet for breakfast at 7:00 and then spend the day together. That is if I could ever get any sleep...

I woke a few hours later, covered in cold sweat. My heart pounding, I raised a hand to the crescent moon pendant I wore. *It was only a dream.*

A dream where I'd found myself running terrified through a dark garden, with Duncan right behind me. He'd caught me by my arm and whipped me around. I'd tried to call up magick, but nothing happened. I'd tried to fight him off, but he was too strong. This time, I couldn't get him off of me, and he'd slammed me against a brick wall and finished what he'd started on New Years' Eve.

"That's a hell of a way to wake up," I muttered. For comfort, I reached over and patted the nightstand for the gris-gris bag. Shannon would probably say that this was my subconscious' way of working through my fears. I squeezed my hand closed around the tiny leather bag and figured that my fears had been given a hell of a refresher course thanks to the events of the evening... it was no wonder I had trouble sleeping and had been rewarded with a bad dream.

I checked the time and scowled at my clock when I saw it was 4:12 am. Giving up on going back to sleep, I clicked on my bedside lamp. I slipped my glasses on, tucked the gris-gris bag in my glass case, and pulled out the journal Gwen had given me out of the nightstand drawer. I scooted up into a sitting position. Merlin muttered and rearranged himself along the side of me. He dropped his head back between his paws and sighed.

"Sorry." I patted him on his back and I settled in, deciding to take notes on everything that had happened in the past twenty four hours. To start, I wrote down my impressions of how the psychic defense technique had worked for me— and then took it a step further— and to pass the time, I jotted down some ideas on what I could do to improve it.

I flipped to the back section of the journal where I'd started a new section for notes on the quest for the BMG (When Ivy had started calling the grimoire that, it had stuck), and went over everything that we did know to date.

The entire family had been meticulously going through the manor, and we still had no idea where to find the final missing piece of the BMG. As far as I knew... no one from the other founding families had any new theories or good news either.

The only person who'd had information was the ghost of my Grandma Rose, and after her last big manifestation and demonstration of power, she'd gone radio silent. There'd been nothing more from her. I re-read the entries I'd made concerning everything Rose had ever told us, and one line seemed to jump off the page at me. 'Begun with three, so it must end with three.'

It must have taken the magick of three Witches' to divide up the grimoire.

Grandma Rose had said three Witches would be required to bring it back together. I searched through my notes and found the particular line from her last visit. "Here we go," I muttered to myself. "'*Three Witches are needed to finish what was once begun; A Maiden, Mother and a Crone will bind what was undone.*'"

I tapped my pen against the pages while I mulled it over. Merlin rose and padded across my lap to paw at the journal. His white-tipped paw pulled it down, and his golden gaze met mine.

"Am I on the right track, Merlin?" I asked him.

The cat let out a soft *meow,* staring at me with unblinking eyes.

"Maybe the question we should be asking is— who was the third person involved with separating the BMG originally?" I said.

Hmmm... David Quinn, Witch or not, must have been one. He'd taken his section and hidden it at his parent's home. I'd found that section by accident last September. My father, Arthur, had most likely been the second since we knew that his mother had helped him conceal another section under one of a trio of her grandmother's old botanical drawings.

Merlin head butted the journal, drawing my attention. "You know, Merlin," I said. "I'm starting to think that if we have any hopes of finding the last missing section, then we need to find out the identity of the third player."

As if in answer, Merlin meowed.

"So, if I follow the theory that it took three Witches to separate the BMG— then how did we end up with four pieces?" Suddenly it hit me, and I sat straight up. "What if the bindings had originally been with the third section?" My stomach tightened, and I knew I was right. The third section wasn't lost at all! Someone had them and was sitting back and waiting as my family put themselves in danger locating the other two-thirds of the grimoire— for them.

I climbed out of bed and began to pace my bedroom floor as I thought it over. "Okay, so 'they' had one of the sections, but they were impatient. I'd come back to town, and maybe they thought I knew about the pages. So maybe to speed things along they'd separated the binding from the last third of the pages, and for some reason sent them to Julian..."

But why Julian? I felt a little rush of adrenaline, and I fought to stay calm as I stopped pacing and closed my eyes to better remember everything I could from last night. I took a deep breath, recalling clearly the visual impression of Julian opening a package and uncovering the red leather binding of the Blood Moon Grimoire. Where had he been, though? I tried again... *His office. It had been delivered to his office at the museum. In plain brown wrappings, and originally he'd set it aside, unimpressed with it.* I opened my eyes and picked up my journal. I sat on the side of my bed and wrote down all the details of the memory I'd gathered and the other impressions from when I'd read Julian.

Going over the information from my reading, I was beginning to get an uncomfortably clear picture of exactly what the bindings of the BMG were capable of inflicting on whoever possessed them. Julian had been a victim of the grimoire's dark magick, and as he'd said — it had ruined his life.

Now Duncan had the bindings, and I had personal experience of how they'd changed him. His magick was thoroughly dark, and his personality had altered into shades of violence and cruelty. On New Year's Eve, when I'd scanned his memories, my original assumption had been that Duncan had received the bindings from his uncle Thomas. But Duncan had snapped at me and said they were a peace offering...

My mind was spinning, and I started to pace again as I tried to make sense out of everything. Merlin began to trot along, back and forth, with me. What if that 'peace offering' had been Thomas's last ditch effort to make sure that his son, Julian, was never exposed to the dark magick of the Blood Moon Grimoire again?

I recalled when Thomas had first approached me at the University Library. He'd said he wanted the book back and described it as having a red leather cover. So Thomas hadn't known the book was divided. And before that, my surviving family hadn't even known the book existed.

I froze. "Which means Thomas Drake probably doesn't have the last section of the BMG." Frustrated, I blew my bangs out of my eyes. "There goes my number one suspect, Merlin," I said.

Merlin rubbed against my ankles in sympathy.

What was I missing? Think, Autumn! If Thomas never had possession of the grimoire, he'd certainly been desperate to have it returned to him. And the more I tried to figure it out, the more confused I became. Thomas had hinted there were 'other parties' that wanted the grimoire the night of the Halloween Ball, *and* he'd warned me about the dangers of reassembling the BMG, but I hadn't believed him.

Then Gwen had died, and after her burial service Thomas had confided to me the cover had driven Julian mad... but Julian was a spoiled, pampered rich boy... he'd been an easy target for the BMG's dark magick. So maybe Thomas had removed the leather grimoire cover from Julian's possession? Had he then given it to Duncan?

Had he thought that Duncan was stronger than his son? On one hand, Duncan had known the risks and the dangers... but on the other he was still falling under the dark influence of the bindings. Duncan had gone into this with full knowledge, and now there was none of the charming, practical, and down-to-earth man I'd once known. His behavior last night was proof.

I stared out my window and wondered what to do next. Take my theory to Bran, to Great Aunt Faye? Or did I wait until I had some proof and not merely supposition? All I had at the moment was a boat load of conjecture, but no actual evidence. I didn't think it was a smart idea to corner Thomas and ask him who the other interested parties were.

Whoever had the third section was *dangerous*. Dangerous enough that they made Thomas Drake nervous, and potentially lethal as they had the power to fatally hex anyone who got in their way.

I scrubbed a hand across my face. I was wide awake now and tense. Checking my phone, I saw that time had passed while I'd been trying to solve this mystery, and that sunrise was in fifteen minutes.

Well, I was awake anyway, maybe taking a quick jog would help me see things clearer. Afterwards, I would know how to proceed. I removed the family crest pendant. It was heavy, and I didn't want it bouncing against my chest while I ran. I slipped the pendant in my jewelry box and tossed on my hot pink running shirt and black shorts. I pulled my hair into a stubby ponytail, laced up my shoes, grabbed my iPod, and got ready to go.

By the time I had let myself out of the gates at the end of the driveway, the sky was brightening in the east, and a few cotton ball clouds dotted the sky in shimmering coral. With my running music blasting in my ears, I jogged towards the riverfront park. I let my mind go blank and enjoyed the scenery. The neighborhood dogwoods were blooming in off white and blush. Bright tulips paraded in neat flower beds, and crabapple trees were fluffy in shades of white, candy pink and red.

I jogged the loop in the park and found myself grinning at my willow tree. My heart lifted as the sun rose above the horizon. Feeling better and more upbeat, I started back to the manor. *Everything would be fine. We'd figure it out as a family. Together.*

I was working my way back up the big gradual hill and into the historic neighborhood, when I realized that I was approaching the Drake's family mansion. Without breaking stride, I checked over my shoulder for oncoming cars. I saw none and crossed to other side of the street to be farther away from the mansion.

I'd no sooner gained the far side of the street, and my iPod crackled and went out. I twisted my arm to check it. *That's weird. It was fully charged when I left this morning.*

I swung my eyes back front just in time to duck under a low hanging crab apple branch that grew straight over the sidewalk. I almost made it, bumping into it only slightly, and white petals sprinkled down like snow. An unexpected gust of wind hit me in the chest, and it was strong enough that I glanced towards the sky. The sky was a clear blue, there was no storm front coming— but oddly, instead of the petals blowing *away* from me on the wind, they seemed to rise up. Shooting forward, the cloud of white petals passed in front and began to spiral around me. Moving with me as I jogged.

Entranced, I slowed my pace to watch as they

seemed to dance and spin, brushing against my face and arms. I raised my hands to touch the dancing petals and laughed joyfully. *It was beautiful... almost like magick!* Then my heart jumped in my chest. I knew a magician who could call and direct the element of air. The last time I'd seen him do so was on the night of Samhain— when he'd made colorful maple leaves swirl and dance.

Duncan.

I glanced nervously over my shoulder. Duncan was jogging on the opposite side of the street, maybe fifty yards behind me. His expression was grim, and he was moving up fast. *Had he been waiting on the Drake grounds for me to pass by?* He crossed the street at an angle, coming over to my side, and the distance between us narrowed dramatically.

I didn't even think— I reacted.

I ran as hard and as fast as I could to get away from him. Now the petals weren't playful. They obscured my vision and the wind blew hard against me as if to slow me down. I raised my arms up in front of my face and kept going. I wouldn't let him use an element against me. I pulled my magick from my gut, casting it up and out. *Element of air, help me!*

I could hear the slap of his shoes behind me on the old brick sidewalk, and I didn't dare slow my stride by looking over my shoulder. I could *feel* that he was getting closer.

Suddenly there was a rush of energy from above. I heard the *kaww kaww* of the crow right before it shot down out of the sky like an arrow. The bird dove close enough over my head that I ducked. Then a second, third, and a fourth crow followed. I risked a quick glance behind me, only to see four large birds flapping at Duncan while he covered his head with his arms. The crows made a terrible sound as they attacked.

"Autumn!" he bellowed.

I could see the manor at the top of the hill, and taking a deep breath, I hauled ass. I ran harder than I ever had before, even with the help of the crows to stall Duncan. My legs were burning as I sprinted up the hill, my chest was tight, my breathing labored— but I kept going. For a few crazy seconds I imagined there was a huge flock of crows behind me. I could almost feel the displaced air from their wings, and that combined with the adrenaline and fear pushed me to greater speeds.

Our wrought iron gate at the end of the driveway was open as I topped the hill. Finally gaining the flat part of the road, I saw Rene and Holly standing on the front porch. *Just have to make it through the gate!* No sooner had I thought it— and the gate began to swing slowly closed all by itself.

Rene swung his head around when Holly ran down the steps and sprinted towards me across the front lawn. "Autumn!" she screamed, stopping where the edge of the lawn met the driveway to point at something above me.

The birds. There really were birds behind me. I didn't waste time answering her, or looking to see. I pumped my arms harder, and blew through the opening in the front gates in the nick of time. The gates slammed shut behind me with a loud bang.

Even inside the gates, I kept moving, "Get inside!" I wheezed at her, but Holly stood frozen, an expression of horror on her face. I saw that Rene was running towards the both of us, and I grabbed Holly by the back of the shirt and yanked her along.

Rene was suddenly there. He skidded, grabbed Holly's arm, and turned to run the rest of the way with us. "Move!" Rene shouted to Holly over the thundering sound of dozens and dozens of crows that had begun to descend on the house. Holly finally snapped out of her daze and began to run.

Together, the three of us pounded up the front porch steps and only then did I look. What I saw blew me away. A massive flock of crows called back and forth to one another. It sounded like a battle cry as they circled the manor. I dropped my hands to my knees, bent over and gasped for breath.

"Where did they come from?" Holly called over the racket the birds were making.

"I don't know... Duncan, he came after me... and they saved me," I panted.

Lexie burst out the front door, with her police gun in her hands. "Get in the house!" she yelled at us, crouching into a firing stance.

"Lexie, don't shoot the birds!" I said.

Ivy ran onto the front porch, digital camera in hand.

"Wow!" she shouted and started to take photos. Bran and Aunt Faye were right behind her.

Bran's mouth dropped open as he witnessed the mass of circling birds. "Who called them in?" he demanded.

"I think Autumn did," Rene said, crouching down in front of me. "Breathe, just breathe. You're safe."

Oh shit, had I called the birds? I nodded to him, but stayed bent over. "You're early," I said to Rene, as I fought to catch my breath, *and* to stay on my feet. Now that the adrenaline was fading I was starting to shake.

"I had a feeling." Rene laid a hand protectively on my arm.

Lexie pointed her gun barrel towards the ground and straightened. "What happened that scared you badly enough to call them in?" she said pitching her voice over the racket.

"She said Duncan was after her," Holly raised her voice to be heard.

"What?" Bran yelled.

Rene glanced at Bran, "Where is he now? Do you see him anywhere?"

Lexie scanned her surroundings. "Negative."

Bran moved behind his wife— on the opposite side of her gun arm, I noticed. "If he's out there you can shoot him!" he said to her.

"Bran." Lexie rolled her eyes.

Aunt Faye was suddenly in my face. She bent over, and her voice was calm and firm. "Autumn, you called them in, now send the birds back."

I held up my first finger, silently asking for time.

"Dear, clear them out and send them away," Aunt Faye said.

"Gimme a second here." I straightened up and walked to the edge of the porch, my chest still heaving from my uphill sprint. Exhausted, and freaked out, I did the first thing that came to mind. "Disperse!" I shouted, flinging my arms up in the air.

It worked. The crows suddenly changed direction, and flew off in a swarm together. Gradually, the noise died down, and I lowered my arms while Ivy continued to take pictures. I felt my knees turn to water. "Huh," I managed. "I see spots," I heard myself say.

Rene grabbed my arm, "Autumn!" his voice was sharp. I'd never heard him use that tone before.

"I think that last spell took it out of me," I said, laughing at my own joke. Everyone was staring at me, and I heard a roar in my ears and the black and white spots returned. "I think I should lie down now," I said, reaching for the floor.

Rene and the entire family were peering down at me. I was flat on my back, staring up at the porch ceiling. "Hey, the porch ceiling is painted blue," I said.

"Autumn can you hear me?" Lexie sat beside me on the floor of the porch, patting my hand.

"Well, yeah." I made a face at her. "I'm okay."

"You went dead white as your knees gave out," Lexie said. "Your color is better now, at least."

"I did *not* pass out," I said, to reassure myself—more than anyone else.

Ivy's face appeared upside down over mine. "I'll say this, you know how to make an entrance."

Rene nudged Ivy back, "Maybe we should take her to the ER."

"What, why?" I frowned at him. "I'll be fine in a couple minutes. It was that uphill sprint at the end of my jog and using magick that wiped me out."

Holly handed me a cool, wet, hand towel. "Here, try this."

To prove that I was fine I eased up on my elbows a bit. I wrapped the cold towel around my neck and shivered. "Man, that feels good."

"Don't get up too fast," Lexie warned me.

"I won't," I said.

"Well somebody help *me* up, damn it." Lexie sighed, holding up her hands. She was at the stage of her pregnancy where she wasn't as nimble as she used to be, and it made her cranky.

Before Bran could get to her, Rene hooked his hands under Lexie's arms and lifted her with one smooth motion. "There you go."

"Thanks." Lexie nodded to Rene and went inside to secure her gun.

I sat up and waited to see if I felt dizzy, but I was good. I wiped my face with the ends of the towel and rearranged it so the coolest parts would be at my neck.

Rene crouched down in front of me. "Do you have

the gris-gris bag that I made you?"

"Shit!" I said. "I left it in my glass case, on my night stand."

"It doesn't do any good unless you have it on you." Rene pointed out. "Did Duncan follow you while you were out jogging?"

"He popped up when I was on my way home," I said as Lexie came back out to join us. "I was jogging past the Drake mansion when I spotted him..." I filled everyone in on what had happened. The flower petals, the wind, me seeing him running behind me, my panicked call to the element of air, the birds— and then the uphill sprint.

"If you will excuse me," Great Aunt Faye said. "I have a few phone calls to make."

Bran opened the door for her. "The High Council?" he asked.

"Yes." She pulled out her cell phone from her robe pocket and stepped back in the house.

Holly stood at the porch rail, staring up in the sky. "The flock is gone."

"Murder," I said.

Holly swung her head around to me. "*What* did you say?"

Now everyone was regarding me as if I were crazy. "Technically, a group of crows is called a 'murder'," I explained. "So that was a murder of crows."

Ivy started to chuckle. "You know the weirdest stuff. What's a flock of ravens called, then?" she wanted to know.

"An unkindness," I said getting to my feet.

"Seriously?" Ivy tipped her head over to one side.

Rene took one of my arms. "Easy does it."

"You're sure those were crows?" Ivy asked.

"Yes, crows are native to this region," I told Ivy. "Ravens are more common where I grew up in the northeast."

"And crows make that *kaww kaww* sound we heard," Holly said. "Ravens sort of croak."

I smiled at Holly. "Exactly. Those were crows for sure." I gave Rene's arm a squeeze. "I'm going to get cleaned up and then we can go to breakfast."

"Are you still up for that?" he asked.

"Sure, let me go hit the showers. I'm starving," I said, realizing that it was true.

"Normally I'd think you should let your system settle after running," Rene said. "But since you pulled out that big magick, you probably *do* need to get your blood sugar levels back up."

"Autumn," Bran called my name quietly. "I think you should come and see this."

I walked over to where he stood with his arm around Lexie. When Lexie pointed, I saw that on a low branch of a redbud tree, one crow perched. Almost as if he were waiting.

I recognized the bird immediately. "That's Midnight," I said.

"Grandpa Morgan's familiar?" Bran's eyes were

wide.

"Yeah, he's been around for months. I need to go tell him thanks, I'm pretty sure he's the guy who led the charge back there."

"Go on." Bran nodded. "We'll wait here."

I went down the porch steps slowly and made my way over to the tree that grew along the side of the porch and the house. I stopped a few feet away from the bird, who cocked his head and ruffled his feathers. "Thanks for the save back there."

Midnight bobbed his head up and down and responded with a quiet *kaww kaww*. I reached out my hand slowly to see if he would allow me to touch him, and Midnight held still. I gently touched his back and ran my fingertips over his wings.

To my surprise Midnight leaned into the touch, not unlike Merlin did when he wanted affection. I chuckled. I'd never pet a bird before. I glanced over my shoulder and saw that Holly and Ivy stood at the bottom steps, with identical expressions of longing on their faces.

"Midnight?" I asked the crow softly. "Would you like to meet the rest of Morgan's grandchildren?"

In response, the crow bobbed his head up and down and moved back and forth on the branch. When I lifted my hand away, he ducked his head under my palm and nudged me.

"Ivy, Holly, Bran..." I resumed my petting and called softly. "There's someone I want you to meet."

I heard them approaching, and Holly and Ivy

arranged themselves on either side of me.

For once, Ivy left her camera untouched and hanging around her neck. "He's gorgeous," Ivy breathed.

Holly slowly ran her hand down my right arm and skimmed her hand on top of mine where I petted Midnight. She waited a moment for Midnight to accept her touch. "Hello," she said, very softly.

Midnight shifted on the branch and turned to Holly, so I gently lowered my hand and let Holly get acquainted with our grandfather's old familiar. I stepped back with Bran and watched as Ivy mimicked what Holly had done, and then she was also skimming her fingers over the bird's back. Midnight seemed to preen as the girls cooed over him.

"I remember you," Bran said to the bird.

Midnight seemed to gather himself, and he flapped his wings, making the twins step back. Midnight hopped off the branch and landed neatly on Bran's shoulder. Bran leaned his head towards the bird and Midnight nuzzled the side of Bran's head.

I couldn't help but grin at my brother. "He knows you."

Bran beamed at me. "He used to do this when I was little." He raised a hand to the bird and gave him a gentle stroke. "Grandpa Morgan used to walk around with him on his shoulder like this. And sometimes, Midnight would want to ride along on mine."

Ivy raised her camera and took a few pictures of Bran and the crow. "Maybe you remind him of Grandpa

Morgan," she said. Midnight cocked his head at Ivy watching her taking his picture. She lowered her camera and grinned at him.

I reached up to pet Midnight again. "Crows are supposed to have excellent memories for faces."

The crow was apparently feeling playful as he stepped off Bran's shoulder and went to mine. Midnight tugged my ponytail holder free and dropped it on the ground. When Holly giggled at his antics, he jumped over to her shoulder, pulling on her long hair and making her laugh.

"This is definitely Grandpa Morgan's familiar," Bran said. "I wonder where he's been all these years?"

Ivy sat on the grass and aimed her camera up to take more pictures. I heard her camera click a few times, and Midnight fluttered down to the lawn and made his way over to Ivy. She lowered to her belly, continuing to take pictures until he began to peck curiously at her camera lens. Ivy squealed a little when Midnight grasped the dangling camera lens cover and gave it a tug.

"Ivy," Holly said. "Show him the lens cover."

Ivy slowly unhooked the silver colored lens cover and held it up to the crow. Midnight cocked his head, grasped it in his beak and took to the skies.

"That," Ivy said, "was awesome."

Rene and Lexie came down the steps and stood with the four of us as we watched Midnight circle around the manor with the camera lens cover in his beak.

Lexie put her arm around Bran. "You realize this

visit was a sign and a message, right?"

Bran tugged her closer to his side. "A good sign. The crow is a messenger from the spirit realm. They offer guidance whenever you come to a crossroads in your life."

"That makes sense, because every time I've had a close encounter with him I've been at a crossroads of sorts," I said.

Holly took my hand. "I think he's the crow that saved us that day... when the car ran the stop sign."

I watched the bird fly off and to the west. "I think so too. He's been hanging around me for months now." I glanced over at Holly and Bran. "Messages from the spirit realm... That makes sense. Because I think he's filling in for Grandpa Morgan."

CHAPTER ELEVEN

Rene and I did have breakfast together, but we ended up staying in. Lexie announced the 'baby' wanted French toast, and so Holly and Ivy had whipped up a big batch. By the time I came downstairs after my shower, breakfast was ready and the family all gathered around the dining room table to loudly discuss the morning's events.

Aunt Faye had gone all out for the family breakfast. She'd added a bowl filled with hydrangea blossoms to the center of the dining room table. Their huge purple-blue blossoms complimented the pale purple cloth napkins she'd set the table with. As I sat down next to Rene, I noted she'd broken out the good china and silverware as well.

We were typically a noisy bunch, and meal times were no exception. As everyone talked over the table there were, as usual, several conversations going on at once. Ivy gestured and the maple syrup slid across the polished table to her, all by itself. "In the Celtic tradition, it's the crow that delivers messages from the spirit world." Ivy poured syrup on her second helping of French toast. "So that means someone from the spirit realm has been staying close and trying to deliver a message."

"Like Autumn said," Holly agreed, spooning blueberries on her plate. "Maybe it *is* our Grandpa Morgan's way of communicating."

"That would be so cool," Ivy added.

"Don't forget the nursery rhyme." Lexie winked at Bran. "One crow for sorrow, two for joy, three for a girl, and four for a boy, five for silver, six for gold, seven for a secret never to be told."

Bran nodded and launched into a lecture on the mythology of the crow in different magickal traditions. I listened with half an ear. Since I was seated next to Great Aunt Faye, I decided to quietly try out my theories on her about the final section of the grimoire not being lost, but held back... and to my surprise that did not go over well, at all.

Aunt Faye shook her head at me. "Not now, Autumn."

"Aunt Faye, I think whoever sent the bindings to Julian has the remaining pages." I kept my voice down, but refused to drop the subject. "Someone set us up to do all the dirty work while they sat back and waited."

"That's ridiculous!" she scoffed at that, and her teacup met the table top with an angry sounding snap.

I set my fork down deliberately and considered her.

"Why are you so angry?"

"Because you're wrong. Arthur and David took the pages." Her eyes blazed a molten silver color. I'd never seen her this wound up.

I lifted my hand to the silver crescent at my throat. "Grandma Rose told me that this *began with three and must end with three*. So it must have taken three Witches—"

"Ghosts have been known to lie!" she hissed.

"So you are implying that my grandmother's ghost is lying to me— us?"

Aunt Faye stood up suddenly from the table. "Trust me when I say, I have more knowledge about the spirit realm than you do. This discussion is over." She tossed down her napkin, and it made an unnaturally loud thud when it hit the table.

I felt the impact the same way you feel the percussion of fireworks in your chest on the fourth of July. "What the hell was that?" I said to Rene.

Aunt Faye stalked out of the living room. A couple of seconds later, I heard her bedroom door slam shut. Now everyone was silent and staring at me.

Lexie, who'd been sitting nearest Aunt Faye, waved off my concern. "It's been a trying morning, Autumn. Let her go."

"But I have a theory about the BMG, and I think the family should hear—"

"It's probably nothing we haven't already considered." Bran shrugged and changed the topic.

I glanced over at Rene, and he was scowling at the family. I opened my mouth to say something, and he gave my hand a little warning squeeze.

"Do you have the gris-gris on you?" Rene asked me very quietly.

"Yeah I do," I whispered back. I'd tucked it in the pocket of my denim shorts before I came down for breakfast. I'd put the family crest back on and tucked it under the neckline of my lacy black top.

"I think the gris-gris is helping you to see a little clearer."

I studied my family who had now launched into a discussion on baby names. "So, how about those crows?" I said deliberately trying to see if they would go back on track.

"Crow?" Lexie frowned at me. "Why would anyone name their baby, Crow?"

And I knew. *Aunt Faye had tossed down magick. Right there in the middle of a family breakfast.* But why? Why would she manipulate the family into not wanting to talk about finding the grimoire?

Rene leaned past me, and using the prongs of his fork, lifted the cloth napkin. He drug it over across the table and let it sit in front of his plate. "Pass the salt," he said conversationally to Holly.

Holly passed the salt shaker, and Rene sprinkled salt over the cloth. No one seemed to notice.

"Containing the magick." I nodded at him. "Smart idea." He smoothly wrapped his own napkin around it and pulled the bundle off the table and into his lap.

"Let's go," I said to him.

"Excuse us," Rene smiled politely at the family.

As Rene and I left the dining room, I glanced over my shoulder at my family. They all sat there having a mundane, pleasant and totally out of character quiet meal around the table. I felt a shiver roll over my skin. Aunt Faye had spelled them all.

If it weren't for the gris-gris- in my jeans pocket I'd be as clueless as the rest of them. *What was going on?*

***

I filled Rene in on my theories about the BMG on the drive over to his place. When he'd parked the car, I stopped talking. After everything that happened I didn't want to take a chance of anyone overhearing me. I remained silent until Rene let us in the back door of Marie's shop. Rene secured the door and I blinked as he flipped on the overhead lights. I never been in the back of the room of the shop before, and what I saw had me looking around with appreciation.

Beautiful and complex designs were drawn in white on the floors, the walls, and even on the back of the door. I touched the design on the inside of the door. The drawing reminded me a little of a fence for some reason... "Wow," I said. "This is a veve, right?"

Rene tapped the metal door. "This is the veve that represents the Orisha, Ogun. He is the Orisha of strength, iron and metal."

"Oh." Admiring the intricate design, I set my bag down to one side of the door. "It's beautiful and a clever magickal link to be painted on the metal door of the shop."

Rene took my hand. "Ogun awards us strength through prophecy and magick."

"The designs are so intricate. They're everywhere and so pretty," I said.

The back room of Marie's shop seemed to be a combination of industrial chic/ practical storage and old world/ magickal work space. At the back of the room, practical metal shelves for storage were arranged. Yet, hanging from the ceiling a vintage metal chandelier with chipped white paint served as overhead lighting. The entire facing wall was taken up with an old, well used wooden workbench, and above that hung rustic wooden cabinets and lots of open shelving.

I approached the workbench, cleverly up-cycled into a magickal work surface, keeping my hands clasped behind my back. There were herbs drying from a rack overhead, and rustic shelves were filled with various supplies. The shelves held dozens of jars in all shapes, sizes and colors. Some were old mason jars in pale blue-green, and others were simple recycled jam and jelly jars. As I walked closer, I saw tiny bottles of essential oils as well as jars of dried herbs, spices, black salt, and large glass containers of Sphagnum moss.

On the far end of the work surface stood a couple of

large mortar and pestles. A terracotta pot held a lavender plant that bloomed lushly despite being indoors. Beside that, a large potted fern was tucked in a copper cauldron. A practical clipboard that held invoices was next to an occult supply catalogue and a computer. Marie was using an old chipped New Orleans mug to hold scissors, pens and pencils in her work area. The shelf above her computer held a wide variety of books on herbs and magick.

"This is amazing," I said, peering at the jars displayed over the center of the work surface in a beautiful wooden cabinet.

The cabinet door was open, and Mardi Gras beads were draped across the shelves. A large Fleur-de-lis was attached to the burlap lining of the back of cabinet, and the bottom shelf held tiny drawers that were lined with more sphagnum moss and held tiny glass jars. I discovered, as I studied this central cabinet, that it held some rather unusual ingredients. Such as an alligator skull that was prominently displayed on the top shelf.

An old bell jar held rusty red powder and was labeled "Red Brick Dust". The large square, glass container next to it read "Snakeskin", and sure enough, I saw a shed snakeskin in that jar. Tucked alongside was a little box of something called 'Blue Anil Balls', and a jar labeled 'White Eggshell Powder'. An apothecary style jar's label announced its contents as "NOLA Graveyard dirt", and I was surprised at what I could see clearly was resting in another jar. "Are those animal bones?" I asked Rene.

"Chicken bones," Rene clarified. "This ain't Wicca, *cher*," Rene grinned at me.

"Well, neither is the Craft that I was taught." I glanced over at him. "The first time I called what Aunt Gwen taught me *Wicca*, I got an hour long lecture on the difference between Wicca and Witchcraft."

"Oh yeah? Tell me about that." Rene began to gather ingredients from the shelves.

I closed my eyes to better recall the details and to keep from tearing up— memories of Gwen always made me a little emotional. "I'd been studying in her turret room, and when I'd said that, she whipped her head around so fast that she caught me off guard." I chuckled, as I remembered. "She'd so rarely gotten mad... she'd even used my full name."

"Uh-oh, your whole name." He set out a few bottles of herbs. "That's how you always know when you're in deep trouble. What did she say?"

"She said, 'I'll have you know, Autumn Rose Bishop, that our traditional family practice is *not* some homogenized, popular culture version of the Craft.'"

"I didn't know Gwen as well as my sister did. I only spoke to her a few times over the years, but I can see that. Bet she put her hands on her hips when she lectured you."

"She did." I blinked a few tears away. "Sorry," I sniffled.

"You need to stop apologizing so much." Rene ran a

hand down my arm.

"Noted." I leaned into him.

"Let's get to work," Rene said. He reached up to a cabinet and removed a carton of salt. He poured a neat circle on the work surface. He unwrapped the dinner napkin and gently let it roll into the center of salt.

Rene opened the cloth napkin that Aunt Faye had tossed down, and there in the center of the pale purple napkin, were the remnants of dried herbs and powder. He leaned over and sniffed, then recoiled. "Asafetida and sulfur, definitely."

I leaned over and got down so I was eye level with the surface of the workbench. "I'm thinking poppy seeds and maybe black pepper..." I frowned at the traces of the spices in the lilac colored napkin.

Rene went directly to the bookshelf and pulled a green book down, he flipped to the index. "Want to check something," he said.

I walked over to him. "What are you thinking?"

Rene set the volume down on the workbench and flipped the pages. He ran a finger down the page. I leaned around his shoulder to see what he was reading. As I observed him, I saw that four out of the five ingredients we'd identified were listed in the recipe he was studying.

My heart dropped to my stomach. "Those spell ingredients are for 'Confusion Powder'." I said.

"Doesn't seem like she added dried hydrangea..." Rene said as he studied the spell.

"She didn't have to. Remember the big blue flowers on the table?" I said. "Those were hydrangea blossoms from the shrubs in the garden."

Rene closed the book. "Well, this is unexpected," he said after a moment.

"Why in the hell would Aunt Faye toss down a 'Confusion Powder' in the middle of the dining room table? What could she hope to gain from that?"

Rene's expression was neutral, as if he were thinking something over. "Asafetida is also called 'Devil's dung'. It's used for other things as well."

"Such as?"

"Banishing spirits," he said.

My mouth dropped open. "Since Grandma Rose's big performance a few weeks ago, her ghost has been MIA. There's been nothing. No scent of roses, no new messages." I leaned against the workbench to think it over. "Aunt Faye deliberately broke the circle that day... and she looked tired afterwards," I said, mostly to myself.

Rene folded his arms. "So she's been banishing ghosts from the house and trying to draw the family's focus away from finding the Blood Moon Grimoire."

"But why?" I stalked across the room. I felt the strangest vibration under my feet and struggled with my temper. "Damn it, this makes no sense!" I said, scowling at the lights in the chandelier as they began to flicker.

"Autumn..." Rene's voice was a low warning.

"What I need is someone to help me find the rest of the damn grimoire. Maybe it's lost, or hidden... who knows? Either that or I need some help contacting the spirit realm—"

"Stop!" Rene shouted at me.

"Stop what?" I shouted back as Rene marched towards me. "This is such bullshit, Rene! How am I supposed to protect my family when all I'm surrounded with are lies—"

"Not another word!" Rene stopped, pointing at the floor. "Look where you are standing."

I cast my eyes to the floor and realized I was standing smack in the middle of a veve. "Oh." *Well, perfect.* "Am I in trouble?" I gulped, staring down at the pattern painted on the floor.

Before he could answer, there was the clear sound of the back door unlocking. Behind me, Marie slammed open the door, hard enough that it bounced off the wall. "What in the name of Oshun are you two *doing*?"

Afraid to move, or say anything, I glanced helplessly at Rene.

"She invoked Papa Legba," Rene said in a matter-of-fact tone of voice.

Marie stalked around the veve and stood side by side with her brother. "You idiot," she shook her head at Rene.

Invoked? That didn't sound good. "I didn't mean to." I hunched my shoulders when I heard how whiney my own voice had sounded.

"Autumn, step over here to me." Rene's voice was flat as he extended a hand.

I went to him immediately. I resisted the urge to scamper over and, instead, forced myself to walk slowly and to stand up straight.

I sniffed the air. "Hey, do you guys smell pipe tobacco?" The identical alarmed expressions on both of their faces made me wonder how badly I had screwed up.

Marie stepped between the two of us and placed a hand on each of our shoulders. "Remember, that I do this out of love..."

"Do what out of lo—" I started to ask only to be cut off when Marie gave me a half hearted smack to the backside of my head.

"Hey!" I glared at her and saw that Rene was rubbing the back of his own head.

"How could you be so careless?" She balled her fists, glaring at Rene. "You brought her here knowing what she's capable of!"

What I'm capable of? My hurt was immediate, and I stepped away from them. *Marie was supposed to be my friend.* Yet there she stood shouting at her brother... About what I was 'capable' of.

"Don't lecture me like some novice," Rene snapped back. "I've seen for myself what she can do!"

Rene's comment stung. So much, that it surprised me. Marie was up in his face, and was gesturing broadly while he argued with her. They were really going at it too. I heard her shout at him about dark magick, and I shrank back. Clearly, Marie thought I was working dark magick. I didn't even want to know what Rene thought of me, now.

I took a step towards the door that still hung ajar. Then I took another. *You don't even see me.* I picked up my bag and pushed out energy. I visualized it, willing that thought into being. I saw heat waves billow out between me and the Rousseau's. *I'll be long gone before you even notice. Just keep arguing.* I concentrated on that thought too, and then slipped out the open back door.

Grateful for my running shoes, I walked silently away from the shop. My heart pounded with the need to get away. Once I moved past Rene's car, I swung my bag over my shoulder and ran. Focusing only on the need to put distance between myself and the shop, I jogged across Main Street, towards the river and down the jogging trail in the park that ran through the woods.

Jogging in denim shorts wasn't ideal, so I slowed to a walk once I was in the cover of the wooded area. There were no people biking or walking this morning on this section of the paved route of the eco-park area. Before I could decide where to go next, I felt something flopping around my ankle and had to stop to retie my shoe. As I was crouched down, I discovered a little dirt path that broke off from the main route and ran down into the woods.

Unless you were small, or bent over, the tree

branches practically hid the path. Elderberry, the small tree sacred to the Crone goddess, grew thick in a clump all around the opening to the path, and I pulled back a few branches to see. The trees along the dirt path were thick, the shade cool, and it was peaceful and sheltered.

Perfect. I could use some shelter for a few hours. Taking the elderberries as a good omen, I ducked under the tree branches and moved quietly down the path. I'd gone maybe three feet when my cell phone started to ring from inside my backpack-style purse. I stopped, shrugged off the fabric pack and yanked the phone out. I checked the read out and saw it was Rene. I clicked my phone over to silent and let the call go to voice mail. I tucked the phone away, discovering I had a half full water bottle in the pack and was grateful for it. I hitched the bag over my shoulders and quietly followed the trail deeper into the woods. I needed to put some distance between myself and William's Ford.

I hiked for a few hours heading north. Little parks ran along the main route, so it was only a matter of time before I ended up in one. Within the first hour, all I saw were a few pre-teen boys riding mountain bikes along the dirt path. I moved out of their way, and with a smile, they zoomed past me. After that, I was blissfully alone.

I used the time on my hike to think about everything I had learned in the past few days and allowed the trees and woods to soothe my hurt feelings and nerves. I didn't start to look for a place to rest until my stomach began to growl. I pulled my phone out of my pocket to check the time and saw it was coming up on noon. The dirt path had led me alongside the Missouri river most of the morning. I had enjoyed some pretty, scenic views as I stood up on high ground, happily following the trail. My intuition had told me to stay on the trail, and to follow it, and I figured after everything else that had happened, maybe I should be silent and listen for a while.

The path veered away from the river, and I walked down a little slope where I spotted the old abandoned cemetery. It brought me up short and made me a little uneasy. I still had problems with cemeteries. I hadn't been back to Aunt Gwen's gravesite since December.

I stopped and studied the old burial ground. It wasn't overly large. It was probably a family plot. It was surrounded with an old, rusted cyclone fence, and the woods had almost reclaimed it. As I walked up to the gate I saw that, while the gate hung crooked, someone had taken the time to care for the old cemetery. The grass was a little high but not disreputable, and there were no trash sapling growing within the perimeter.

An old tree had fallen and lay along side the fence surrounding the cemetery. It was clear with no poison ivy growing on the trunk, and was as good a spot as any to rest for a while. I pulled my purse to my lap and opened it. I sipped from the water bottle and checked the contents of my bag. My wallet, a package of gum, a granola bar, and old mashed candy bar were the extent of the contents.

I ate the granola bar and took slow sips of the water. As I sat on the fallen tree, I realized I could hear the sounds of people and cars. A road was somewhere close. I hadn't gone very far on my walk— maybe four miles, but I knew I was outside the city limits of William's Ford. I'd give myself a bit more time before I started to head back. I gazed up at the sunlight filtering through the tall trees and connected to the earth. I took a few deep breaths and grounded my energy.

I'd taken a few hours for myself. I'd sorted through things, and now it was time to face Rene and Marie, and of course to return to the manor. If I was going to counteract the magicks Aunt Faye was working on the family, then I needed to think outside the box. And for that, I would need the Rousseau's help.

"Hello, child."

I startled, dropping my bag and almost fell off the log. I found an elderly black man leaning against the gate of the cemetery. He was thin, wearing old jeans, a faded red shirt, and a straw summer fedora shaded his eyes.

"Hello," I studied him as he leaned there casually and grinned at me in a friendly way. I hadn't heard him approach, but I didn't get a sense of any danger or malice from him.

"You paying your respects to the dead?" he hitched a thumb over his shoulder towards the cemetery.

I tucked my wrapper and water bottle away, and

stood to face him. "I don't have any relatives buried here." I had to clear my throat against the emotions that had welled up and surprised me. "I was just out for a walk."

"But you buried a loved one someplace else recently. Haven't you child?"

I studied his weathered face that was handsome still besides the winkles. "Yes sir, I have."

"It's hard losing loved ones." He sighed and ran his hand along the gate.

"Yes it is." I stood up and shifted my bag over my shoulders.

His eyes met mine. "Still, you should pay your respects. A graveyard is a sacred place."

"I don't like cemeteries."

"Is that a fact?" He chuckled. "Well then, what you doin' sitting by one?"

"Thinking about stuff," I said.

He tipped his hat back slightly. "Such as?"

"Family, trust, and power." The words had popped out before I thought them through.

He gave me a long and considering look. "Power is a tricky thing. Some folks chase after it their whole lives, others throw it away, and others must learn how to use it wisely."

"That's true." I nodded to him. *What a strange conversation.* I studied the man thoughtfully. He stood quietly and waited. I wondered how far he'd walked by himself. "Can I walk you back to your car?"

He let loose a loud and bawdy laugh that had me smiling in response. "No car, child. I walked. It's a pretty day for a walk," he said, leaning heavily on his cane and making slow progress. "You have a good day now," he said as he moved past me.

Before I could respond in turn, his shoe caught a rock and he stumbled. I reached out to steady him. I made up my mind and looped an arm through his. "Tell you what, why don't I walk you back to the road where the pavement is flat and easier to navigate."

"Don't fuss, I'm fine," he said his voice gruff.

"It's no bother at all." I patted his arm and steered him back towards the sound of the people and the road.

He pointed his cane up a slight hill. "That way is quickest to the park."

We walked in companionable silence, and a few minutes later we came out into a clearing of a small park. I blinked, spying a little league baseball game in progress and a concession stand that was doing a bustling business.

I had escorted him as far as the playground when he gave my hand a pat. "I'd like to rest on the bench for a little while," he said.

"Sure." I steered him towards it and hovered nervously until he sat down. "Can I get you something to drink?"

"Well, a coffee sounds nice." He removed his straw hat revealing white hair and waved it towards his face.

"I'll be right back," I promised.

"Don't you worry about me."

I hustled over to the concession stand and waited in line. I turned to check on him and there he sat, waiting in the shade. I bought a bottle of water, a coffee, and a candy bar. I tucked my wallet in my bag, snapped a lid on the coffee, and started back to the playground.

I dodged a couple of kids that ran past me screaming and playing. I looked up and discovered that the old man was gone.

I swung around searching for him, and concerned, I jogged to the bench where I'd last seen him. There was no one around except a half dozen kids and a few parents. I stopped a woman pushing a baby stroller past me. "Excuse me, did you happen to see where the elderly black gentleman went to?"

"No. I didn't see any other adults, well besides you, walking out of the woods a bit ago," she said.

"What?" I said. "You would've had to have seen him. He was walking *with* me, he had on a summer hat, was wearing a red shirt, and had a cane. I left him sitting on the bench a few minutes ago."

The woman's eyes were wide as she stepped back. She whipped her baby stroller away. "I think you're confused." She rushed away from me, and I let her go.

"How could she have seen me, but not him?" I muttered. *Oh god, had I encountered another spirit? But he'd felt real! I'd held his arm and walked with him...*

Shaken, I dropped to the bench, carefully sat the

coffee and candy bar down, then twisted the cap off the water bottle and guzzled it.

CHAPTER TWELVE

"Autumn." A hand dropped on my shoulder, and I jolted, choked, and did my best not to spit water all over the place.

A short, stocky older man with curly hair and familiar twinkling blue eyes patted my back. "Mr. Jacobs!" I gasped between coughs. "What are you doing here?"

Oliver Jacobs, Sophia and Chloe's grandfather— and the best doughnut maker in town— moved around to the front of the park bench. "I'm taking in a ball game." He hunkered down in front of me, concern written on his face. "Honey, what are you doing out here and all alone?"

I managed to stop coughing. "Hiking?" I shrugged.

"Faye called me this morning." He stood, and moved over to sit on the bench next to me. "She told me what happened." He rested a foot on his knee and leaned back. "So, you unleashed a whole flock of crows, eh?" he chuckled. "I'd have liked to have seen that."

"Ivy took pictures." I sighed and felt mildly embarrassed. "I'm sure she'll show them to you." *If she even remembered they were in her camera after Aunt Faye's magickal whammy.*

He sat beside me in companionable silence for a moment or two. "So, were you really hiking? Or were you running away from everything that happened today?"

I studied him. He sat there wearing a *Cardinals* baseball t-shirt, khaki shorts and a ball cap was pulled over his curly hair. Seeing him dressed so casually, I had to remind myself that Oliver Jacobs was not only the head of his family line, he was also a member of the High Council. If he said 'everything' he probably knew about the incident at Marie's. "Am I in trouble with the council?" I asked.

"Trouble? No. But there are a whole lot of worried people out searching for you right now."

I raised an eyebrow. "I bet my family aren't among them."

"No, they aren't, and that concerns me. Do you want to talk about it?" he asked me casually.

"I'm sorry Mr. Jacobs, but I don't know if I should." I said, turning to face him.

He leaned forward a bit, "Call me Oliver," he invited.

"Okay, Oliver," I said, meeting his eyes.

Those kind blue eyes locked on to mine. "Gotcha." I heard him say, and I felt a falling sensation. He was in my mind and scanning my memories before I could blink. Unlike the time Bran had scanned my memories, this wasn't uncomfortable at all. Oliver Jacobs was a pro. I felt his energy, but it was nimble and lightning fast. A couple of moments later, and he was finished. He sat back on the bench and blew out a breath.

I'd thought I was good at scanning people's memories, but wow, he wasn't simply good, he was *scary good*. I'd seriously misjudged the baker. Oliver Jacobs came across with this affable, modern grandpa vibe... but it was an excellent cover that disguised a very strong, very talented Witch. I frowned at him anyway. "You could ask a person."

"Don't worry. What I saw stays between you and me. And besides, sometimes looking for yourself expedites matters— especially when a person's safety is at risk."

"I've done pretty well protecting myself so far..."

Oliver rolled his eyes at me. "Girl, you're more like your father than you know." He patted my knee in a paternal way. "Trouble seems to find its way to you. No matter what."

"You knew my father well?" I blinked in surprise. "What was he like when he was young?"

Oliver jiggled his foot up and down as he spoke. "Arthur? He was talented, reckless, and defiant. He ran your grandparents ragged. Like father, like daughter."

I hunched my shoulders, not sure if that was a compliment or a criticism. "I'm not defiant," I muttered half-heartedly.

Oliver raised his eyebrows at me. "What do you call a young woman who was stalked, and chased only this morning, disappearing for hours to go off *hiking* on her own?"

"I'd call her fed up, hurt and pissed off," I snapped back.

Oliver said nothing in return but the mildly disapproving expression on his face had me fighting not to squirm.

Finally, I sighed and gave up. "I learned some things today, and I'm not sure I can trust even my own family right now."

"Your Great Aunt Faye? I *saw* when I scanned you." Oliver leaned forward resting his elbows on his knees, seeming to think it over.

"Why? Why would she do that to the family?" I asked him.

Oliver tugged his ball cap off and scrubbed a hand through his hair. "I don't know, and I admit... it troubles me as well."

"I know I eventually have to go back to the manor. But first I need to speak to Rene and Marie."

"Especially since you stepped in a veve and invoked a Loa today." Oliver whistled between his teeth. "The council is going to *love* that."

"Did you get that from my memories or from Marie and Rene?"

"Rene told me the basics. When I scanned you I got

the full picture." Oliver steepled his fingers. "Be assured, you have invoked Papa Legba."

I tossed up my hands. "In my defense, I don't even know who Papa Legba is."

Oliver shot me a look. "You should. You just took a walk with him. He was the old man you came out of the woods with."

My heart jumped in my chest. I tried to make words form. I failed.

Oliver grinned at me. "I saw it in your memories just now. That old man you thought you helped? He was Papa Legba— and I'd say he was testing you."

"I thought he was simply an old man who needed help. I even offered to go get him a coffee…" my voice trailed off.

"That's smart," Oliver said. "Coffee is a traditional offering."

I blinked. "I had no idea."

"Papa Legba often appears as an old black man wearing a straw hat, red shirt and he carries a crutch—"

"Or a cane?" I asked.

"Exactly." Oliver beamed at me.

"Wow. Do you think I passed the test?" I managed after a moment.

"You showed him kindness and you brought an offering. I'd say yes, you passed his test. He will more than likely help you find what was lost," Oliver said.

"Wow," I said again, blowing out a breath.

Oliver patted my head. "You over-achiever, you."

I sighed, covering my face with my hands. "Well, I suppose I better get this over with." I peeked through my fingers at him. "I wish..."

"Yes?"

"I'm not ready to face Marie and Rene quite yet," I admitted.

Oliver bounced to his feet and held out a hand. "Come on, let Rene and Marie know you are safe. They can call off the troops. Let's get you some lunch, and that will help you stall a little longer."

I took his hand, stood up and saw that I was at least four inches taller than the man. "So where are we going?"

He gave my fingers a friendly squeeze, then let go. "Ever been to *The Old World Pub* on Main Street?"

I reached for my bag and decided to leave the coffee and candy on the bench in case Papa Legba came back. "Ah, no I haven't." I pulled out my phone, and winced at the read out. Twelve missed calls and several messages from Shannon, Marie, Violet and Rene.

But none from my family.

I hustled to keep up with him. He might not be tall, but he could move quickly. "I'm going to send a quick text, and let my friends know I'm okay." I followed along behind him scrolling through my messages.

"That's good." He nodded. "I'm going to call the Missus... let her know where I'll be." He pulled a cell phone out. "Darlin' I found what we were looking for." He turned, hooking his arm through mine giving me a tug so I was walking with instead of behind him. "Yes, safe and sound. I'm taking her for a bite to eat. Love you too." He disconnected and tucked his phone in a clip on his belt.

I felt suddenly guilty as I walked along with Oliver. He gave a wave to some people sitting in the stands. "Am I interrupting your plans with your wife for the day?" I asked.

"Nope, changing them a tad," he said. "Not interrupting."

I followed him to a white, late model mini-van with the logo of his bakery painted on the side. He opened the door for me and I hopped in. As he walked around to the driver's side, I sent a quick group text to Shannon, Violet, Marie and Rene. I wasn't sure what to say, especially after the magickal faux pas, and the *you know what she's capable of,* comment of Marie's.

So I kept it simple: I'm fine. Went for a walk. Needed some space. Going with Mr. Jacobs to get lunch.

Before I could put my phone away, Rene responded: On my way.

A little surprised at his instant response, and wondering how the hell he would even know where we'd end up for lunch, I shot back a snarky response only to him: You sure you want to? You know what I'm capable of.

Rene texted back: Stay with Oliver. See you soon.

My breath huffed out at the nerve of the man. *Did he think I'd sit there and let him be all domineering? I'd given control of a relationship over once before, and it had led to disaster. That was never going to happen again.*

When Oliver chuckled, I glanced over at him. "What? I didn't say anything."

He cleared his throat. "Has anyone ever told you that you broadcast your thoughts very loudly?" Oliver started up the van, and I could see he was trying not to laugh.

"Yeah, I get that a lot."

"I'm thinking you need a pint," Oliver decided. He flipped on the radio and classic rock pounded out of the speakers.

"I don't like beer," I said over the music.

"What? A nice Irish girl like you?" He sounded scandalized. "That's a crime against nature!"

"Got sick on it my Freshman year at college. Never touched it again," I said.

"Bah! Frat boy beer." He dismissed that with a flick of his hand. "You need a Guinness, my girl."

As Aerosmith throbbed out of the van's speakers, I leaned back and started to relax for the first time that day.

***

The Old World Pub lived up to its name. It had an Irish Pub vibe and boasted dark wood paneling, a massive carved wooden bar, and a television on the wall that broadcasted a soccer game. Oliver was apparently a regular, as he walked in and was hailed by no less than five different people. The waitress showed us to a corner booth, and I slid in and made sure my back was to the wall and my eye was on the door. I'd had enough surprises for one day.

"We'll have the lamb stew and two Guinness," Oliver ordered before I'd even picked up the menu.

"And a water for me," I told the waitress.

"Sure thing," she flipped her order book closed.

I tucked the menus back in the little holder on the table and noted the cover design was a smiling Green Man face. I raised my eyes to the walls, and I counted several versions of leafy faced Green Men smiling or scowling down on the patrons from the walls. "Nice place," I said to Oliver.

We chatted politely for a few moments about his granddaughters, Sophia and Chloe, and the waitress came back with a small loaf of brown bread on a wooden board, two small plates, and a dish of butter. She set my water down in front of me, told us to enjoy and scurried off across the room.

My stomach growled loudly when the scent of the warm bread hit me.

"Allow me." Oliver took a knife from the board and sliced off a section.

I took a bite and groaned. "Oh, wow... This is really great." I reached for the butter and slathered it on my slice.

When the Guinness arrived, I took a cautious sip and

discovered it was actually pretty good. When I said as much to Oliver, he grinned at me.

Oliver kept me entertained with stories of Chloe's first loose tooth, and when our food arrived, I dug in. I stuck with water for the most part, but I managed to drink about half of the Guinness. I was finishing up the stew when I saw Rene stride in the Pub door. And he didn't seem pleased.

"Aw, hell," I said, bracing myself for the apology I needed to make.

His body language read neutral, but it was the lack of emotion on his face that had my heart beating a little faster. Which made me wonder: *Was there a male equivalent of 'resting bitch face'?* If so, Rene was working it, which made me realize that he was using his training as a model to hide his emotions.

Everyone stopped speaking, both women and men turned to stare as a gorgeous, six foot five inch tall, caramel-skinned god in ripped jeans and a snug t-shirt stalked across the pub floor, straight for me.

I found it a little unnerving that he never once took his pale green eyes off me, not even when he made his way through the maze of tables to our booth. For such a large man, he moved well, and with a poise I would *never* achieve in this lifetime. In a moment, he stood beside our table, glowering down at me, then he slid into my side of the booth, giving me no choice but to move over and make room.

Oliver nodded to him as he took his seat. "Rene,

good to see you."

"Oliver, thank you for finding her for me."

For me? Any apology I would have made, slipped away as my temper started to raise its head. *Why, the arrogant son-of-a-bitch.*

"No trouble at all." Oliver grinned at me from across the table. He was probably picking up on my inner monologue again.

"Now look," I began, but didn't get to finish as Rene reached out hooked the back of his fingers around my neck, pulling me close.

He was right up in my face, but still holding me gently. His body was rigid, and tension came off him in waves. "You spelled me so you could run off." He took a breath. "Don't *ever* do magick on me again." His voice came out in a deep growl.

"I'm sorry..." I began softly, and he caressed the back of my neck. He smiled at me, clearly assuming that I had given in to him. *Oh baby, are you in for a surprise.* I yanked my head away from him. "I'm sorry that you'd think that I would ever— for one minute— take orders from you."

Oliver leaned back in the booth across from us as if to enjoy the show.

"Are you defying me?" Rene's eyes widened in surprise.

I rolled my eyes. "Ding, ding! He got it right on the first try!"

Rene clenched his jaw and glanced over at Oliver.

"Would you excuse us for a moment?"

Oliver slid out of the booth, fighting a grin. "Sure, I'll head over to the bar for a few." He grabbed his empty glass and strolled away whistling.

"Autumn..." Rene began, then stopped and frowned at me so hard his forehead scrunched up. He took a breath, and seemed to be choosing his next words with care.

"You're going to get wrinkles if you keep furrowing your brow like that..." I said sweetly. "Then your modeling career will be shot to hell and gone."

His eyes blinked in shock.

Before he could say anything else, I let him have it. "Listen, I was prepared to apologize for making you worry, but then you strutted in here acting all domineering, and it's seriously pissing me off!"

He blew out his cheeks. "I'm pissing *you* off?"

"So, I tossed down a little reluctance to get away from you? Big deal. Because from where I'm standing, that was self-defense." I struggled to keep my voice low and checked to make sure no one was eavesdropping. "Don't act so surprised. You're the one who pointed out to me on the night of the High Council meeting that my magick isn't always ethical."

Rene rubbed his chin. "You don't trust me," he said.

"About as much as I trust anyone these days. But I'll remind you that it was *you* who decided to take things slow with our relationship because *you* don't trust *me*. Or what I'm capable of."

"Is that what you think?" His voice rumbled low and deep.

"Why should I think anything different?" I said to him. "I was drawn into this world, not even a year ago... I'm trying to learn as much as I can as quickly as I can. When Duncan taught me magick, I lapped it up. It never occurred to me that it was manipulative. It worked, and I used it. Simple as that." I caught myself and made an effort to keep my voice down. "I only had a few months to train with Gwen before she died. Now, I study and practice mostly on my own. But truthfully, half the things I do? I conjure on the fly. Calling in the crows this morning, then summoning a Loa at the shop, I didn't even plan those... It just happened."

Rene slid his hand down my arm. "Bottom line, you put yourself at risk, running off like that." His touch was gentle and non-threatening— almost as if he were trying to calm me down. "I was worried for you, especially after this morning." He patted my hand like I was a child.

I snatched my hand away. "Well how *nice,* you were worried. Was that before or after you discussed with Marie "what I am *capable of*?" I tossed his own words at him again and watched his smile drain away.

"Damn it." Rene kept his voice low, but I could feel the frustration coming off him. "I know you didn't intend to invoke a Loa. Marie panicked that you had done so on purpose, and that's why we argued."

I picked up my water glass and took a sip. "Did it

ever occur to you that knowing you don't trust me when we are alone together *and* hearing her say that hurt me?"

"Did it ever occur to you to stay and stand your ground, instead of running away and behaving like some frightened child?"

I glanced meaningfully at my water glass. "You wanna see child-like behavior?" I asked quietly.

"Put the glass down, now." Rene's voice was deep and flat.

I heard and *felt* the compulsion in his voice, but I was angry enough that it didn't have much of an effect on me. For a split second, I almost gave into the urge to toss my water at him, simply to see what he'd do, public restaurant be damned. I set my glass down on the table very slowly, but I kept a hold of it and lifted my eyes to his. "You really wanna play mental domination games, big guy?"

I could see by his little smirk that my challenge had been accepted. "You'd lose the game, but you'd *enjoy* it," Rene whispered, and brushed a hand over my knee.

The promise of his soft words had my mind careening off into dark sexual fantasies. The desire to submit to his will was so strong that for a moment, I trembled with it. *I had totally underestimated his magicks. Talk about your double whammy. First, I'd misjudged Oliver Jacobs and now Rene. I'd thought Rene was simply a root worker— like Marie.*

But Rene was more... much more. I caught myself

and leaned back a bit from him.

Rene's magickal power was based in physical attraction, glamour, and sex appeal. It was how he smoothed things over to get his way, and how he had become so successful. And he was damn good at it. Being this close to him, the strength of his physical beauty made me break a sweat.

I held myself very still and resisted his allure with every bit of my own magick. "You fight dirty, Rene." I worked to keep my voice even.

"*Cher*, you don't want to fight with me," Rene said in the sexiest, most compelling tone of voice I'd ever heard him use. He cupped my chin in his hand and leaned in closer. I felt the punch of his power in my gut, and my hormones jumped up and applauded.

Running out of options, I fell back on *my* superpower: Sarcasm. "I bet that shit works a lot for you, doesn't it?" I said softly, right before his lips touched mine.

"What are you talking about?" He frowned at me and withdrew. No longer touching me.

I remained perfectly still, keeping my voice even and my tone polite. "The whole, drop-dead gorgeous, Alpha male routine. You strut in, glower a bit, use that deep rumbling voice for effect, and women fall all over themselves, quivering at the thought of being told what to do."

Rene seemed surprised at my comment. And his magick, thankfully, faltered. "Your will is strong," he said. "Stronger than I knew."

"I've had to be strong." I rubbed the heel of my hand over my heart. There was an ache there— from the cost of resisting his glamour. I blew out a quiet breath. "And Rene? Don't ever throw sexual glamour at me again. You won't like how I'll retaliate."

Rene stared at me for a few moments, almost as if he was seeing something he didn't expect. "You're the first person to ever resist or to call me out on it." He leaned back against the booth and a slow smile spread across his face. "Damned if I know why that makes me want you even more."

I lifted one eyebrow. "Because you're perverse?"

He chuckled, and the atmosphere lightened. I took in the pub and the customers. A few people were staring, mostly women— probably at Rene— but for the most part it seemed business as usual. I saw Oliver glance over, and he went back to his conversation at the bar.

"Did we just have our first fight?" I asked, as the waitress strolled over in our direction with a few water glasses on a tray.

"We did." Rene stretched out his long legs, and tucked his hands behind his head. His biceps rippled, straining against the short sleeves of his navy t-shirt.

"You should save the 'gun show' for the tourists," I smirked at his posing, and I wasn't the only woman who'd noticed. There was a gasp as the approaching waitress bobbled the tray, and then a crash as the glassware hit the floor.

"Oops." Rene grinned at me, and it was full of mischief and fun.

"Knock it off, Rene." My lips twitched, but I refused to smile. It would only encourage him.

"Had to make sure my mojo was still working. Since it doesn't seem to have much effect on my girl."

I shook my head at him. "For Goddess sake."

Rene sat forward and took one of my hands. "Please don't run off like that again." His voice was quiet but in his normal tone, with no compulsion behind it.

Since he wasn't pushing magick at me, I apologized. "I'm sorry that you were worried."

He gave my hand a gentle squeeze. "I was. Taking off after Duncan came at you this morning was reckless."

Reckless. *Like father, like daughter.* Oliver's words about being like my father came back to haunt me. I picked up my glass from the table and took a sip of my water before I answered Rene. "I needed some time alone to think things over. And to decide what to do."

"And have you?" He reached up and toyed with a lock of my hair. "Decided what to do?"

"I have an idea on how to minimize the effects of the spells Great Aunt Faye has cast against the family," I said. "But I'll need both you and your sister's help."

Rene smiled. "What did you have in mind?"

***

I got a crash course in Hoodoo, or root-working, that afternoon and evening from both Rene and Marie. While we worked with the various herbs and roots to create specific powders, potions, washes, and gris-gris bags for the family at the manor, Marie and I spoke and cleared the air.

Violet O'Connell had popped in that evening with a bag of rose petals for Marie and to bring me five amethyst points with instructions to hand them out to the family for added defense against manipulative spells. Apparently at home working magick with the herbs, Violet had pulled up a stool and created two small herbal sachets. She called them 'dream pillows', and she crafted them out of felt in her trademark color, purple. As she sewed them together by hand, she explained to me that they were for the twins' beds, to help break the spell cast on them.

Maybe it was my earth element connection, but I felt a connection, or an affinity, to the root-working. It was practical and hands-on, and I focused on it completely. When we finished, I had the dream pillows from Violet and little red gris-gris bags for the twins. I was now equipped with washes and powders to sprinkle across the thresholds of everyone's bedrooms for protection and to limit their exposure to any more mental confusion spells from Aunt Faye.

I arrived home late that evening at the manor after everyone was already in bed. Only Merlin seemed to be waiting up for me. He sat at the top of the second floor landing, his tail twitching as I approached. I scooped him up with one arm and carried him and my bag that was heavy with supplies and a book from Marie. After my magick was finished here tonight, I had orders to read as much as possible about the Loas A.S.A.P.

I went directly to my room, set Merlin on my bed, and began to unload my supplies. First order of business was to get the jar candle that Marie had given me working. The tall "Seven Powers" candle featured seven different stripes of colored wax, and the jar was covered in symbols drawn by Marie and then empowered by Rene.

I set the candle inside the fireplace in my room. The fireplace may have worked at one time, but since I had lived at the manor, its use was strictly ornamental. I secured the candle in the little stack of pretty logs that were arranged in the grate and then lit the wick. Rene had told me this particular type of candle was often burned to resolve complex situations. Especially when there was no easy solution to the problem.

I stayed hunkered down in front of the fireplace and decided to improvise a charm to go with the big spell candle. I held my hands out and focused. "By the element of fire, may my magick be blessed. Protect my cousins, my brother, his wife and child from any more magickal manipulation and from any harm. As I will, so mote it be." The candle popped and crackled for a few seconds and then settled down with a steady flame. Merlin gave me a kitty head butt in my back to get my attention.

"Time to go to work, Merlin," I whispered to him. I took off my shoes and tucked the two little dream pillows in my shorts pockets. I gathered up the blue bottle Marie had called 'Peace Water', and as quietly as possible, walked out into the hall. Merlin followed, padding silently along with me.

I wasn't sure what I was expecting when I sprinkled drops of the blue tinted water over Lexie and Bran's threshold— but hearing a little hiss as the potion made contact with the ground was *not* it. Figuring the peace water was working, I poured a little more of the liquid in the palm of my hand and flicked it on the door itself where the liquid disappeared immediately.

As I moved from one doorway to another, there was a noticeable reaction each time as the droplets of liquid hit the doorframe and the floor. I smelled roses and lavender as I worked my way along the second floor, and a sense of, well, *peace* settled over me. Feeling bolder, I nudged the twins' bedroom door open and then dropped to my hands and knees. I cast a quick reluctance on myself hoping to lower my chances of being seen, and Merlin stayed glued to my side, slinking along with me as I crawled across the floor and over to the foot of Ivy's bed.

My hands were shaking, but I was determined to finish this up. I gingerly tucked one little purple dream pillow Violet had made between Ivy's mattress and the box springs. I slowly moved over and added the second sachet to the end of Holly's bed. According to Violet, by morning Aunt Faye's enchantment on the girls would be weakened, and my cousins would begin to remember.

I was counting on their recollection as I slowly made my way over to Ivy's desk. Once there, I stood and picked up her digital camera. I resisted the urge to check the photos, knowing it would make too much noise. I looped the camera strap around my neck and eased out of the room, closing the door behind me.

Only after I had flicked peace water over the door and threshold of the twin's room did I consider my job done for the evening. I headed back to my own room, and promptly tripped over the carpet runner in the hall. I caught myself on the banister with one hand, and secured the camera with the other. I held my breath, half expecting someone to bust me standing out in the hall with Ivy's camera. But no one did, and I let out a shaky breath and moved as quickly as possible to my own room.

Merlin scampered in behind me before I shut the door, and I sagged against it with relief. "I did it, Merlin," I said to the cat.

Merlin rubbed against my ankles in a sort of congratulations I suppose— I'd only tripped once. Which, basically, was a true act of magick in and of itself.

I decided to cover my bases and used some of the Peace Water to draw a large pentagram in the middle of the inside of my door. "Earth, air, fire, water..." I quietly named four of the points of the star, then finished with the top and fifth point. "And spirit."

I drew a circle around the upright star, visualizing all the elements represented by the pentagram— to be with me. "I now create a sacred space, no one can enter who wishes me harm," I chanted. "The five elements shall spin around, and surely bind this charm." I shook my hands as I finished the spell, and more droplets of the Peace Water scattered around my room.

I wiped my hands on my shorts and quickly began to scroll through the photos on Ivy's digital camera. The photos from this morning's encounter with the flock of crows *were* all there. Even the close ups she had taken of meeting Midnight. Relieved that I had the proof I would need to convince them something was going on with Aunt Faye, I hid the camera under my bed.

I decided to stash the rest of the occult supplies from Marie and Rene inside of an old suitcase, in the back of my closet. Come morning, I'd talk to the girls and give the twins the protective gris-gris bags I had made for them. At the first opportunity, I'd hide the protective charms in the baby's room and Bran and Lexie's bedroom.

As for Great Aunt Faye, and her room downstairs... I had other things in mind.

I had a poppet with her name on it.

CHAPTER THIRTEEN

I was rewarded for all of my covert protection work with another sleepless night. When the sun rose, I rolled out of bed and staggered into the shower. I got dressed for my day of classes and mentally prepared myself for the work I still had to do in order to break the lingering magick Aunt Faye had cast over Holly and Ivy. As soon as I heard that the girls were up and moving, I snagged them before they left for school to try a version of the spell Ivy had once worked on me. The one that had broken my father's enchantment that had muffled and bound my magick.

Explaining briefly what I wanted to do, I handed out the little red gris-gris bags, and the crystal point from Violet. "You'll need to place these items so they have direct contact with your skin," I said.

"On it." Ivy immediately tugged down the neck of her green shirt and tucked the little bag and the crystal into her bra.

"Okay." Holly shrugged and followed suit.

The girls had been suspicious when I locked my bedroom door, but once the three of us had joined hands, a rosy pink light began to glow from the center of our circle. The light spread and spread. The fragrance of roses and lavender bloomed in the air, and then the light bulbs in the ceiling fixture, my night stand lamp, and my desk lamp all blew out in succession with soft pops.

Holly was the first to release hands. "Oh my Goddess!" Her voice shook and her eyes were huge in her face. As she began to remember, she trembled.

Ivy dropped her butt on the floor, taking in huge gulps of air, as she tried to center her energy. "How could she have done that to us?" Tears filled her eyes. "*Why* would she do that to us?" Ivy whipped her head up. "Where's my camera? Do I still have the photos of the crows?"

I stroked my hand over Ivy's brown hair. "Shorty, I have lots of theories and none of them look very good — and yes, I've got the camera, and all the photos are still there." Quickly, I filled them in on what I had worked out about the BMG, the mysterious third player, and Aunt Faye's reaction to my theories.

Ivy leaned her head against my leg. "So someone has been using us to find the other two sections?"

"I believe so," I said. "They've sat back, let us do all the dirty work, *and* take all the risks."

Ivy shuddered. "So the family's been the magickal equivalent of cannon fodder."

I bent over and cupped Ivy's face in my hands. "Well, we won't be anymore." I met her eyes and let her feel my resolve.

Holly walked slowly, shakily to the edge of my bed. She sat, carefully smoothing her pale pink dress down. "Have you told Lexie and Bran?" she asked.

I straightened and faced her. "No, and I don't think I'm going to. Lexie's a couple months away from having the baby. I want her to be safe."

Ivy held up a hand to me, "If Bran knew, he'd be hell on wheels trying to protect us all," she said as I hauled her to her feet.

I nodded in agreement. "Which is why I don't think we should tell him either."

For once Ivy was quiet, I could practically see the wheels turning in her mind as she kept her hand in mine, thinking everything over.

Merlin jumped up to sit next to Holly. He batted at her long red curls as they fell all around her. "So we're alone then, dealing with all of this." Holly closed her eyes, and pulled Merlin to her lap for comfort.

"No, we aren't alone. The High Council knows." I began to tick off names on my fingers. "All of the Rousseau's, Violet, Oliver Jacobs and the rest of the Council members will be watching Aunt Faye. And they are all searching for any information on the BMG."

Holly set the cat aside. She stood up and her hands were clenched into fists at her side. "I want out of

William's Ford so badly." She practically spit the words. "By the gods, I can't *wait* to get out of this town."

I blinked at her. "What do you mean?"

Holly braced her hands on the mantle. "I mean that I have accepted a scholarship to the University in Kansas City. I'll be leaving home in August to attend."

Ivy whipped her head around to stare at her twin. "You would've had to send an acceptance letter *months* ago... and you are only telling us now?"

"It never seemed the right time..." Holly trailed off, and her knuckles went white as she gripped the wooden fireplace mantle. She glanced over her shoulder at us. "Now with all of this happening, I know my decision has been the right one."

I considered Holly as she stood there. "Kansas City is what, four hours west of here?"

"It is." Holly shifted her eyes to mine. "I want to go where no one has even heard of the Bishop family of Witches. Somewhere I can be anonymous, and an ordinary student like everyone else."

Ivy moved like lightning. Reaching out, she grabbed her twin's shoulder and whipped her around. "You're going to leave us, *and* abjure the family legacy of magick?" she said, sounding appalled.

Holly knocked Ivy's hands away. "I have the right to choose my own path!" she snapped, clenching her hands into fists again. Suddenly the framed photos on my mantle began to shake. A sure sign that Ivy was losing her temper.

I hurried over to get between them. "Hey!" I tugged Ivy back a couple of feet. "Take it easy. Both of you."

"It's my life. I have the right to choose," Holly said, while the framed photos shook more violently.

"Yeah and you're choosing to be an *idiot*!" Ivy snarled at her twin, and Merlin let out a howl, as if he agreed.

A picture frame went flying across the room and I ducked. "Damn it! Control your telekinesis, Ivy!"

Ivy glared. "That wasn't me!" She pointed at her twin. "That was Holly!"

Well shit! I knew this morning wouldn't be easy, but I hadn't expected the possibility that Holly might whip out a new power. "Holly," I said as calmly as possible. "You need to focus, you're losing control of your temper and your magick."

"You're right. I'm sorry." Holly closed her eyes and inhaled. She gracefully lifted up her hands to eye level. With a fluid movement she flipped her hands over, exhaled and pushed her palms down and towards the floor.

The framed photos stopped shaking.

"You got ahold of your temper now?" I asked her, keeping a wary eye for more flying objects.

Holly drew in a couple of steadying breaths, and opened her eyes. "This— my losing control— is one of the reasons I've decided that I need to take a break from the Craft," she said, turning to me. "I have to see if I can live without magick for a while, and then I'll decide if that's something I'd like to be permanent."

"Okay," I said, trying to placate her. "I understand that, but right now is maybe not the best time for you to go cold turkey on the magick. We need as much firepower as we can get to finish this quest."

"Fine. You have my word," she said. I'll do whatever I can physically and magickally to help protect the family, and to help with search for the grimoire until August." Holly crossed her arms over her chest, and her eyes blazed a brilliant aqua-blue. "Then I'm out."

"Until August..." Ivy's voice sounded small and hurt. "When you are leaving us, to move clear across the state. Because you can't wait to get away from this town and our legacy."

"That's right." Holly's voice was cold and final.

Ivy stared at her twin for a few moments. "I never knew an empath could be so insensitive and selfish." The emotion behind Ivy's statement hit Holly like a slap. Holly's eyes widened at the insult, but she stood still, staring at her twin, saying nothing.

"Ivy!" Shocked, I reached out for my cousin.

"Leave me alone." Ivy jumped towards the door, whipped it open and ran down the hall. A moment later I heard Ivy run down the main staircase.

Holly raised tear filled eyes to me. "I'm wasn't trying to hurt her, or anyone else." She seemed to steady herself. "I'll help you for as long as I can, but then I *have* to go."

"It's your life and your decision." I reached out and gathered her close in a careful hug. When she began to sob against my shoulder, I felt my own eyes prick with tears. "Holly, I understand that better than you think."

"You do?"

"Yeah. I do. When I left New Hampshire, a part of me knew that everything would change... But I had to follow my own path."

"I don't leave for another three months," Holly said, sighing against my shoulder. "A lot can happen, maybe we'll find the grimoire and this will all be over."

"There you go," I said as if I agreed, but I suddenly *knew* this would all have to end at the fourth blood moon within the tetrad cycle. And that final lunar eclipse wasn't until September.

"Three months seems like forever," Holly said, her voice shaking.

"I'm grateful to have your help for as long as I can." I eased back and wiped her tears away. "The time will pass sooner than you think."

***

The time did pass, so much faster than I would have wished for. The twins graduated from high school in June. Holly went back to work as a lifeguard at the country club for the summer, while Ivy took as many shifts as possible at *Enchantments* to build up her college fund.

Ivy printed up a series of stunning photos for me from the day the crows had come to call, and she put them in a big envelope which she'd labeled "Message Of The Crow." I tucked it away with the hopes that eventually I'd be able to show them to Bran some day. And she did win the photography scholarship, as Julian had told me she would.

That scholarship allowed Ivy the luxury of living on campus. Whereas before she had planned on saving money by living at home and simply making the short commute across town— now she could live in the dorms.

In an interesting coincidence, but more likely teenage magick, Ivy ended up being assigned Cypress Rousseau as her roommate. My father had always said that everything happens for a reason, and maybe the girls being away from the manor would be the best thing for them.

I had spent the last two and a half months keeping an eye on Aunt Faye for any other signs of manipulative magick, and watching over Bran, Lexie, and the twins by working protection magick. All kinds of protective magick.

The morning Holly dropped the bombshell about going away to college, I'd dashed into Aunt Faye's room on the first floor as soon as the woman had left the house. I searched through her personal items trying to find any clues for further magick, but came up with nothing. I did grab a little of her silver hair from her brush, then added it to the poppet Marie had made for me.

The poppet was made of plain cotton and had a rough gingerbread man shape. But inside of it was a sample of my great aunt's handwriting, and now some of the older woman's hair. I wrapped the poppet representing Aunt Faye in white ribbon to safely bind anymore negative intentions or manipulative magick from her. Afterwards, I placed the poppet in a shoe box and buried it in the rose garden under the statue of Diana. There the poppet would stay until I got to the bottom of whatever her magickal intentions were.

I also placed hex-busting charms in my great aunt's room in case there were any more confusion charms in the works... I tied an herbal sachet designed to limit her powers under her bed. Finally, I sprinkled red brick dust on the carpet right inside Aunt Faye's room to try and bind any negativity and to keep it contained within her own personal space. There may have been a time when I would have balked at such magickal maneuvers, but I was done playing. We'd already lost Gwen, and my family's safety was on the line.

I continued my grad school classes, putting in my assistanceship hours in the archives at the museum with Professor Meyer, *and* I worked part-time at the shop. Between customers I studied for school. I also studied root-working with Marie and Rene whenever I was able. My relationship with Rene had slowly progressed over the summer, and while we weren't lovers yet— we were still together. Building trust took time, and we were both willing to put the work in.

I didn't go out jogging or walking on my own anymore. I took Rene with me when I jogged, or I went for a walk in the summer evenings with Lexie. You couldn't get much safer than walking with a cranky, very pregnant, armed police officer. At any rate, I never saw Duncan. I thought I'd sensed his magick a couple of times, but I never physically saw him.

I continued to secretly use the floor washes and protective powders from Rene and Marie all over the house once a week. I tucked the remaining crystal points from Violet under Bran and Lexie's bed, and the final point in the corner of the baby's room.

Violet had assured me that amethyst was good for turning away manipulative witchcraft, and all of my efforts seemed to be working, as Aunt Faye was subdued. Between the twins and the occasional intelligence gathering from Marie— always disguised as a casual visit to the manor, we didn't think she was doing any more magick on the family. Which was good, as the focus at the manor had shifted from worry and death to the happiness of a new life.

As Grandma Rose had predicted, Lexie went into labor the morning of the last day of July. Morgan John Bishop was born at 9:34 pm under the second full moon of the month— a blue moon. Weighing in at eight pounds and eleven ounces, my nephew had a head full of red hair and a temper to match.

The new family was settling in at the manor, and Morgan John, or MJ as I'd started to call him, seemed to like his soft, neutral nursery that was all decked out in vintage teddy bears and shades of soft cream and buff.

I let myself in through the garage door, sighing in relief at the coolness of the air conditioned manor. I strolled through the potting room and stopped to grab a bottle of water. Merlin sat on the kitchen counter watching the back door, as had become his habit most early evenings. He seemed to have taken on the duty of feline sentry for the past few months.

"Hey Merlin." I rubbed his ears for a moment and then twisted the cap of the bottle and drank deep. I hitched my book bag on my shoulder, left Merlin to his security detail and began to cross to the family room. What I saw there gave me such a happy and warm feeling of déjà vu that I stopped to lean against the archway and watch.

Lexie sat in a big comfy chair nursing Morgan. She smiled down at the baby as he busily got down to eating his dinner. Bran knelt at her side and ran his hand over his son's hair and adjusted the baby's pale blue summer weight blanket. They spoke quietly to each other, and I couldn't help but grin at the picture they made.

Behind them, the mantle of the family room was still decorated for the last sabbat of Lughnasadh. Yellow and white pillar candles were grouped at one end of the mantle, opposite a large fern spilling out of a copper container. In the center of the mantle, a large arrangement of sunflowers, courtesy of Violet— a gift for the new parents, was displayed.

Exactly as I'd seen in my vision on Yule. The flowers, the red haired baby in the blue blanket... I blinked away a few happy tears and stepped into the room to join them.

"How's my nephew?" I asked.

Lexie glanced up at me. "He's hungry tonight," she said as the baby made little noises while he ate.

"He's always hungry." I yawned. "And he lets everyone know it. No matter what time it is."

Bran looked concerned. "I'm sorry, did he wake you up last night?"

I rolled my eyes. "Bran, he's only two weeks old, I'd be surprised if I didn't hear him cry at night. Besides, I don't mind... I was teasing you."

Ivy came in through the main foyer with several take-out bags. "Hi guys!" She was all smiles when she spotted the baby. "Be right back." She headed towards the kitchen, and I heard her flip the oven onto warm and stuff the bags in the oven. She came in and plopped down beside me on the couch. "How's MJ doing today?" she said.

"Morgan John," Lexie and Bran corrected in unison. They'd named him *Morgan* after our grandfather Morgan and *John* after Lexie's dad.

Lexie shifted the baby to her shoulder and patted his back, and after a few moments Morgan John let out a mighty burp and squirmed against his mother's shoulder.

"Let me hold him." I held out my hands for the baby. Bran took the baby and passed him to me while Lexie rearranged her shirt. I settled the baby in the crook of my arm. "Hello handsome." I grinned down at him.

The baby stared up at me with bright blue eyes. He waved his arms happily for a few minutes, then he grimaced— and proceeded to fill his pants.

"Whoa!" I had to laugh.

Ivy bounced up from the couch. "I'll change him!" She dashed over to the powder room where Bran had stashed some diapers, wipes and changing pads. Ivy came back and rolled out a changing pad in the middle of the sofa. I laid the baby down, and Ivy quickly and competently changed his diaper.

"I'm going to miss your diaper changing services next week when you're living at the dorms," Lexie told Ivy.

Ivy snapped the baby back into his sleeper and wrapped him lightly in his blanket. She bent over to gently nuzzle his belly and laughed when the baby grabbed at her hair. "I'll be right across town, only ten minutes away." She eased back and gave a light kiss to the baby's chin. "I have to come home to spend time with the cutest red-haired baby in the world, don't I?"

"Of course," Bran agreed. "And he's going to want to see his Aunt Ivy."

Ivy grinned at Bran and then scooped up the baby.

"I'll drop by as often as I can to see him."

"I'll keep the diapers at the ready," Lexie teased, and stood up to stretch. "Actually Ivy, will you keep an eye on Morgan for a few minutes?"

"Sure." Ivy never glanced up from the baby.

"Great," Lexie said. "I didn't get a chance to take a shower today, Morgan was a little cranky, and maybe it's silly, but I wasn't comfortable leaving him alone, even to take a bath."

My stomach tightened. Lexie was a very down-to-earth and relaxed new mama. *If Lexie was uncomfortable not having the baby out of her sight, then something was wrong.*

"You could have asked Aunt Faye," Bran said. "She could have helped you for a few minutes."

"She hasn't been home," Lexie said. "She left a note on her door saying she would be out of town for a few days."

"Really?" I asked, perking up at this unexpected and new information.

"I've got him," Ivy said. "Go hit the showers, and then we can all have dinner. I brought Chinese food."

"Thanks." Lexie headed upstairs, and Bran excused himself. Ivy and I grinned at each other as he followed Lexie up the steps.

"Guess he's gonna help scrub her back?" Ivy slanted a look over at me.

"That's about all he *can* do right now..." I laughed.

"So how long is a woman supposed to wait before

she has—"

"Let's not go there," I said, cutting her off. "I'm more interested in where the hell Aunt Faye went to."

"She's seemed a little quiet for the past couple of months."

"Distant, more stiff with us, maybe." I nodded.

"Yeah *stiff* is a good word. If it wasn't for the fact that Bran and Lexie seemed to have completely forgotten the visit from the crows, you'd never know anything was off."

"Be right back," I said, getting up to check out the note. I walked through the back section of the house to the rooms Aunt Faye had claimed almost a year ago. Taped onto her door was a handwritten note.

I'll be out of town for a few days, visiting friends in Hannibal
and taking care of an unexpected business matter,
If you need anything, call my cell.
Faye

I carried the note back in the room with me and showed it to my cousin. "Is Holly joining us for dinner?" I asked Ivy. "Maybe she could use her clairtangency and see what emotions she picks up."

"Good luck with that," Ivy said. "She leaves for Kansas City tomorrow morning with Kate and her family, and she's been shutting down her magick more and more over the past few days."

I studied Ivy. She was trying to hide how hurt she was, and wasn't quite pulling it off. "I really wish she'd let one of us help her with the move to school. She shouldn't do that alone."

Ivy shrugged. "When I found out Kate from the cheer squad was going to the same college, I felt better. I mean, Kate's clueless as to the family's legacy of magick— always has been. Still, she's a nice girl, and at least Holly will know someone on campus."

As if Ivy's words had conjured them up, Holly and Kate walked in the front door. They juggled several empty cardboard boxes. Holly set the boxes down, took the ones from Kate and gave her a quick hug.

"See you in the morning!" Kate said, and with an excited wave to Ivy and me, let herself back out, shutting the door behind her.

Holly stacked the boxes over to the side of the foyer and then came over to join us, holding out her hands for the baby. "My turn," she said, happily.

Ivy handed the baby to me instead. "I'll go set the table." She walked out of the room without so much as a glance at her twin.

Holly watched Ivy walk away, and for a moment she seemed unbearably sad. "She's still angry with me." She sat on the couch and ran a hand through her hair.

"I think she's more *sad* than mad," I said, holding out Morgan to her.

Holly took the baby. "I need to do this, for myself. People go away to college all the time... This college has a great program for Art History, it's what I've always wanted to study." Her voice was soft as she spoke, but her eyes were hot. "I mean, she's going to be living in the dorms with Cypress. How is what I'm doing really any different?"

"It's different because you hid all of it from me," Ivy spoke up from the archway. "It's different because you are turning away from your Craft *and* your family when we need you the most. I'm going to be right across town, where you will be four hours away."

"Why can't you be happy for me?" Holly asked her twin.

"I *am* happy for you," Ivy said, stepping into the room. "I'm happy that you are got a partial scholarship. Happy that you were accepted in the program you wanted... However, I am sad that my sister, my twin, has shut me out of her plans, and is shutting me out of her life." Ivy's eyes welled up with tears, and her voice went up. "Admit it, the real reason you don't want any of us to help you move is because you are embarrassed by us! You're afraid that someone will figure out you come from a family of Witches."

"I *never* said that," Holly gasped.

"You didn't have to!" Ivy snapped back.

Silence hung in the air for a good ten seconds as the twins stared at each other. Finally, Holly cleared her throat. "I am not embarrassed by the family. I was thinking *of* the family."

Ivy crossed her arms and rolled her eyes. "Oh,

Really?"

"Really. Autumn is in graduate school, Bran and Lexie just had their baby, you move into your dorms in a few days... That leaves Aunt Faye. Who spelled us a few months ago and is seventy-four years old!" Holly finished with a shout. "Damn it Ivy, what was I supposed to do, ask an old Witch of questionable ethics to haul boxes up and down the dormitory steps?"

Morgan scrunched up his little face and began to cry at the raised voices.

"Hand him over," I said reaching for the baby. I took Morgan from Holly, eased him over my shoulder, and stepped back out of the line of verbal fire.

Holly stood up, and Ivy marched down into the family room. They faced each other and let their argument rip. They yelled, they cried, and they argued, but no magick was thrown, and that relieved me.

A moment later Bran came running down the steps. "What's going on?" he called over the girl's shouting.

"Twin fight," I said, rubbing the baby's back, who must have decided to join in. He was really howling now.

"So much for our quiet family evening." Bran took the baby and began to rock him back and forth trying to calm him down— it had the opposite effect.

"Hello? Are you new?" I said over the girls' argument and the wailing baby. "Since when have evenings been quiet in this house?"

Lexie appeared, her hair still wet from her shower.

"Well shit." She rolled her eyes at the girls. "I really wanted that Chinese food."

"God damn it." Bran frowned as Morgan cranked up the volume. He tucked one side of the baby's head against his chest and covered Morgan's other ear. "Don't make me get the hose!" he yelled at the twins.

The uncharacteristic sarcastic comment from Bran silenced both girls. The baby stopped crying, and I felt inappropriate laughter bubble up. "Guess he told you," my voice broke on the laugh.

"Wow honey," Lexie purred. "That was kind of hot. You being all manly, forceful and stuff." She batted her eyes at him. "Do it again."

Ivy snorted out a laugh, and Holly giggled. Bran let loose a belly laugh, and soon all of us were laughing and smiling instead of crying and shouting.

CHAPTER FOURTEEN

A week later and the number of people living at the manor had gone from seven to four. Aunt Faye was still out of town, and I had to admit, I was becoming very suspicious by her absence. Lexie was puttering around the manor enjoying her maternity leave, and I'd never seen Bran so content. Being a husband and a new father suited him, if anything it made him relax and loosen up a bit.

Holly was settled in her dorms across state and had started her classes. The girls had called a truce that night, and the next morning when Holly started packing up her car, Ivy, Bran and myself had all been there to help. We all gave her a hug and wished her good luck as she left to caravan out to Kansas City with Kate and her parents.

A few days later, Rene and I helped Ivy and Cypress move into their dorm room at William's Ford University. Which was actually fun, probably because after everything else— this seemed so blissfully normal. We'd hauled boxes, helped the girls hang curtains, and rearrange their room into bunk beds so they would have more floor space.

Seeing Ivy and Cypress standing arm in arm and grinning at each other as they began their college adventure made me feel sentimental. It also really made me wish that Holly would have changed her mind and let us drive out to see her campus and help her get settled in. Once again I was thankful that the girls were away from the manor. Because even though things were quiet, I was uneasy.

On one hand, my life was going well. I was in the home stretch to getting my Master's Degree. This final semester of evening classes were as intense as the first two had been, but my grades were excellent, and come December I would graduate.

On the other hand, time was running out. There was only a little over a month left before the fourth and final lunar eclipse in the tetrad. And I still didn't have any answers. Somewhere out there that third person held the final section of the grimoire, and they were waiting. But what the hell were they waiting for?

I stepped outside into oppressive heat and humidity. I was the last person to leave the museum after class since my program director wanted a word about an upcoming exhibit I'd been assigned to display. By the time we were finished, everyone else had already left. The cicadas were making a huge racket, and my footsteps were muffled as I walked across the parking lot. A waxing crescent moon peeped down and clouds were gathering in the northwest. I flipped my phone off of silent and checked the weather app. It was muggy, sticky, and sure enough, the app announced that the local temperature was 92 degrees and the area was under a severe thunderstorm watch. *Damn Missouri weather...* I thought, tucking my phone in my pocket.

I unlocked my old truck, slid my laptop and book bag across the bench seat, and quickly climbed in. I slapped the locks down, started up the engine and cranked the a/c. I rolled a window down slightly and waited for a moment, allowing the air conditioning to do its thing. I leaned back as the air washed over me and stared out the windshield. My phone chimed, alerting me to a missed call. I pulled it out of my pocket, glancing at the read out. I looked again in disbelief.

The phone read: 1 Missed Call: Gwen Bishop.

The phone slipped out of my suddenly numb fingers. *Was this some kind of sick joke?* The phone had landed face-up on the seat next to me. The sound of my breathing was loud to my own ears as I struggled with shock. I reached for the phone again with a shaking hand. "I misread it, that's all." I tapped on the icon to listen to messages.

"Autumn, it's Gwen," my Aunt's voice came loud and clear through my phone. And I cried in astonishment hearing her voice. "Stupid cell phone... never works when you need it to," she muttered. Then her voice was louder. "Honey, listen to me... You're not safe, tell Bran and the girls. Don't trust *anybody*. I'm on my way, and coming home as fast as I can. If you get the message call me back. I love you."

The message ended, and I immediately hit play to listen again. "Oh my god." I pressed my fingers to my mouth as I listened for a second time. *How was this possible? We'd buried Gwen eight months ago, how could I receive a voice message from her phone now?*

Before I could figure out who could have sent the message, a crow landed with a thump on the hood of my truck. It wasn't a graceful landing. I jumped in reaction to the bird crashing on the car and waited... hoping that the bird would hop up and right itself. But it sprawled there. Its wings misshapen and feathers all messy. My stomach lurched as I realized that the bird was dying.

"What the hell?" I said, and then a second bird crashed into my windshield. I screamed as the windshield cracked. Then a third bird, a fourth, and a fifth, and then two more birds fell from the sky and right onto my truck.

Seven. I stared while my heart pounded. There were seven dead crows. I knew this was significant, and out of nowhere, that old child's nursery rhyme popped into my mind. *Seven crows for a secret that should never be told.*

I didn't think. I reacted. I slammed the truck in gear and spun out of the parking lot and drove away as the birds rolled off the hood of the truck.

My windshield now had several cracks in it, but I could still see as I whipped across town. I knew better than to try and use my phone and drive when I was so scared, so I shoved my phone in my front pocket, keeping my focus on getting back to the manor and staying alert for anymore birds. I screeched to a halt in the driveway of the manor, grabbed my things and sprinted up the front steps. I reached for the front door only to find it already open. It hung crookedly on the frame and stopped me in my tracks.

Oh god, had there been a break-in? Then I remembered. *Lexie and the baby were home.* "Lexie!" I shouted as I shoved the door aside. I dumped my things on the floor of the foyer and rushed through to the kitchen, but it was empty. I checked the other rooms on the first floor, calling for Lexie, but there was no answer and the rooms were empty. *I could feel it in the air though. Something was horribly wrong.*

Nothing appeared out of place, but Merlin wasn't coming out to greet me, and the manor *felt* wrong. I stopped and listened hard. I walked over to the counter and pulled a big butcher knife out of the knife block. My gut told me that whoever had been here was now gone, but I wasn't taking any chances. I heard a rustling sound behind me and spun.

Midnight flew down the stairs past me and circled the kitchen. "*Kaww, kaww,*" he cried, landing on the newel post on the back stairs. He cocked his head to the side and then flew back up the stairs.

One crow for sorrow... I remembered, rushing to follow him. I reached the second floor landing and heard the pitiful sound of a baby crying. As I watched, the crow flew straight towards the baby's room. He landed in front of the door and made a loud squawking noise.

"Bran?" I called. "Lexie?" But there was no answer. The scent of roses hit me. Strong and sweet. My grandmother's ghost must have returned, and I hurried to the baby's room, but found the door locked. Which made no sense as there was no lock on the door. I shook the door knob and felt the knob grow hot. With a gasp I yanked my hand back. *The door had been spelled.*

The baby was still crying, and that spurred me to action. I dropped the knife and placed both of my hands flat on the door and raised up as much magick as I had. "Open up!" I said. The door rattled on its hinges, and I visualized whatever enchantment placed on the door thinning out and weakening.

I took a deep breath and tried again, this time I closed my left hand around my family crest pendant and laid my dominant hand on the door. And I called for back up. "Grandma Rose, Aunt Gwen, I call on you to help me break this spell and get to Morgan," I said.

It took effort. I shook as I pushed my magick against whatever spell had been cast. The fragrance of roses intensified, and I could have sworn I felt a hand on my shoulder... Merlin appeared and brushed up against my ankles. He leaned his head against the door, and without warning, the door swung open. I fell forward and landed hard on my hands and knees. Merlin scampered away, and I discovered that the sash on the window in the nursery was open, and a breeze had the curtains billowing into the room.

I was shocked to see three crows perched on the end of the baby's crib. They seemed to chatter back and forth to themselves, and I knew they were literally on sentry duty. No one else was in the room but the birds, the crying baby and me. I felt the air around me shift, and Midnight flew past. He landed on the railing of the crib, looking down at the baby.

Four crows for a boy...

I scrambled up to find little Morgan lying in his crib, shaking angry fists in the air. I reached past the birds for my nephew. "It's okay baby." I cradled him. "I've got you."

Morgan began to quiet, but his cry was soft, almost tired sounding. Not the top of the lungs cries he typically made. Midnight nudged my hand where I held it against the baby, then he launched off the end of the crib and flew across the hall. The other three crows flew silently out the open window. I followed the crow to Bran and Lexie's room, and when I reached the door, my heart stopped in my chest.

The bedroom was trashed, books were everywhere and papers lay scattered all over the floor. My grandmother's ghost stood there plain as day in the doorway to the room's walk-in closet. Her bright pink sweater stood out. And she wasn't alone. Aunt Gwen stood side-by-side with her mother.

I gasped. "Aunt Gwen, you're here!"

My aunt's ghost smiled at me. She seemed to glow from within. "I told you. I was coming home as fast as I could."

My grandmother's ghost pointed inside the closet. "Your aunt, grandfather and I did what we could to help... but you need to hurry," she said. Grandma Rose turned and, with Gwen, they vanished inside the closet.

I ran to the closet door with little Morgan in one arm and stopped in my tracks.

The spacious walk-in closet, usually so neat, was destroyed. I saw in seconds that the panel that hid the collection of Bishop family grimoires, journals and spell books was wide open. The old books were flung on the floor, and the locked lead box that Bran had kept the BMG pages in was missing. But what scared me worse than that was finding Lexie.

Lexie was lying on the floor inside the large closet sprawled on her back, her service weapon was next to her, and she wasn't moving. "No!" I went down to my knees and reached to check for a pulse with my free hand. I dropped my head in thanks when I found one.

"Lexie, can you hear me?" I pressed my ear to her chest. She was breathing, and her heart beat sounded strong. I ran a hand over her, searching for wounds. Her hands and shirt were smeared with blood, and her knuckles were torn up. She'd obviously put up one hell of a fight. As I looked for other injuries, I smoothed her long hair back from her face, saw blood in her hair, and a purple bruise forming along one side of her hairline.

As if Morgan knew his mother was nearby, he began to cry again in earnest. "It's going to be okay, Morgan," I said, my voice breaking. "I'm going to get help." I yanked my phone out of my pocket, but my hands were shaking so hard that I dropped it.

I scooped it up and tried again. As I knelt there, Aunt Gwen seemed to materialize right next to me. She ran her hand over the top of the baby's head. "Hush now, sweetheart," she crooned, and he began to quiet.

"There are two words." I heard my grandmother's voice as if she were whispering in my ear. "Two powerful words that guarantee every police officer on duty will respond, dear."

"I know," I said, feeling stronger with the ghosts of my relatives beside me. They smiled at me as I made the call. Then they faded away.

The operator picked up on the second ring. "911. What's the nature of your emergency?"

"Officer down," I said.

***

I sat in the waiting room of the emergency department with my brother, his in-laws, Nancy and John Proctor, Ivy and my nephew. Little Morgan had been checked out by the doctors and was fine, besides being hungry. His grandmother Nancy held him now, and she had gotten the baby to sleep after giving him a bottle. She sat in a big wooden rocking chair in the waiting room rocking the baby, and was hanging in there. I could tell she was worried, but Nancy was a cop's wife, and I imagined taking care of the baby was helping.

John, still in his police uniform, had been one of the first responders to arrive when I'd dialed 911. He paced the waiting room back and forth, and occasionally spoke to a fellow officer or two while he waited. The waiting room was filled with cops, and Witches.

Marie, Rene, Cypress and Violet were there. Cora O'Connell stood speaking quietly on her cell phone to Holly and was filling her in. Zach and Theo brought everyone some water and went and sat with Nancy.

Bran sat silently between Ivy and me. His eyes were too large, his skin too pale. I reached out and laid my hand on his, and without a word he held onto mine, tightly. He was watching down the hall for a doctor to come out and tell us something, anything new. It had been quite a while since they'd gotten the results of Lexie's tests. While the news had been good, and the scans showed only a concussion, Lexie was still unconscious. The fact that she'd been unconscious for so long was worrying, and they were setting up to admit her.

"This can't be happening, there was magickal

protection in place at the manor," Bran said under his breath.

I squeezed his hand. "Bran, your mom *and* our grandparents were there at the manor tonight. Grandpa Morgan's crows protected the baby, and Gwen and Grandma Rose were both guarding over Lexie."

Bran blinked at me, "You saw Mom?" he whispered.

"I did, she was with Grandma Rose." I smiled and told him what she'd said and done.

Ivy cried, even as she smiled while listening in. She wiped her eyes, put her arm around Bran and held on. "Lexie's strong," Ivy reminded him. "She fought back and did damage to whoever broke in."

John was suddenly there and hunkering down in front of my brother. "Bran," he laid his hand on Bran's arm. "We know that her gun was fired, and that she got in a few good punches."

"That's right," I said, "her knuckles were all torn up."

John nodded. "Bran, the blood on her clothes and hands— it wasn't hers."

"So you're saying that she shot the intruder?" Bran asked his father-in-law.

"Put money on it," John said. "I know my girl, she's an accurate shot. There was a blood trail out of the manor, we are following up on that."

Ivy leaned her head on Bran's shoulder. "Lexie kicked their ass." She smiled, but it turned wobbly.

John patted Ivy's knee. "Damn right she did. The

officers at the crime scene and the doctors here took samples. Now we have DNA. That can only help us identify and convict who did this."

"It's my fault," Bran said. "I kept the pages of the grimoire at the manor."

"It's not your fault!" I squeezed his hand hard to make him focus on me.

"How many people knew the grimoire was there, behind the panel in the closet?" John asked Bran.

"Only the family," Bran said with a shake of his head.

"Is your Great Aunt Faye still out of town?" John asked quietly.

Bran's head whipped up. "You don't think she had anything to do with this, do you?"

"I'm going to make a few calls, see if we can verify your great aunt's whereabouts." John stood and left.

Ivy and I exchanged significant glances. We both knew Faye was capable of manipulative magick, but could she really attack a new mother? I stood up, hitched my bag over my shoulder and started to pace myself. I walked from the large windows that showed a little planted outdoor area and back towards the wall where several photos hung of various hospital board members.

My breath caught in my throat as I saw the portrait of the serious face of Thomas Drake, and I remembered. *Duncan knew the pages were in the house. That night the manor had first been broken into and the girls room trashed*, I'd said in front of him *"How's Bran's tie collection looking?"*

"*Cher*," Rene's hand dropped on my shoulder. "What are you thinking?"

I tilted my head up to him. "I'm thinking that I may have accidentally tipped Duncan off to where the pages were stored," I said, keeping my voice down.

He slipped an arm around me. "You think Duncan did this?" Rene asked quietly, so no one would overhear.

I leaned against Rene's shoulder. "I don't know. If Duncan connected the dots and figured out where the pages were being stored... I don't know if his exposure to the leather bindings could have made him violent enough that he would've attacked Lexie."

"What about Faye?" Rene asked.

"John Proctor is checking into her whereabouts right now," I answered, but was distracted by Thomas' portrait, and weirdly I kept getting flashes of the Drake family mansion in my head. "Rene," I said softly so the rest of the group wouldn't hear me, "the day we buried Gwen, Thomas Drake claimed he wanted to help us. He tried to warn me about the danger of the grimoire... he insisted that the Bishops and the Drakes had to work together. That if we worked together, then we could bind the grimoire's destructive power."

"He did?"

"Yeah, he did. But before he could tell me anything else, Aunt Faye showed up and blasted him." I met his silvery-green eyes. "At the time I thought she was being protective... Now, I'm not so sure."

Rene pressed a kiss to the top of my head. "What can I do?"

An idea was forming in my mind. "Step outside with me for a minute, will you?"

"Of course." Rene ushered me over and out the glass door to the little outdoor seating area.

I sat down on a bench facing away from the windows. "Can you be my psychic anchor?" I patted the bench next to me.

"You're going to try and scry? Future or the past?" Rene sat beside me and offered his hand.

I took his hand and leaned my arm against his. "I'm going to try a remote viewing, a seeing of the present in another location."

"Astral projection?" Rene asked. "You sure you are up for that?"

"I want to try. But, I'll need to have someone that I trust here to guide me back. Will you do that?"

"Of course," Rene said.

I took a deep breath and gave his fingers a gentle squeeze. "Wish me luck."

Rene dropped a kiss on my mouth. "*Bon chance.*"

I shut my eyes and visualized myself firmly tethered to the earth, even as my spirit began to float free. *Show me where to find Thomas Drake.* I focused my will and let The Sight loose.

I found myself standing in a brick courtyard. A tall

solitary oak tree grows up in the center of the enclosure. I tip my head up to study the tree, and see that all of the oak leaves are brown and ready to fall. A wind tugs at my hair, but the leaves above me do not rustle on the branches of the tree. There is no noise. No rustling leaves, crickets, or cicadas. I see the sky illuminate with lightning but there is no thunder... It is totally silent, and the silence is discordant and unnatural.

A feeling of déjà vu sweeps over me. Have I dreamt of this? Is this why this place seems familiar? Deep green ivy covers the brick walls of the courtyard, and I see old fashioned gaslights flickering on ornate black metal posts. They lead the way to the house.

Now I see the house, and I know this place.

I know exactly where I am.

The mansion looms three stories tall and is built of gray stone. The ivy covered courtyard should make this place inviting and charming, but it is forbidding. Still I am drawn to the house itself. I move closer and find an arched wooden door set in the gray stone of the house. The door is red, and ornate. Heavy and old metal lanterns flank the red door. I reach for the door and try to open it.

Suddenly the silence breaks. Now I can hear the sounds of the night as they rush in around me. The leaves of the tree are rustling in the wind, thunder rumbles low and angry in the distance. A crow calls out and the door swings open easily with a sigh. I hear voices from within the house. They are muffled and distorted, but familiar to me. The answers I seek are here.

I step forward alone and into the old stone house.

I felt myself return to my own body with a thump. My eyes snapped open and I inhaled deeply as if I'd come up and broken the surface of a lake. I made a real effort to ground my energy and to remind myself of where I was. *Outside. With Rene. Still at the hospital.* I leaned against him for a moment, thankful for his strength.

"Autumn?" Rene's voice sounded concerned. "Take whatever energy you need." He squeezed my hand.

"You're sure?" I blinked up at him.

Rene swooped down and kissed me. When he did I felt a jolt of his power, and I grew warmer and felt steadier. After a few seconds he pulled away.

He smiled at me. "Did it work? What did you see?"

"It did work. But it was hard to make sense of, really," I said, stalling for time. "Rene, would you mind going to get me a soda from the vending machine out in the hall?

"Sure," Rene said. "You'll need some sugar and caffeine after that, I'll bet."

I smiled, and hoped he wouldn't notice how false it was.

"Be right back." Rene headed towards the door.

I gestured to a small ornamental tree over in the corner. "Take your time," I said. "I think I'm going to go sit under that and ground my energy for a while. Reconnect to the earth."

"Good idea, give yourself a little bit to make sense of what you saw." Rene stopped and studied me for a moment, then he left.

I took a few steps towards the tree and shifted to watch him go back inside. I felt guilty for lying to him, but I knew *exactly* where I was in that vision.

It was the Drake family mansion.

With a growing sense of determination, I studied the people, *my family* that were gathered together inside the waiting room. Enough people had suffered, and enough lives had been lost. It was time for someone to step up and put an end to all of this once and for all.

I had to go now, and I had to go alone.

My mind made up, I eased towards the tree in the corner of the little outside area and to a set of stairs that were marked as an exit. Once I made the stairs, I ran.

No sooner had I run up the steps, and a cab had pulled up to the curb to drop someone else off. I hopped in and gave the cab driver the address. I held my breath, half expecting Rene to come running around the corner in pursuit, but the cab smoothly pulled away from the hospital curb with no drama. I had gotten very, very lucky.

I stared out the cab window and watched as the thunderstorm rolled in, and I wondered if fate was playing its hand tonight. Or if there were other mystic forces at work. I needed a ride, and one had magickally appeared. However, the cabbie became so nervous when he dropped me off at the Drake mansion that he refused to let me pay him. I'd barely gotten the car door closed before he was pulling away. Hard to blame him, really.

The Drake family mansion was a horror movie aficionado's dream. Three stories tall and built of somber gray stone, it was set back from the street and surrounded by tall, gnarly, old catalpa trees. The predicted thunderstorm had arrived, the winds were picking up, meaning the rain was not far behind.

I could see that a few windows on the ground floor and the top floor were illuminated. So someone was home. Determined to get some answers, I swung my bag over my shoulder and marched up the path to the ornate front door.

Alone on the long brick sidewalk in front of the house, I thought about everything that had led me to this place and time. The accident that claimed my grandparents, my father running away from his home and his family. Ivy sitting in the ER with her eye swollen shut while she related to the police the details of her abduction.

I stalked forward recalling baby Morgan crying alone in his crib, and my aunt's and grandmother's ghost leading me to find an injured and unconscious Lexie. I could easily see my brother's pale face and his fears while he waited for news on his wife... and I remembered too clearly holding the twin's hands while we stood by Aunt Gwen's casket.

This ends tonight. I knew it like I knew my own name.

I'd worked myself up into a fine righteous anger by the time I approached the wide covered porch. I raised my hand to knock on the front door, but before I could, I felt a brush against my ankle. I flinched, and looked down. A crow gazed up at me with bright, intelligent eyes. "Well hello, Midnight," I said, totally thrown off-guard.

Midnight took off, flying off down a side path. He stopped, landing on a tall shrub as if he were waiting for me to follow. I felt a strong pull, a tug at my solar plexus, so I followed my instincts. I ran around the side of the mansion and towards the back. By the time I reached him, the crow was waiting on top of an ornate, black metal lamp post. A gas lamppost like I'd seen in my vision. Beside the post, a curved archway led to a courtyard, and the walls were brick and covered in ivy.

Raindrops started to fall and the bird took off, flying through the entrance. I hurried to follow. What I saw once I entered the courtyard had me skidding to a halt. A tall dying oak tree was centered in the courtyard, its leaves brown and shriveled.

The rain started in earnest, and I ran for cover towards the house. I tripped when I realized the back door was red and heavy, and flanked by lantern-like sconces on either side. *Damn, my vision was right on the money.*

I knocked briskly. And huddled under the narrow overhang.

A moment later, the courtyard door opened slowly, with a creaking sound.

"What the hell are *you* doing here?" Julian Drake stood staring at me, his eyes wide and his mouth slack.

CHAPTER FIFTEEN

"Julian," I nodded. "I need to speak to your father." A crack of thunder punctuated my words, and the storm increased. I pushed my way into the house and out of the lashing rain.

"Are you crazy?" He stepped back, throwing out his arms as if to block me. "You have to get out of here!" he hissed at me.

"No," I said calmly as I dripped on the parquet floor. "Either you tell me where he is or I'll go find him myself."

An incredibly loud boom of thunder shook the house, and both Julian and I jumped. The winds outside howled and the lights inside flickered out.

"The power's out," Julian whispered.

I froze in place, waiting for my eyes to adjust to the darkness. I'd only had a few seconds to get an impression of the interior of the mansion. I had no idea where to go. The lightning created a strobe affect against the windows, and I saw Julian reach for a drawer from a table in the entry way and pull out a flashlight.

"Got it." He clicked the flashlight on, but Julian's hands were shaking. He swung the flashlight towards the floor and the light bobbled.

"What has you so terrified?" I said.

Before he could answer me, I heard the voices. As the storm bashed against the house, I couldn't make out who was speaking or what they were saying, but raised voices were coming from above us, and the tone was urgent enough to make my hackles rise.

Julian shoved the flashlight at me. "If you're smart you'll go. Get out and save yourself." He backed up from me and was lost in the darkness of the house.

I swung the flashlight's beam around the foyer, but he was gone. There was a curving set of stairs across from me. Following the voices, I slowly made my way to the second floor. Stained glass windows lit up from the storm and went dark again as I cautiously climbed up the stairs. I skimmed my hand over a newel post, the carving was elaborate enough to make me shine the flashlight on it. It was the carving of a dragon.

The newel posts of the Drake mansion were carved into dragons. *Creepy.*

Any other time I might have appreciated the beautiful gothic architecture, the stained glass, the paneled walls in deep, rich wood, but now that I'd gained the second floor, the voices were clearer. After listening for a few seconds, I knew I still had another flight to go, so I eased back against the heavily paneled walls and continued up to the third floor.

As I made my way up the stairs, a calm descended over me. Every witchy sense I'd developed since moving to William's Ford shouted that I was in the right place at the right time. That made me feel bolder. Was I in danger? Probably. But I was also revved up, pissed off, and I *knew* that I was close to putting an end to this curse of the Blood Moon Grimoire that had haunted my family for generations.

The staircase narrowed as I reached the third floor. Dropping to my knees at the last of the steps, I crawled my way onto the third floor. I shut my eyes and listened hard to the people as they cursed and shouted back and forth. I felt my stomach heave as I recognized one of the voices for sure and prayed that I was wrong about the second voice.

There was flickering light coming from a room at the far end of the hall. It was candlelight— a part of my brain registered. I clicked off the flashlight stuffed it in my bag and left it at the top of the stairs.

Best to go in low and as quietly as possible, I decided. I stayed on all fours, creeping down the hall on my hands and knees, getting closer to the voices. I stopped and wrinkled my nose at the stench of sulfur. *Whatever was going on it that room was dark, very dark magick.*

I eased my way around the doorframe and saw two people. One sitting in a chair and another pacing back and forth.

"You bitch!" Great Aunt Faye snarled. "If you've done *anything* to hurt that girl, our deal is off!"

I shut my eyes against a huge feeling of betrayal. I'd hoped it wasn't true, but there sat my great aunt. I forced my eyes open in time to see Duncan walk past Aunt Faye and out of my line of sight, deeper into another part of the room.

"That's enough!" he said, obviously to Aunt Faye. In a completely different, gentler tone I heard, "You're hurt. Bleeding. Let me help you."

A hideous floral sofa was blocking my line of sight to the rest of the room and the other players: but it also blocked their view of me. I didn't dare raise any magick with other Witches so close— they'd feel that in a heartbeat. With my heart pounding in my ears, I eased my way into the semi-dark room and huddled against the back of the couch.

"I'm fine. It's only a flesh wound," said yet another familiar voice.

I couldn't stand it. *I had to see everyone in that room. I had to know for sure.* I squinted in the darkness and leaned my head out around the sofa. I almost didn't recognize the Witch that stood behind the desk in the center of the room.

A fire burned low in the grate, and several candles were lit across the mantelpiece back-lighting the Witch. The Witch wore a long ceremonial black robe with flowing sleeves and was staring at the surface of the desk.

Lighting flashed against the windows, allowing me to briefly see what was spread all over the desk. It was the red leather binding and the pages of the Blood Moon Grimoire. I could hardly believe my eyes. Duncan stood beside the Witch and as I watched, he rolled up one of the sleeves of the robe, competently tying a makeshift bandage to his mother's bleeding arm.

He too wore black, a flowing black shirt. His beard had grown out more since I'd last seen him, and the fanatical look in his eyes as he smiled down at his mother had me cringing back a bit. His eyes were glowing orange.

"Finally," Rebecca Drake-Quinn ran her hands lovingly across the loose pages of the grimoire. "It's been over twenty two years..."

"And now you have all of the pages again." Duncan's voice soothed.

"At last." Rebecca breathed the words with reverence. "The Blood Moon Grimoire and all its secrets are mine."

Rebecca? My mind reeled. *Rebecca?* I tried to accept the reality in front of me compared to the composed, soft spoken woman that I'd thought I'd known. *But Rebecca had been so kind to me. She'd helped us, had told me about my father and my brother... she'd been Gwen's friend... and she stood by my side at Gwen's funeral.*

And it had all been a lie. I suddenly understood. It had all been an act. A way to use my family to flush out the damn grimoire pages. Thomas had been telling me the truth after all. There had been another person after the grimoire. And that person was Rebecca.

Everything started to click into place for me, and rage took over. It roared through me, but I fought not to let it win. I channeled that anger into determination—and let it fill me up with power. Determination I could use, because one way or another I would see to it that this ended tonight.

"You idiots!" Aunt Faye snapped, drawing my attention. "You can't reassemble the pages now, there has to be a lunar eclipse for the book to be re-bound successfully."

"Silence!" Rebecca shouted.

The magickal vehemence behind the word caused Aunt Faye's head to snap back. A low sound of pain came from the old woman.

I tried to stay calm as I squinted at her in the darkness. *Why was she sitting so oddly?* A crack of thunder shook the house, and lighting illuminated the room at the same time. In those few seconds, I saw my great aunt's long silver hair was down and tangled around her face. A trickle of blood ran from the corner of her mouth, and I was shocked that my habitually flawlessly groomed relative was disheveled and wearing rumpled, stained clothes.

She'd been treated badly, and it showed. More

lightning lit the room, and now I could see that Aunt Faye was actually tied to the chair, not merely sitting in it as I'd assumed. Whatever they'd tied her up with was glowing. She was bound with magick. *Why would they bind an accomplice?* I quietly shifted my position so I could better see the room, and all the players.

"You've got the grimoire, all of it," Aunt Faye rasped. "Now live up to our bargain. Release my family from your curse."

"Be quiet, old woman." Duncan didn't spare her a glance as he set the loose pages inside the leather binding.

"You promised me if I helped you locate the pages, that my family would be safe!" Aunt Faye raged. "Enough lives have been lost! My brother Morgan and his wife Rose, your own husband, and Gwen, they were all innocents—"

Rebecca appeared behind my aunt's chair faster than was humanly possible. She'd blurred her movements and yanked Aunt Faye's head back by her hair. "They weren't innocent." She sounded pleasant, even as she pressed a long thin knife to Aunt Faye's throat. "Not innocent at all," Rebecca said. "Because they were all guilty of hiding pages from me at some point in time."

I held my breath, stuck in my hiding place like a cornered animal, praying that Rebecca was not going to slit my great aunt's throat while I watched. Rebecca was more than capable... she'd killed at least four people already.

The thunderstorm was still howling outside, and rain pounded against the windows of the house. When Faye stayed silent, Rebecca withdrew the knife. But she made a shallow slice across Aunt Faye's ear. My great aunt flinched from the pain, and I winced in sympathy. Rebecca tossed her head as if she found the whole situation amusing and slowly limped back over to the grimoire.

I was psyching myself up to be a hero when I heard Aunt Faye's voice in my mind. *Autumn, don't do anything stupid. Get out of here! I made a terrible mistake, I underestimated Rebecca. Don't you do the same!*

Aunt Faye, I projected my thoughts back. *I'm close. Hang in there.*

Before I could act, the lights came back on. I shielded my eyes from the lamp that blinked to life directly above where I'd been hiding, and it was then that I felt a hand on my arm as Duncan hauled me out from behind the sofa.

"Leave her alone!" Aunt Faye shouted.

I fought him with everything I had. Screaming, I went for his unnaturally lit eyes, and he yanked his head back just in time. When he wrenched me around by my arm, I spun into him and kicked. My running shoes make contact with his legs, and he winced, but before I could get a shot at his groin, he had me turned in his arms. My back slammed against his chest so hard it knocked the wind from me. His arms clamped down.

"Stop fighting me!" he growled in my ear.

"Fuck you," I managed, and slammed my head backwards. I felt a satisfying crunch when the back of my head made contact with his nose, but I saw stars. Duncan dropped me to the floor. I shook my head and got to my feet as quickly as I could.

I hadn't realized how much that little maneuver would hurt *me*.

Duncan had his hand cupped over his nose. It was bleeding badly. "You goddamn bitch." he spat.

"Children, children," Rebecca tsk-tsked "No more fighting, I need the both of you to help me reassemble the grimoire." She sounded so pleasant that it made my stomach lurch.

Hurting, but proud, I backed up from them both. "I'll never help you," I said, ranging myself next to Aunt Faye. "Not after everything you've done to my family..." I trailed off when I caught Julian out of my peripheral vision.

Julian stood off to the side in the hallway, out of his cousin's and aunt's line of sight. I shifted slightly so I could see him more clearly, and he flared his eyes at me in warning. Julian held up one hand. "*Stall*." He mouthed the word.

Rebecca stood behind the desk, her hands on top of the grimoire. The fact that she wasn't concerned enough to come around and confront me had to be bad. "Well, well, aren't you spunky?" she said absently, fastening the leather bindings of the grimoire. "You certainly didn't inherit *that* from your father." Now that my eyes had adapted to the light, I could see that Rebecca was looking a little roughed up herself. One of her eyes was puffy. Compliments of her run in with Lexie, I was sure.

Duncan pulled a handkerchief out of his pocket and pressed it to his nose. He hissed in pain, and it seemed to remind Rebecca that her son was bleeding. She waved her hand towards Duncan's face, and the bleeding stopped. "Thank you, mother," Duncan said as he mopped up his face.

Julian had asked for me to stall, so I started talking. "It was *you* who convinced David and my father to steal the grimoire from Thomas. Not to keep it away from your brother— but so you could have it for yourself," I said to Rebecca.

"Your father was easy to manipulate. So foolish and so very gullible." She narrowed her blue eyes at me. They were a gorgeous color— like her son's used to be. "For a time you were naïve yourself." Patting Duncan's shoulder as if she were proud of him, she winked at me. "We couldn't have done this without your help. You were the one who found the missing sections of the grimoire and told my boy. Why, I should thank you."

Internally, I cringed from her comments. I bore down and worked hard to even out my breathing and to calm my heart. My rage wouldn't work on her. She'd soak it up like a sponge. I grounded myself in order to pull up the strengthening power of the earth.

"So all those years ago," I said, "you sold my father a sob story— like the tale you told my family last year." I kept chattering, trying to give Julian time to get help. "You manipulated everyone. You used my father, and even your own husband, to get what you wanted."

"Go ahead child, put it all together." Rebecca made a 'go ahead' motion with her hand. "This is actually quite entertaining."

What a narcissistic bitch. I sent the thought to Aunt Faye and wondered if Duncan would pick up on our psychic communication. He didn't even glance at us.

He's not a problem. Trust me. Aunt Faye sent telepathically. *Keep her distracted, I'm sending out a psychic distress call to the Coven. They should be able to pick it up.*

"Okay, here's how I think it went down..." I said to Rebecca. "It was your husband, David, who figured out that you wanted the grimoire for your own personal gain. He was afraid that you were using dark magick, so he went to my father and, together, they stole it back from you."

Rebecca glared at me, her chest heaving up and down in anger as she listened.

Keep going, Aunt Faye's voice was clear in my mind. *I'm almost free.*

"They each tore out a section," I continued, "knowing the grimoire was useless unless it was whole, and they took those pages to hide them from you." I stopped and flashed an overly sweet smile at Rebecca.

"I bet that pissed you off when your precious grimoire didn't work anymore."

"When Duncan told me that you and he made the pages rearrange themselves into their proper order, I knew..." Rebecca's voice was almost a growl. "*Finally,* I understood."

"Understood what?" I asked.

She slammed her hands against the desk. "It would have taken the magick of three Witches to separate the Blood Moon Grimoire, and David was no Witch! Arthur and David used Duncan's magick and *yours* to divide up the grimoire!" Rebecca seemed to lose it. She began screaming and beating her hands against the desk in time with her words. "They used my own son against me!"

Aunt Faye surged to her feet behind me, dropping a hand on my shoulder. "Take her down, my girl," Aunt Faye whispered, squeezing my shoulder. The power she pushed into me made me feel taller, greater, and powerful enough to take on the world. I sucked in a breath— hard— as her magick rushed through me.

Rebecca stopped her tantrum abruptly and focused on Aunt Faye and me. "They *paid* for their betrayal. Make no mistake..." She began walking slowly, and very deliberately, towards us. "David deceived me, and he paid for that with his life. And as for your father..." She smiled at us. "I took *everything* away from Arthur: everything that he held dear, and watched him live with his grief. Doting mother and father— dead. Best friend

— killed trying to rescue his parents... then your mother threatened to leave him unless he abjured his Craft. Arthur lost *everything*. His parents, his home, and his legacy."

Wait until she's close. Aunt Faye sent her thoughts to me. *Then hit her hard.*

I nodded subtly, shifting my weight, to prepare myself.

"I never could get to you though..." Rebecca tapped a finger against her lips. "I'd always wondered why." She stopped directly in front of me. "But when Duncan told me how the pages had rearranged themselves when the two of you touched them at the manor... I realized that you had to stay alive, because I needed both you and Duncan to reassemble the grimoire."

"That's never going to happen," I said, and slammed my hands against Rebecca's chest. I put every bit of my own power, and what Aunt Faye had lent me, behind the strike. When my hands hit her, I saw a vivid dark green light, and Rebecca blew back across the room, past Duncan who didn't react in any way. She lay sprawled on the floor, tangled in her black robes. And she wasn't moving.

"One crazy, power-hungry bitch down," I said, blowing out a breath.

"She may not stay down long," Aunt Faye warned.

"I'm on it." I rushed to the desk with Aunt Faye hot on my heels. I scooped up the grimoire, but before I could take more than a few steps, Duncan clamped a hand on my arm.

"No, don't go," Duncan said.

"Duncan, have you been listening to your mother?" Aunt Faye said urgently. "Do you understand that your mother cursed your father and caused his death?"

Duncan stood statue-like next to the desk, but his eyes flickered. For a second I thought I saw the blue color that I had once loved. Pity for him stirred within me. "Duncan, let us go." I laid a hand on where he gripped my arm and pushed a little magick into him, the way I used to do.

To my surprise, he released my arm. "Get out, Autumn. Hurry."

I handed the grimoire to Aunt Faye. We rushed towards the hall. Before I could reach the door I bounced off of Rebecca, who was suddenly right in front of me.

"Power mad bitch?" she said and hit me across the face. The magick she put behind the strike had me shooting backwards, hitting the floral sofa, and flipping over the back. I heard her laugh. "I'll show you *power*."

I lay on the ground, blinking up at the ceiling for a moment. I'd taken enough spills in my life to know when I was hurt, or merely dazed. Fortunately, while my cheekbone hurt, I was only reeling from the magick. I rolled slowly to my side, searching for Aunt Faye.

"Rebecca." I heard Aunt Faye's voice. "You are a pathetic fool." My great aunt moved into my line of sight. Aunt Faye held up the grimoire like a shield with both hands as I crawled to my feet.

"You are the fools." Rebecca stalked the older woman, smiling— and it was full of malice. "Please don't try and run, a woman your age won't get far. Give me the grimoire."

"Never," Aunt Faye told her.

"Do you believe you can stop me?" Rebecca threw back her head and cackled. "There is *no one* who has the power to stop me now."

"Did you issue a challenge, sister dear?" Thomas Drake calmly stepped into the room. "Consider that challenge accepted." He set his briefcase down.

Standing there in his immaculate dark suit, Thomas Drake petrified me. More than Rebecca and her raving ever had. Seeing a chance to get to Aunt Faye, I ran behind Thomas and towards my great aunt. She reached out and linked an arm around my waist, pushing the grimoire towards me. I tucked it under my arm like a football.

"We've got to get out of here," Aunt Faye whispered to me.

Thomas spared us a glance and adjusted his cuffs. "You must stop this, Rebecca. You drove Julian mad to try and flush out the pages, and then you killed Gwen Bishop when she wouldn't give you what you wanted. Do you even begin to comprehend the karma you have unleashed upon yourself?"

"Why, I had no idea Julian would be so affected." Rebecca's shrugged it off. "As for Gwen, well... that was a simple hex really. It was so sad that her brakes just happened to go out while she was driving in an ice storm."

The cavalier words about Gwen's death hit me hard. "You *bitch*." I couldn't help but react, and Aunt Faye tried to hold me back.

Thomas didn't even glance at me. "Autumn, take Faye and leave," he suggested.

I caught myself. *Rebecca was trying to bait me.* I eased us back towards the door. Duncan began to struggle. It was horrible to see. Spellbound, he stood shaking beside his mother, his eyes flickering from orange, to blue.

"Duncan?" Thomas said. "Can you hear me?" Duncan slowly twisted his head towards his uncle. His mouth worked— but no sound came out.

Rebecca snapped her fingers, and Duncan's gaze whipped back to her. "I've held a third of the grimoire for two decades, Thomas. You have no idea of the powers at my command." Rebecca snarled at us all, and with a gesture— the book was torn away from me. The grimoire flew across the room to her waiting hands.

As soon as she had it in her hands again, lightning flashed and thunder cracked. Rebecca's hair began to blow back from her face as she pulled power from the grimoire.

"We have to go," Aunt Faye whispered to me, tugging on my arm.

"Not while that bitch has the grimoire," I said under

my breath.

Thomas merely tilted his head as he watched his sister. "Rebecca, you have no idea what you're playing with," he said in a soft, deadly serious tone. "If you do not stop drawing power from the Blood Moon Grimoire, you'll end up dead."

With a flick of a wrist, she had all of the candles in the room leaping. The flames shot up, tall and straight. "You can't stop me. You simply don't have the magick that I do, brother." The fire in the hearth behind her leapt and shot out sparks.

"Your magick is undeniably superior." Thomas stared her down. "It doesn't mean I won't hurt you if I have to."

"You and our father always underestimated me. I was passed over, ignored all my life! You can't stand that *I'm* the one with the power!" Rebecca shouted.

"No, Rebecca, I'm the one whose heart is breaking, seeing you poisoning your own son with dark magick." Thomas looked pointedly at Duncan.

"My son *loves* me!" Rebecca snarled as Duncan stood struggling in place. "I gave him every opportunity, every luxury and comfort."

I couldn't stand it any longer. I yanked free from Aunt Faye and stood next to Thomas. "Oh, we can all see that," I said. "Yeah, mother of the year for sure. Especially since you've got him spellbound to the point that he can't even move or think for himself."

Rebecca focused on me. Her eyes brightened with a

strange red glow. I didn't even have time to blink before a bolt of light and magick shot out from the grimoire and straight at me.

Thomas threw out an arm to block me, and I felt the impact of his magickal shield lift me up and off my feet. The sound of Rebecca's magick hitting her brother instead of me was earsplitting. I went down hard, skidding across the hardwood floor. I didn't stop moving until my head bumped against the doorframe. But it was a soft bump. Something had slowed down my momentum.

I lay there, dazed. Thunder boomed through the room, and I frowned up at the ceiling, feeling sore and confused, *Where had all of the colored lights come from? Was the storm inside the house?*

"Stay down," a voice hissed in my ear.

I turned my head and found that I was nose to nose with the last person that I ever expected to see: Julian Drake. I blinked at him. "Julian, what's happening?"

"Shit, we don't have time for this," he said. I could barely hear him over the sounds exploding within the room. He ran his hand over the top of my head. I felt a warmth emanating from Julian's hand. The warmth spread and ran down my body in a whoosh. It filled me with energy and awareness.

Suddenly, I remembered what was happening and the danger we were in. "Where's Aunt Faye?" I whispered, rolling over to my hands and knees. I glanced back to the room, and my jaw dropped.

Thomas and Rebecca were in a massive, magickal battle. Thomas threw out his arms and a sizzling blue light fired at his sister. Rebecca held up the glowing red grimoire, and the blue light bounced off and ricocheted around the room.

An energetic explosion hit the wall above us, and pieces of plaster rained down. "Come on!" Julian said. I covered my head, leaving the Drakes to their battle, and crawled out with him and into the hall.

Julian tugged me to my feet, and I tried to run to Aunt Faye, who stood waiting at the top of the stairs. I scooped up my bag while Julian looped an arm around Aunt Faye's waist. The three of us lurched our way down the staircase, away from the sounds of the magickal combat, and then out of the house and into the rain.

Julian and I half walked-half carried Aunt Faye across the courtyard. We had almost made it to the dying oak tree when a neon green ball of light streaked across the sky. All I saw was a flash. The light was blinding—the sound deafening.

Before I could understand what was happening, I was face down on the bricks, and the stench of ozone filled the air. I shook my head to clear it. I saw Aunt Faye and Julian lift their heads, and I rolled over and looked back at the mansion. Lightning had struck the peak of the mansion, and smoke poured from the top of the roof.

I was picked up off the ground by a pair of very

familiar arms. "*Cher.*" Rene held me close.

"Rene!" Relieved, I hugged him back. "You *heard* Aunt Faye's call."

"Let me see you." His hands ran down my face and arms.

"I'm all right. Help Aunt Faye," I said.

"She's being taken care of. Be quiet now, and let me look at you." Rene ran a gentle finger over my cheekbone. "You really have to stop running off on your own to play the hero." Rene sighed, and lifted me off my feet, pulling me close again.

From over his shoulder I saw police, EMT's and firefighters pouring into the courtyard, heading for the mansion. There was a police officer hovering over Aunt Faye. She sat on the ground next to Julian, who seemed a little dazed. While the officer spoke to them, he motioned for the EMT's. Aunt Faye was arguing, loudly, that she was fine.

"Aunt Faye," I called, as Rene set me back on my feet. "Let them check you out."

She crossed her arms over her chest glaring at me. None of the first responders paid any attention to her arguments. They gently began to examine her injuries.

Rene wrapped a blanket around me. "Here, take this."

I smiled up at him, but stayed focused on Aunt Faye and Julian. "Thank you, Julian for helping us," I said, pulling my blanket closer.

Julian took the blanket they had offered him and

tucked it around Aunt Faye instead. Before he could move back, she brushed his dark hair from his brow. "You did a good thing in there, young man. We owe you our lives."

Julian blushed. "You don't owe me anything, Ma'am."

Aunt Faye inclined her head. "Nevertheless," I expect you to come see me. I assume I'll be allowed visitors after you admit me?" She scowled at the EMT's.

The closest paramedic spoke soothingly to her patient. They helped Aunt Faye onto a gurney. A police officer helped Julian up. He wobbled but was able to stand on his own.

Rene touched Julian's arm to get his attention. "There's your father," he said.

"Dad!" Julian whipped around and ran towards the mansion.

Thomas and a firefighter were helping Duncan out of the house. Thomas had one arm around his nephew's shoulders while carrying his briefcase. Thomas handed his nephew off to the EMT's. He grabbed Julian, hugging him hard. Tears welled up in my eyes as I watched the Drake men embrace.

Thomas met my eyes from over Julian's shoulder. "Come on, Rene," I said, and we walked over hand-in-hand to the Drakes. "Is that everyone?" I asked Thomas as gently as possible.

"Yes, it is." Thomas held the briefcase out to me. "I

trust you will find a safe place to store this, until it can be reassembled?"

I cautiously took the case and opened it. The Blood Moon Grimoire rested inside. "Yes sir, I will." I knew that if Thomas was giving this to me, then Rebecca was no longer a threat. I shut the briefcase and handed it to Rene.

"I want no part of that book," Thomas said, watching as Duncan was being helped to a stretcher. "And I want it well away from my family."

I nodded. "I understand." I held out my hand to him. "Thank you, Thomas. Thank you for everything."

He took my hand, smiling down at me. The change was startling. He was almost handsome. "I did it for Gwen."

"You loved her." I realized.

There was a commotion coming from the mansion. I heard firefighters calling back and forth, something about a 'DOS', and the chief called for a recovery squad. The fire department descended on the house in earnest. The police ushered us all back for our own safety. Rene scooped me up, and I could see flames licking against the majority of the windows on the third floor.

We all filed out of the Drake's courtyard in the thinning rain and to the waiting street. People had started to gather around to gawk and stare. I huddled close to Rene, ignoring them.

Duncan was taken to a waiting ambulance, and

Julian and Thomas rode along with him. I was about to ask Rene to take me to my family when the female paramedic who'd been taking care of Aunt Faye approached me.

"Excuse me, are you Autumn?"

"Yes?" I said, concerned that something had gone wrong with my great aunt.

"Everything is fine," she was quick to assure me. "But our patient, Miss Bishop, refuses to leave unless she knows you are safe."

I sighed, resisting the urge to roll my eyes. No doubt she had her hands full. "I take it my great aunt wants me to ride along with her?"

"Yes, she does," the paramedic said.

"Rene, put me down," I asked.

"Not happening." He grinned down at me. "Lead the way," he said, falling into step with the nice paramedic.

We approached the ambulance, and I could clearly hear my great aunt's raised voice. Rene set me on my feet, and handed me the briefcase. "I'll ride in front. You help with Faye." He lowered his head and pressed a kiss to my mouth.

Rene and a police officer helped me up. I caught the tail end of Aunt Faye's rant as I climbed in the back of the ambulance, hauling the case.

"...very well be dehydrated, but young man, I am *not* mentally incapacitated!" Aunt Faye lectured the poor paramedic, who was simply trying to do his job.

I sat on the bench where the paramedic directed,

tucked the case by my feet, and checked on my great aunt. They had her hooked up to oxygen, and a heart monitor was taped to her chest. "I'm here," I said. "Now *please* shut up." I had to grin when she snapped her mouth closed.

"Thank you," The EMT breathed in relief.

Aunt Faye narrowed her eyes at me. "Well it's about damn time," she snapped. "I needed to tell you... I was only trying to *protect* the family. I didn't betray you... I thought if I could bargain with Rebecca that she'd end the feud and stop the curse—"

"Hey," I cut her off, seeing the EMT frown over her words. "I figured that out for myself when you dumped all of your energy into me." I smiled at her. "Now relax, please lie back and let them take care of you."

"Very well," Aunt Faye grumbled. She reached out for my hand. "I love you. I am so very proud of you, my girl."

The doors of the ambulance were shut, and we were on our way. "And I love you, you old Witch," I said over the sound of the sirens.

"Well of course you do," Aunt Faye tossed her head. "What's not to love?"

CHAPTER SIXTEEN

The damage from the fire on the third floor of the Drake mansion had been extensive. The fire department concluded that the blaze had started from a combination of the lightning strike to the roof and the burning candles on the mantle that must have been knocked over.

Rebecca Drake Quinn did not survive that night. The official report said that she had died from the combination of a massive stroke and smoke inhalation. However, the real cause of her stroke was likely due to a deadly overdose of dark energy. Between her duel with Thomas and abusing the laws of magick by drawing on the powers of the Blood Moon Grimoire, she'd fallen by her own hand.

It wasn't a coincidence that Lexie regained consciousness at the precise moment that Rebecca had been pronounced dead at the scene. Lexie came to with Bran, Morgan, Ivy and her parents all sitting by her side. She bounced back to her old self within days.

Aunt Faye spent a few days in the hospital due to exhaustion and dehydration. She and Lexie received plenty of visits from the family and the Coven. Julian Drake *did* come to see Aunt Faye. I was surprised when I walked into Aunt Faye's hospital room and discovered that he was smiling and chatting with her. Clearly enjoying himself. I was touched that Julian had brought her a huge box of chocolates and a dozen multi-colored roses.

Holly called and sent flowers to Lexie and Aunt Faye, but did not come home from her college to visit. When I spoke to her she'd confided to me that she was relieved the drama was past, that everyone was safe, and now we could all settle back to a normal life.

I didn't have the heart to tell her that I was absolutely positive that *normal* wasn't ever going to be possible, not in William's Ford, anyway.

Lexie and Aunt Faye had come home from the hospital together. I heard from Violet O'Connell that there had been no memorial service for Rebecca Drake-Quinn. They had simply and quietly had her remains cremated.

With the assistance of the High Council, the coven, *and* the Drakes, the Blood Moon Grimoire was rebound. During the final lunar eclipse of the tetrad in late September, a Grand Coven was convened within the privacy of the courtyard at the Drake mansion. The ceremony started as the eclipse began. I watched the moon darken in the south-eastern sky and thought about the sacrifices made by my grandparents, David Quinn, my Aunt Gwen, and even by my father.

Determined that this chapter would be permanently closed, and that the rest of my loved ones would finally be safe, I sucked it up and did my duty. Duncan and I were called upon to stand on opposite sides of the altar. We avoided eye contact with each other and, at the appointed time, placed our hands on either side of the grimoire. As the earth's shadow cast a blood colored light across the coven, the grimoire flowed together while everyone watched.

I was relieved to be able to remove my hands from the cover of the grimoire, and turn it over to the chosen trio of Witches to finish the task. Following the prophecy of my grandmother's ghost, the three Witches chosen to bind the grimoire once and for all were Ivy, who represented the Maiden, Lexie as the Mother, and Aunt Faye, who acted as the Crone.

My part in the ritual complete, I happily went to stand with Rene and Marie. I saw that Duncan's hands were shaking as he walked back to his place in the circle. I understood his reaction completely. The personal cost to him had been high as well. His father had been killed by his mother, Rebecca, and he had watched his mother destroy herself with dark magick. Very nearly taking him with her. If not for Thomas, Duncan would have died along with his mother that night. Nevertheless, he stood next to his uncle and cousin for the remainder of the ritual and was stoic.

I leaned my head against Rene's strong shoulder and reminded myself that it was almost over. Once the ceremony was complete, the Blood Moon Grimoire was then entrusted to the Proctors, who fulfilled their roles in the community as guardians and protectors. The ritual circle was finally opened and the group broke into a spontaneous cheer. I accepted a hug from Marie and heard a crow call. I looked up to see a pair of crows watching over us all, high up in the branches of the oak tree in the courtyard.

Two crows for joy, I thought and nodded my head at the birds, acknowledging the message from the crows.

***

October had arrived, and the trees were a glorious explosion of color. I had left Merlin snuggled in the blankets at the foot of my bed and was out enjoying an early morning run. I was on my way back home, jogging my favorite route through the neighborhood, as dawn broke. I had changed things up today and was without my iPod.

With no music blasting, I was able to listen to the sounds of the birds singing. The rising sun made the sky seem a rosy color, brightening up the deep blue. Feeling my muscles warm, I tugged the long sleeves of my bright orange running shirt up to my elbows and enjoyed the sensations of peace, security, and freedom.

Pumpkins were arranged on porches, and a few

decorative scarecrows were guarding various flower beds in front yards. I tried to pay attention to my footing on the old brick sidewalks, but there was so much to see, smell and enjoy. A new planting of chrysanthemums along my route distracted me. The mums were blooming away in such bright happy colors of gold, red, orange. I glanced down as I jogged past them and— I snapped my head up. A man had stepped out right in front of me.

"Hey!" I tried to step to the side to avoid him, but I was in mid-stride and we smacked solidly into each other.

"Shit!" he swore.

I felt myself falling to the bricks. An intense feeling of déjà vu washed over me. I automatically put my hands out to stop my fall, and, fortunately, the man managed to wrap his arms around me. He aimed us towards the grass, and we landed— with me directly on top of him.

My breath rushed out in a solid thump as our chests knocked against each other. I blinked down at the latest victim of my klutziness, and found myself in Duncan Quinn's arms. Our eyes met and held for one heartbeat and then two.

I lifted off him and eased over to my hip in the grass. "We really have to stop meeting like this," I said, before I thought better of it.

He lay there and blinked at me. "Woman, you are a menace." He shook his head and actually chuckled.

I squinted over at him lying on his back in the grass. He seemed good humored and relaxed in casual work clothes— his beard was gone, and there was no trace of dark energy around him either. His eyes were bright blue and clear.

I cleared my throat and tried for a casual, slightly snarky tone. "Hey, I was jogging wearing a bright orange shirt *and* neon green shorts. That ought to be warning enough for anyone," I pointed out.

"Well, you've got me there." Duncan sat up and turned to me. "How's your family?" he asked politely.

"Good," I said, and struggled not to feel awkward. "The family's doing great."

Duncan stood up and offered me a hand. "Are your classes going well?"

I accepted the hand. "Yes, I'll graduate in December." I was pulled up. We were now facing each other. I stepped back and tried to let my hand slip away.

He didn't let go. "Are you still seeing Rene?" he said, our eyes locked on to each other.

"Yes. Are you still seeing Angela?"

"No." He shook his head. "No, I'm not."

"Oh." I discovered I was standing on the lawn of the Drake house. Quinn construction trucks were parked in the long driveway. "How goes the repairs to the mansion?" *There, that sounded almost normal. I congratulated myself. Just two people having a casual conversation.*

"The repairs are going well." Duncan slowly let go

of my hand. We both took a step back. "We're giving the old place a decent facelift while we are at it."

"I heard that you are living with your uncle and cousin now," I said next in my bid for adult, polite conversation. "How's that working out?"

"Better than I'd thought." He tucked his hands in his pockets. "My mother had always tried to keep us apart from each other, but they're trying. And they are all the family I have left... so I think that we'll get there."

I felt sympathy for him and touched his arm. "I understand."

"Yeah, I know you do." He smiled down at me. "You had to build a new family for yourself too, didn't you?"

Over his shoulder, I saw Julian dressed in jeans and a t-shirt. To my surprise he was carting five gallon buckets of paint along with the guys on the crew. "Family can surprise you..." I said tilting my head towards his cousin.

"Oh yeah, Julian," he said as he followed my gaze. "I've got him helping with the painting. It's good for him. I told him, chicks dig callouses on a guy's hands."

I snorted out a laugh at that. "I'm pleased for you, Duncan," I said, meaning it. "It's wonderful that you are re-connecting with your family."

Duncan's eyes were suddenly haunted. "Do you think *we* can ever re-connect? Find our way back to each other?

Caught off guard by the shift in the conversation I blinked up at him. "Duncan, we aren't the same people any longer. I don't know if that's even possible."

Duncan reached out as if he would touch me, but hesitated. "There's a lot I need to say to you. If I'd have listened to my heart a long time ago... we wouldn't be standing here like this now." He dragged a hand through his hair. "But I couldn't find my way out from the influence of that damn grimoire... until I almost died."

My feelings were all twisted up inside. I searched his eyes. The Sight hit me like a ton of bricks, and I 'saw' him.

There he was. The man I'd once loved. *Humbled, but brave, and a better man for all that he'd been though.* My breath caught in my throat, and I felt my heart crack.

"I once asked you to read me, and I'm doing so again." Duncan held out a hand. "Take a good look at me. See who I am now."

I tucked my hands behind my back. "I don't have to touch you. I can see who you are... It's right there in your eyes." I swallowed hard, willing myself not to cry. "Welcome back," I said, a few tears escaping anyway.

"I know you coming back to me is a long shot..." he said quietly, and to my surprise, he wiped my tears away with his thumbs. "But I'll be waiting right here."

"I don't expect you to—"

"Waiting right here," he said, gently cupping my face in his hands. He kissed me, his lips pressing softly to mine.

It took everything I had to stand still. "Duncan," my voice shook. I eased back. A thousand emotions tumbled through me, leaving me confused and hurting.

He let me go. "I love you," he said. A corner of his mouth lifted even as tears shone in his eyes.

He'd never said that to me before. It caused an ache around my heart. "I need to go," I said after taking a few seconds to try and compose myself. "I'm not running from you, I simply need to go." I tried a smile. "Be happy, Duncan." I walked back to the sidewalk and started up the hill towards the manor. I glanced back at him. There he stood by a cluster of chrysanthemums, arms crossed over his chest as he watched me walk away.

I blinked to clear the tears from my eyes, swiped at them when that didn't work, and began to jog up the street. I gained the top of the hill and stopped to catch my breath. I stood, studying the manor and wondered about my future. The truth was, I had no idea what the future held for me... because it was always harder to *see* for yourself.

If I'd learned anything in the past year, it was that power and magick, like nature, are neutral forces. Awesome, raw, and untamed though they may be, the true magickal practitioner works respectfully and in harmony with these natural forces. Works with— but never tries to control. In the end, a Witch can only control their own actions.

That's the thing about power, magick, and love; you

have to respect it for the awesome force that it is. Only by walking our own paths and following our own hearts do we grow and become wise.

My heart lifted, and I smiled as I gazed at my home. Two stories tall, the Queen Anne style house was painted in a warm gray, with fancy burgundy gingerbread trim. At the peak of one of the Witch-hat shaped towers of the manor, a crow perched.

I jogged across the street and through the gates at the end of the driveway. Like magick, they swung closed behind me all on their own.

The End

The *Legacy of Magick* Series continues…
Turn the page for a preview of book #4 in the Legacy of Magick series.

Beneath An Ivy Moon

I was minding my own business in the University library when I got my first inkling that something was wrong. I sat up straight in my chair, all my spidey senses on alert. It was nothing I could physically see, hear, or touch with my own two hands... but I *felt* it in my gut nonetheless. A foreboding feeling that pushed me to move. To do something, to scan my own surroundings for danger, and to check on my family and friends... Something was coming, and everything would change.

As the premonition rolled over me I shivered, tugging my short black jacket closer around me. Waiting to see if I got a 'hit' in my solar plexus, I silently ran down a mental list of the names of my nearest and dearest: *Great Aunt Faye, Bran, Lexie, Morgan, Autumn, Rene, Marie, Cypress, Holly...* I was searching for a sort of 'energetic tweak', as my cousin Autumn called it, something that would let me know where to pinpoint my focus.

And there it was— *Holly.* I got the energetic hit on my absent twin sister. I sighed, pushing my laptop away from me, and sat back to think. Things had been pretty quiet (magickally speaking) in William's Ford for the past year and a half... ever since the big magickal show down between the Drake family and mine.

The crazy, evil practitioner who had caused so many problems was dead and buried, and the Blood Moon Grimoire was safely under the protection of the Proctor family— Lexie's family. I was happily finishing up my Sophomore year at University, and Cypress Rousseau and I were still roommates, and still witchy BFFs.

So life was good, but I'd be lying if I said there wasn't a big emotional vacancy in my world. And her name was Holly. My twin sister Holly had moved away, choosing to go to a college clear across the state two years ago. I hadn't seen her since January at the end of our Winter break. Besides the occasional text, email or phone call— that I always instigated— I rarely heard from her. I hoped she was happy in her new life, studying Art History at her college in Kansas City. While I missed seeing and talking to her every day, there were *other* ways, magickal ways, of keeping in touch with my fraternal twin.

I looked around, making sure that I was unobserved in the little glass-walled study room I had rented. All I saw was my own reflection against the glass walls. I lifted a hand to my hair. *Yeah, the new cut and chunky blonde streaks had been a good choice.* The light blonde stood out against my brown hair, and it drew attention to my angular cut and choppy side bangs. It was fun and kicky, and I was happy with it. Sometimes I missed the crazy purple and blue I used to dye my hair back in the day, but the natural brown suited me better. Plus, it helped to make my green eyes more noticeable.

I dropped my hand, smirking at myself for primping. I checked again to see if anyone was paying attention to me. No one was, and the coast was clear. I propped my feet up on the desk, smoothing my short black dress with white skulls all over it down over my thighs. *Don't want to accidentally flash the campus boys, Ivy.* I reminded myself.

I tipped back in my chair, shut my eyes and reached out energetically to my twin. I found the psychic bond we shared, and visualized that unbreakable energetic silver cord that connected me to her. I gave it a good hard yank on the astral plane. Ha! That would get her attention. *Holly, what's up, sis?* I called out to her on the astral.

I felt an answering tug at my solar plexus. *I'm studying for finals, Ivy. I'm fine.* Came Holly's annoyed reply.

Mentally I rolled my eyes, and I let my sister 'feel' that. *Why... do I not believe you?*

Because you like to create drama where there is none.

Hey, I sent back, a little hurt at the dismissive comment. *I had a premonition and it felt like something was wrong. I was worried about you.*

I'm fine. But I do have to get back to my studies. Gotta go now.

I felt the link lessening between the two of us as Holly tried to dissolve our psychic communication. Before I lost her I sent out: *I'll see you soon for summer break. Love you Holly.*

Her response came back. *Love you too Ivy, stay out of trouble.* Then after a moment's pause she added. *Be safe.* Then, there was nothing else.

Our psychic communication over, I opened my eyes and dropped my booted feet to the floor, setting the chair back on all four legs. Taking in a deep, steadying breath, I held it for a four count, then blew it out slowly and reconnected my energy to the earth. I'd expected to feel better after checking in with my twin, but if anything, a stronger feeling of unease rolled over me. I gathered up my things for the walk back across campus to my dorm.

As I left the library I figured that whatever *it* was, was coming from somewhere within the campus itself. I moved over to the edge of the sidewalk, squinted my eyes and turned my head to use my peripheral vision to 'see'.

The library felt clean, but now that I was aware of *it*, it kind of made sense that the energy had been muffled while I'd been inside the building. Almost as if whatever was 'out here' had been energetically barred from the library. Which would be my brother Bran's doing. He'd keep the University library locked down good and tight with his magick. After all, he worked there full time. But still, I wondered about Holly's closing message. Why would Holly have told me to 'be safe'?

Well, I could damn sure find out. I may be a college sophomore, but there was more to me than most folks realized. I am Ivy Bishop. The gothic-fabulous and youngest female Witch of my generation, from the Bishop family line.

As the sun set, I walked quickly back to my dorm. However, instead of enjoying a pretty spring night, all of my physical and witchy senses were on full alert. The feeling of 'wrongness' seemed to tease the edge of my awareness. But I knew it was there, waiting and gathering strength.

Obviously the last eighteen months of peace and quiet William's Ford had been blessed with— were over.

Beneath An Ivy Moon By Ellen Dugan
Coming Summer 2016

Made in United States
Troutdale, OR
07/02/2025